D1508825

JENNA'S COWBOY

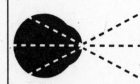

JENNA'S COWBOY

SHARON GILLENWATER

THORNDIKE PRESS

A part of Gale, Cengage Learning

GALE
CENGAGE Learning™

Detroit • New York • San Francisco • New Haven, Conn • Waterville, Maine • London

Copyright © 2010 by Sharon Gillenwater.
The Callahans of Texas Series #1.
Thorndike Press, a part of Gale, Cengage Learning.

LIBRARY OF CONGRESS CATALOGING-IN-PUBLICATION DATA

Gillenwater, Sharon.
  Jenna's cowboy / by Sharon Gillenwater.
    p. cm. — (Thorndike Press large print Christian romance)
  ISBN-13: 978-1-4104-2674-1
  ISBN-10: 1-4104-2674-2
  1. Texas—Fiction. 2. Large type books. I. Title.
PS3557.I3758J46 2010b
813'.54—dc22   2010005972

Published in 2010 by arrangement with Revell Books, a division of
Baker Publishing Group.

Printed in the United States of America
1 2 3 4 5 6 7 14 13 12 11 10

To my husband, Gene, who served his country as a helicopter pilot in Viet Nam. My hero then. My hero still. I thank God that he brought you home to me.
And to the members of the United States Military, both present and past, and to your families. Thank you for your service and your sacrifice. May the Lord bless you and keep you and give you peace.

ACKNOWLEDGMENTS

A special thank-you to Bill and Doris McClellan, recently retired from the Renderbrook Spade Ranch, for answering my questions about the large cattle ranches in "our" part of West Texas. I hope I didn't mess anything up, but if I did, any mistakes are mine. Y'all are the best!

While I was researching combat-related post-traumatic stress disorder, my agent, Steve Laube, suggested I look at the books written by Chuck Dean. What a blessing! Thank you, Steve.

Nam Vet by Chuck Dean
Down Range: To Iraq and Back by Bridget
   C. Cantrell, PhD, and Chuck Dean
Once a Warrior: Wired for Life by Bridget
   C. Cantrell, PhD, and Chuck Dean

I only wish my husband and I had found *Nam Vet* twenty years ago. With God's help, we muddled through on our own, but I suspect things would have been much easier and different if we'd understood what we were dealing with.

I strongly urge anyone who has served in combat — no matter what the war — or who has a loved one who has served, to read these books. They will help you understand PTSD and give insights on healing, both medically and from a Christian perspective.

If you think you or a loved one might be suffering from PTSD or any other potential service-related disorder, contact the Disabled American Veterans (www.dav.org). They will assess your situation, and if appropriate, serve as your advocate with the Veterans Administration.

The Spirit of the Lord GOD is on Me,
because the LORD has anointed Me
to bring good news to the poor.
He has sent Me to heal the
brokenhearted,
to proclaim liberty to the captives,
and freedom to the prisoners.

Isaiah 61:1
(Holman Christian Standard Bible)

1

Callahan Crossing had changed some while he'd been gone. But then, so had he. A man couldn't fight for his country and not be affected by it. Nate Langley had served with honor, and according to his army commanders, courage. Which he figured really meant he was as bullheaded as his father had always said he was.

But some things ran deeper than love of country, such as family loyalty and duty. It was time to protect those he loved by tilling the land his family had owned for almost a hundred years. Time to help his father, who could no longer handle the load of running a farm alone.

Thumbing through the latest issue of *Western Horseman* magazine, he glanced down the aisle of Miller's Grocery toward the deli. The roasted chickens were still turning in the rotisserie, so he'd have to wait awhile longer. He'd already picked up the new battery for his truck, and it would be at least twenty minutes before UPS delivered the tractor part his dad had ordered from the farm implement store. Killing time at Miller's was preferable to listening to long-winded fishing tales any day.

Halfway down the aisle, two elderly ladies stopped by the birthday cards for a chat, their West Texas twang bringing a smile to his face. At the other end, two high school boys stopped while one of them scribbled on some paper attached to a clipboard.

Nate's smile widened into a grin. It was the last week in September, traditionally the time for the local newspaper subscription drive. It was usually handled by two or three clubs at the high school as a fund-raiser, but he hadn't heard which ones were competing this time around. It was also homecoming week, and judging by the boys' appearance, Costume Day was still part of the celebration.

One was dressed as a stereotypical TV geek — pants a couple of inches too short, white socks and black loafers, white shirt with a plastic pocket protector holding pens and a short ruler, slicked-back hair, and dark-rimmed glasses. The other guy, who probably played tackle on the football team, wore a purple tie-dyed loose cotton T-shirt, yellow flowered bell-bottom pants, and sandals. An orange flower painted on his cheek clashed with a shoulder-length, cheap pink wig.

Pinky glanced up toward the checkout counters and tilted his head, giving somebody the eye. "We haven't asked her."

"Quit staring at her like that." The Geek made a face. "Dude, she's old, and she's got purple hair."

"Just a couple of stripes for school spirit. So she's cool."

"Well, yeah . . ."

"She may be old, but she's still lookin' good." Pinky moved out of sight. The Geek rolled his eyes and followed.

Curious to see who they were talking about, Nate tossed the magazine into the cart and moved down the aisle. He stopped and peeked around an end display of hot dog buns, canned chili, and baked beans.

Jenna Callahan Colby.

Pinky was right about one thing. She did look good. Nate supposed that to a teenager, twenty-eight was old. Since he was a year older, he didn't have a problem with it. She was still slender, with an athletic build. Her red hair, short now instead of shoulder length, was cut in a simple layered, flattering style. She wore a short-sleeved shiny gold top, close enough to the school colors to count. Her slacks and the purple stripes in her hair were a perfect match to the letterman's jacket hanging in his bedroom closet at the farm.

He drew back and watched her between the shelves while she teased the boys.

Her turquoise eyes sparkled as she gave Pinky the once over. "So are you in the drama club?"

He shook his head, the pink hair flopping across his face.

"Is there a hippie commune around here that I don't know about?"

Pinky chuckled and shoved a clump of wig out of his eyes. "No, ma'am. At least I haven't heard of one."

"How about you?" Jenna turned to the Geek. "Science or math?"

The kid grinned, but his face turned bright red. "Looks like I should be in one of those, huh?" He tipped his head toward his friend. "We're in FFA."

"No! Well, you certainly fooled me. Great costumes."

A wave of nostalgia swept over Nate. The Geek was right — he and Jenna were old. He'd been in FFA a lifetime ago. For years, the letters had stood for Future Farmers of America. About the time he hit high school, the organization changed the name simply to FFA since there were many more facets to agriculture education than farming. He supposed that was progress, but he'd always think of farmers like his dad when he heard the name.

Out of the corner of his eye, he noticed the lady at the deli waving at him. She held up a couple of packages. The roasted chickens were ready. He nodded, then absently picked up a can of chili and some hot dog buns and started toward the deli, hoping nobody had noticed that he had been watching Jenna.

Nate had fallen in love with her the summer he was fifteen when his horse threw him into the big, water-filled dirt stock tank, and she hadn't laughed. She'd watched him with a tiny frown of concern as he sat up, sputtering muddy water and dying of embarrassment. Then she asked if he was all right. Momentarily hurting too much to move, he stayed put and forced a grin. When he plopped his wet Stetson on his head, she dismounted, took off her boots, and waded in to cool off.

Between the time she got off her horse and sat down beside him in the water, he was a goner. He'd been crazy about her all through high school, although he never told anyone, not even her. He'd tried hard to keep his feelings hidden whenever he was around her and especially at her father's ranch, where he sometimes worked.

He'd slipped up once his senior year, watching as she walked to the house from the barn. Her father, Dub, noticed and flat-out told him that he wouldn't take kindly to a part-time cowboy making a move on his little princess. Though Dub liked him, the tough rancher didn't pull any punches in letting him know he wasn't good enough for his daughter. When she married, it would be to someone who was going places. And they both knew he wasn't. He was a cowboy at heart, and working the farm came in a close second. Neither occupation would earn more than an honest living.

Nate had only nodded in acceptance. It would have ruined a good friendship if he told her how he felt. By then she'd been crazy in love with Jimmy Don Colby, a high school football star who was being pursued by a dozen colleges.

After graduation, Nate went to work at a ranch in far West Texas and convinced himself that he was over her. That it had been a bad case of puppy love.

Then 9/11 happened, and Nate felt a call that ran deeper than anything he'd ever known. Less than a week after that fateful day, he joined the army. He was in Afghanistan when his mom wrote that Jenna and Jimmy Don had gotten married, and Jimmy had been drafted into pro-football by the Dallas Cowboys. Nate was in Iraq when he heard that she'd had a little boy. Another letter from his mom several months later said that Jenna and Jimmy were getting a divorce because Jimmy had found someone new.

Nate had thought of her often during the lonely nights camped in the windswept sands of the Middle East. Picturing her face, he had silently prayed for her and her son as he drifted off to sleep. In his dreams, he'd seen her smile, heard her whisper his name, felt her fingertips brush his cheek.

He caught another glimpse of her through the store window as she walked to her pickup. A familiar ache tightened his chest, one he thought he had vanquished long ago.

Maybe things hadn't really changed at all.

Jenna took a deep breath and jumped up in the air a little, pushing on the tire iron with all her strength as she came back down. It didn't budge. The guy at the service station had gotten carried away with the impact wrench the last time he rotated the tires.

She released the tire iron and straightened, huffing out a frustrated breath, silently threatening to wring his neck. She had specifically told him not to tighten the lug nuts so much that she couldn't get them off herself. He knew she lived fifteen miles from town and probably figured he'd make good money driving out to fix a flat. "No way, mister," she muttered.

She decided to call her brother Chance. Reaching through the open pickup door to the passenger seat, she took her cell phone from the outside pocket on her purse and hit the speed dial for his construction company. As she expected, his secretary answered. "Hi, Pat. This is Jenna. Is Chance available?"

"Sorry, he's way out north of town meeting with some potential clients. Do you want me to have him call you when he checks in?"

She could always call him directly, but she didn't want to interrupt his business meeting over a flat tire. "Yes, please. On my cell. Thanks."

Frowning, she considered her options as she hung up. It wouldn't do any good to call the ranch. Her dad and her other brother, Will, had gone up near Lubbock to pick up a new stallion. The ranch hands were wandering across sixty thousand acres on horseback, looking for a wayward bull. Even if she were fortunate enough to reach one of their cell phones, it would be stuffed into a cubbyhole or console in a pickup. By the time they returned to the truck and got her message, Chance probably would have the tire changed.

At least she'd stopped by one of the few trees next to the road, so there was a little shade. She tucked her phone into her pant's pocket and rearranged some of the groceries, putting all the cold stuff into a couple of bags with a frozen package of meat in each one. Normally, she kept a small cooler in the pickup, but she had taken it out to clean a few days earlier and had forgotten to put it back.

Tapping her fingertips on the edge of the truck bed, she glanced at her watch: 3:00. Her mom wasn't expecting her for another hour, so she didn't need to call and make her worry. Mom had assured her that she was free to babysit all afternoon, so Zach was in good hands. He loved having Grandma spoil him.

She plucked the water bottle from the holder by the driver's seat and took a long drink. The weatherman had predicted eighty degrees by mid-afternoon. She figured he had it pegged about right. And she had a carton of ice cream sitting in the backseat melting.

Shrugging, Jenna walked around the extended cab pickup and opened the glove box, rummaging through the odds and ends stashed inside until she found a couple of plastic spoons still sealed in clear bags, remnants of a stop at Dairy Queen.

Taking one of the spoons and the carton of ice cream, she found a comfortable spot in the dry grass beneath the pale green lacy leaves of the mesquite tree and sat down in the shade. She pried the lid off the ice cream and took her first bite. Double chocolate fudge brownie on a hot day. "Mmm . . . thank you, Lord, for small blessings."

In the pasture across the road, two Black Angus cows and their calves lay in the green grass beneath a stand of mesquites, swatting at flies with their tails, resting in the afternoon heat. Away from the trees, amid grass baked golden by the summer sun, stood a large valve and gauges on a natural gas pipeline. The gold and green rangeland stretched as far as she could see, ending with a brown mesa on the horizon. The field behind her was full of bright green plants a couple of feet high covered with green bolls of developing cotton.

She'd eaten enough to spoil her supper when she spotted a pickup coming down the road. Debating whether or not to retrieve her pistol from the console between the front seats, she waited a few minutes to see if she recognized the truck. If she didn't, she'd get the gun. A lot of strangers traveled the highway. On rare occasions there had been trouble. A woman stranded alone miles from the nearest house had to be careful.

A few minutes later, Jenna relaxed. It was Tom Langley's pickup. He and his wife, Chris, lived on a farm near the Callahan Ranch. He'd had neck surgery a month earlier, so she was surprised that he was even driving. The challenge now would be to keep him from trying to change the tire.

She went back to the ice cream, watching as the truck slowed and pulled off the road, stopping about ten feet behind her pickup. Jenna stared at the driver, dropping the spoon into the carton.

Nate! She hadn't heard that he was coming home for a visit. Her heartbeat kicked to double time. She had lived elsewhere for several years and never made it to Callahan Crossing when he was home on leave. He still had the same affect on her that he'd had when she was fourteen. Unfortunately, if he'd ever had any romantic ideas, he certainly hadn't given her any hint of it. And she'd never been the kind of girl to chase a guy.

He turned off the engine and opened the door. Was he all right? She'd heard that he'd been burned on the arm and been hit in the leg by shrapnel four months earlier in Iraq. His mother said neither wound had been bad enough for the army to send him back to the States. But he'd been awarded a Purple Heart, so it must have been more than a scratch. He'd earned a Silver Star that day too. There had been a write-up in the local paper about how he saved two badly injured soldiers even though he was also hurt.

Jenna held her breath as he climbed out of the pickup and slowly walked around the front of it. *Wow* . . . He wasn't the six foot tall, rangy cowboy she used to know. This man was all muscle. Not the overdone Mr. Universe type, but either he'd been working with weights or carrying a lot of military gear around. Probably both. His snug, blue, short-sleeved T-shirt emphasized his physique. She had to force herself not to stare at his broad shoulders and thick, solid arms.

He moved fine, so he must not have suffered any permanent injury to his leg. A pink scar on the back of his forearm stood out against his dark tan, but it didn't seem to bother him. And it wasn't bad enough to freak anybody out. He crossed his arms and leaned against the truck fender with a smile, his bright blue eyes twinkling.

Jenna's heart skipped a beat. How could his eyes have gotten even more beautiful?

He scanned the jack waiting near the right rear of the pickup, the tire iron still hanging on a lug nut, and the spare tire lying on the ground. He brushed a strand of light sandy brown hair off his forehead, and his gaze flickered to the ice cream before meeting hers. "Refueling?"

She laughed and stood, walking over to meet him. "I couldn't get the tire off, and the ice cream was melting. Didn't see any sense in wasting it." Setting the carton in the truck bed, she swallowed the sudden lump in her throat. "Welcome home."

Something flashed in his eyes, then he lowered his arms and straightened, taking a step closer. "Don't I get a hug?" Was his voice a little thicker?

Jenna hesitated for a second, then chided herself. This was Nate, her friend. And he was home safe and sound. Quick tears stung her eyes. *Thank you, Lord.* "You bet."

She slid her arms around his waist and

hugged him, resting her face against his chest. He wrapped his arms around her too. What did it matter if he held her a little tighter and a little longer than was customary? She wasn't going to complain.

Still, if she had any sense, she would end it quickly and not risk him thinking she might be open to anything other than friendship. She was a complete failure when it came to romantic relationships. Getting involved with anyone was unthinkable.

When he finally released her and she stepped back, tears stung her eyes. "I'm glad you made it okay."

He gave her a lopsided grin. "Me too." He walked to her truck, but instead of checking the tire, he looked over the tailgate at the ice cream. "You gonna share?"

Jenna laughed, feeling back on solid ground. "Help yourself. If I eat any more I'll make myself sick."

He picked up the carton, grinning when he read the flavor. "I should have known it would be chocolate."

"Is there any other kind?" When he reached for the spoon, she touched his arm to stop him. "There's a clean one in the glove box."

"Do you have anything contagious?"

"Not that I know of."

He scooped up a bite of the quickly softening ice cream and ate it. "Considering the germs I've been exposed to the last few years, I doubt yours will give me a problem." A tiny smile hovered at the corner of his mouth. "I like your hair that way. Though I'm surprised the purple doesn't clash with the red."

She laughed and smoothed her hair as the breeze ruffled it. It was a losing battle. "It does clash with some of my clothes. They're hair extensions, so nothing permanent. I'll have my stylist take them out next week. Are you here for a short visit or a long one?"

He swallowed, his gaze skimming the countryside. "Neither. I'm home to stay."

"I thought you were going to make the army a career."

"I was seriously considering it. But after Dad had surgery, I decided I needed to be here to help him. So I didn't reenlist."

"I'm sure your folks are thrilled to have you home."

He ate another couple of bites, then stuck the spoon in the carton and held it out to her. Regret shadowed his eyes. "Mom cried and Dad got all choked up when I told them. Every time I'd talked to them before, they'd brushed his neck and back problems aside, saying it was nothing to worry about.

I think they were trying to prove it by flying out to see me when I got back from Iraq instead of me coming home then. I could tell he was in rough shape. But they both insisted that the neck surgery would fix him up. Maybe they really thought it would.

"But I wasn't convinced, so I called his doctor after he had the operation. Dad had given the doctor permission to talk to me, but I don't think he really thought I'd call him. He said Dad would be fine as long as he didn't work so hard, but that his neck and back are a mess. Several compressed discs and arthritis from the top to the bottom of his spinal column, some stenosis causing pressure on the nerves. The doctor said he shouldn't run the farm by himself and especially not do any heavy lifting. Dad admitted last night that they'd been debating selling the farm because they couldn't afford to hire anybody."

"Then it won't support them and you, will it?" Frowning, Jenna walked a few feet away and dumped the ice cream in the grass. The ants were in for a treat. She straightened and looked back at him in time to see a fleeting grimace.

"In good years it wouldn't be too bad, but this isn't a good year for cotton. I'll have to make sure I don't eat too much." He smiled,

26

but his expression was strained. "And live at home."

Putting the lid back on the carton, she pulled an empty plastic grocery bag from behind the backseat and wrapped it up. "That isn't going to be easy. You've been on your own a long time. So have they."

"It will be a patience builder all the way around. I'll look for something else part-time." He bent over, gripping the tire iron, and pushed down. The muscles in his arms flexed until the lug nut broke free, and Jenna silently thanked the Lord for sending her a strong Good Samaritan.

Placing the tire iron on the next one, he paused and glanced over at her. "Know of anybody who's looking for a slightly rusty cowboy or farmhand?"

"I do." She tried to tamp down her excitement. They could help him, and she'd get to see him a lot more often than if he were holed up at the Langley farm all the time. Not that she wanted to delve into why the thought of having him around made her so happy.

"Who?" He broke another lug nut free.

"We are. Virgil White has been semi-retired for the last year. He officially quit the end of August on his eightieth birthday. He and Nadine bought a place outside of

San Antonio so they can be closer to the grandkids. They finished moving out last week.

"We'll need somebody to work three to four days a week, sometimes more, depending on what's going on. The house comes with it, if you want to live on the ranch. You'd only have to pay for the electricity and phone."

"You sure Dub doesn't have somebody else in mind?"

"We've talked to a couple of people, but we weren't all that impressed."

Nate was quiet as he quickly loosened the rest of the lug nuts. He moved around to the back and slid the jack into place, easily working the handle to raise that side of the pickup off the ground. Spinning off the lug nuts one by one, he set them in a little pile on the ground nearby. He lifted the heavy tire from the hub and laid it in the pickup bed with an ease that Jenna envied.

"That could be a real answer to prayer. But the days would have to be a bit flexible, depending on what I need to do at the farm." He rolled the spare around to the side of the pickup and lifted it onto the hub. "I'll give your dad a call tonight."

"You're hired if you want the job."

He stood, a tiny frown wrinkling his

forehead when he looked at her. "Don't I need to ask him about that?"

"You should talk to him, but I know he'd be glad to have you back." She grinned at him. "I still have Daddy wrapped around my little finger. And I'm a partner now, so I have some say in things."

Nate arched one eyebrow. "So you'd be my boss lady?"

"Got a problem with that?"

He knelt down to finish mounting the tire. "Not unless you get all uppity on me. I'm used to taking orders." He glanced up with an impish smile. "Used to giving them too."

"I bet you are." Smiling ruefully, she watched him spin the lug nuts in place and tighten them down with the tire iron. They'd be about as hard to remove next time.

Lord, thank you for bringing him home safely. Jenna had prayed for him while he was overseas, and she would continue now that he was home. She prayed for those she cared about. And she cared about Nate Langley.

She just hadn't realized how much.

2

Jenna didn't have an opportunity to talk to her father about Nate until supper. They usually ate dinner around noon with a lighter meal in the evening, but because her dad and Will had been gone, a roast had been cooking in the Crock-Pot all day. She waited until the food was passed around and everyone, including their housekeeper Ramona and her husband, Ace, filled their plates.

Having sudden reservations that maybe she had been too hasty to tell Nate that he was hired, she diced up some peaches and placed them on Zach's plate. Her almost-two-year-old son grinned at her from his booster seat and picked up several chunks of fruit, shoving them into his mouth.

"Use your spoon, Zach." When the little boy obediently picked up the spoon and tackled the peaches, she turned toward her dad.

She watched him cut up his slice of roast beef and glanced at her mom, who had heard all about her seeing Nate and her impulsive job offer. Her mother gave her an encouraging smile and nod. Jenna took a deep breath and automatically caught Zach's hand before he threw peaches at his uncle Will.

A twinkle lit her son's eyes. "No-no."

"That's right. Throwing food is a no-no."

Zach grinned, first at her then at Will. "Sor-ry."

"Are you teasing us?" asked Will, giving the little boy an indulgent grin.

Zach nodded, making them chuckle.

Jenna tried to be stern, but it was hard when the kid looked so cute. "You need to quit playing and eat your supper, young man."

"Yeah." Zach shoved the peaches into his mouth.

Satisfied that his moment of mischief had passed, Jenna focused on her father. "I hired someone to replace Virgil today."

Dub's hands stilled, and he looked down the oval golden brown mesquite table at her, his expression mildly surprised.

"Whoa! Gettin' a little big for your britches, aren't you, sis?" Will's wide-eyed grin told her that he thought she was in big trouble.

"I'm a partner," she said defensively, then grimaced because she'd let him bait her.

Her dad finished cutting up his meat. "Who?"

"Nate Langley."

Her father's brows practically met in a frown.

"Nate made it home?" asked Chance with a smile. When Zach pointed at his sippy cup, he handed it to him.

Jenna nodded. "He changed a flat for me this afternoon on the way home from town. He got in a couple of days ago. So you knew he was coming back?"

"I talked to him about three weeks ago, and he said he wasn't going to reenlist."

"Why didn't you tell us?"

"He wasn't positive the army would release him. He'd had some friends whose tours were extended even though it was time for them to get out. So he didn't want Tom or Chris to hear about it until it was a done deal. He didn't want to get their hopes up and then disappoint them." Chance moved the sippy cup farther back on the table.

Jenna nodded in understanding and turned her attention back to her father. "His folks didn't say anything until after he'd decided to come home, but they were thinking about selling the farm because Tom can't handle the whole job and they can't afford to hire anybody. Nate plans to do all the heavy work, but he needs something part-time so he has some income."

"Chris said she wasn't going back to work at the clinic for another month, not until she's reassured Tom is doing okay," said her mother. "So their finances will definitely be stretched thin for a while." A look passed between her parents. Jenna might be able to sway her father on many things, but the person he trusted the most for advice was his beloved wife, Sue.

Zach reached toward her. " 'Tatoes."

She put some mashed potatoes on his plate, added some carrots and squished them, then mixed a dab of gravy in with the vegetables. Cutting up some small bites of roast, she added them to his plate and smiled when he successfully put a bite into his mouth with the spoon. "Good job."

Zach gave her a potatoes-and-gravy-tinted grin.

"Nate needs a place of his own," added Sue, looking at Dub. "You said yourself that a man needs some breathing room." Which was why her father had Chance build a house for himself and one for Will, each an acre away on either side of the main house.

Will winked at Jenna. He had confided that he sometimes felt an acre wasn't quite enough distance. "You know, Dad, I never have figured out whether you thought Chance and I should have the breathing room or whether you needed it."

Dub chuckled and dabbed a roll in the gravy, sending his wife a mischievous glance. "Both."

Jenna felt a twinge of guilt, suspecting that her parents might like to be empty nesters again. It was past time to talk to them about her and Zach moving into her grandparents' house, which had been built in 1910. She loved the twelve-foot ceilings and numerous tall windows that made it bright and sunny. Her folks had remodeled it fifteen years earlier as a guesthouse, but it hadn't been used much since her brothers had moved out. Dub and Sue enjoyed having their company stay with them in the ranch house.

She wasn't sure how much peace, quiet, and privacy they'd really had before she and Zach moved back home. With the exception of breakfast, Will ate most of his meals there, and Chance joined them in the evening several times a week, more often if he was between building projects. They enjoyed the food and the family, and being there was expected. She didn't think it was a hardship on her mother, since Ramona did most of the cooking. But she expected her parents would enjoy more time alone.

Jenna wiped potatoes off Zach's face and a bit of carrot from his hair. Her food was getting cold, but that was normal. She picked up her fork. "Nate's going to call you tonight."

"You think he's up to the job?"

"He said he's a little rusty. But I think he'll do fine."

"Does he look fit?"

"Very." Her cheeks grew warm when she realized what she'd said and how she'd said it.

Will hooted and Chance grinned.

"William, don't tease your sister." But the amusement in her mother's eyes told Jenna that she liked her answer.

"Yes, ma'am." His laughter settled into a grin.

Jenna peeked at her father and almost groaned. He didn't seem one bit happy with what she'd said. "I meant he appears all healed up from his injuries. His leg didn't bother him at all." She cleared her throat. "And he's added a lot of muscle."

Will snickered, and she tried to kick him

beneath the table. She missed. He really was a responsible and intelligent thirty-one-year-old, except when it came to giving her a hard time. Why did his teasing turn her into a kid again, wanting to get even?

"I'll talk to him." Dub pinned her with his gaze. "But the final decision is mine."

"Yes, sir." She should have known better than to act so impulsively. She might be a partner, one who could give input into ranch affairs along with her brothers and mother, but ultimately, her father made the decisions. She needed to remember that. Everyone around called it Callahan country, and Dub Callahan was the reason.

Will and Chance had some power over various aspects of the ranch — certainly more than she did — but her father was the reigning monarch. She was his princess, and that's all she would ever be. "I'm sorry if I overstepped my authority. It was so good to see him home safe and sound, and when I heard about their situation, it seemed right to help them out."

"You know he'll make a good hand," Chance said quietly. He and Nate had been best friends since first grade. They'd kept in touch since graduation, although Nate's access to email had been sporadic when he was overseas.

"So that's three votes," said Sue.

"Four," Will added quietly. "We owe him the opportunity, if for no other reason than for helping keep us safe."

"I agree with all that, but I still want to talk to him face to face." Her father's expression softened as he focused on Jenna again. "War changes men, honey. Sometimes for the better. Sometimes not."

Oh, he's better. But she didn't think she should express that opinion out loud.

An hour later, Nate pulled up in front of the light tan brick, one-and-a-half-story Callahan ranch house. He'd expected that Dub would want to discuss the job in person, check him out for himself. He would have done the same if he were in the rancher's boots.

He walked up the stone steps to the wide porch that encircled the house. Chance threw open the door before he could knock and crushed him in a bear hug. When he released him, his friend took a step back and playfully slugged him on the upper arm. "Why didn't you call and tell me they'd turned you loose?"

"The colonel waffled until the last minute. Then I was scrambling to deal with all the paperwork. I only got here day before yesterday. Spent the time hashing through stuff with the folks and running over to Abilene to see the grandparents."

"How's your dad?" Chance clamped an arm around his shoulders and ushered him into the house.

Nate noted that Sue had redecorated. Red was the predominate color, along with southwestern patterned throws, pillows, and pottery. She'd added more Western paintings and a brass statue of a cowboy riding a wild bronc. But the old, worn Western hats still hung on the antique hall tree, and Dub's grandfather's scuffed cowboy boots remained on the floor beside it.

"I think he's still way too weak and pale, but they both insist that he's getting stronger. It's hard for him to accept that he can't work as much as he's used to, so he overdoes it."

"Then it's good you decided to come back home," said Sue, holding open her arms.

"Yes, ma'am." Nate hugged her gently. "It feels right." He knew she was pushing sixty, but there wasn't any gray in her hair, even if it was a little lighter than it used to be. More strawberry-blonde than red. Jenna had inherited her mother's hair and her turquoise eyes, but not her height. At five-three, she'd gotten shortchanged a few inches in that department.

When Nate stepped back, Dub held out his hand. "Welcome home. Looks like the army agreed with you."

"Can't complain. They treated me fair and square." He shook hands with Jenna's father, keenly aware that the man was sizing him up. Dub's hair had turned silver, but he still stood straight and tall, topping Nate by a couple of inches. The boys had taken after him in height and with their dark brown hair. But only Will had his dark eyes. Chance's eyes were green, which had prompted his brother to try to convince him that he'd been adopted when they were kids. They were a striking bunch, both in looks and with an air of confidence that came from being the most powerful family in the area.

"But it's good to be back in West Texas." No bombs. Nobody shooting at him. No wondering if the person walking toward him was friend or enemy.

Will was next to greet him, shaking his hand and slapping him on the back. Out of the corner of his eye, Nate saw Jenna step out of the kitchen carrying her son. Seeing her with the little boy triggered an unexpected wave of longing. With pale blond hair, Zach was as cute as could be, especially as he looked up at his mom in adoration and patted her cheek.

He smiled as Jenna joined them. "So this is the man in charge."

Dub laughed. "You got that right."

"And you love every minute of it." Jenna winked at her dad, then smiled at Nate. "Zach, this is Nate. He's an old friend."

The little boy watched him carefully. His eyes were dark blue with light gray starbursts radiating from the center. Nate decided he had the second prettiest eyes he'd ever seen. Zach glanced around at the others. Nate had the impression the kid was trying to gauge how his family felt about him.

As the boy's gaze came back to him, Nate said quietly, "Glad to meet you, Zach. Your mama was braggin' about you this afternoon. She said you were the cutest, sweetest, and smartest boy in the whole world."

"Not that she's prejudiced," mumbled Will with a chuckle.

"And I have every right to be."

Zach still studied him intently. What was going on in that little mind?

"He's okay," Jenna said softly. "He's a good guy."

Her son looked back at her, his serious expression making Nate a little nervous. She had mentioned earlier that Zach loved to kick his Nerf soccer ball around the house. "And I play soccer."

"Since when?" Chance asked.

Nate glanced at him. "First tour in Iraq." He turned back to Zach. "Maybe you and I can kick the ball around sometime."

Zach held out his arms to him. "Play ball."

Nate noted surprise flash across Jenna's face. "Is it okay?"

"Sure. He just doesn't normally go to someone new right away."

He lifted Zach carefully and settled him on one arm, holding him securely across the back with his other hand. Nate liked kids and had spent as much time as he could with the neighborhood children in Iraq. He had also visited a nearby orphanage whenever he had an opportunity. The boys there had taught him to play soccer.

Zach rested one arm on Nate's shoulder and pointed across the room. "Play ball."

"Now you've done it. Looks like our meeting will be postponed for a few minutes." Dub's eyes twinkled as he glanced down at Nate's boots. "Worth the wait to see you scramble around in cowboy boots."

"Sorry, sir." He frowned at Jenna. "We're only going to kick it back and forth, right?

He doesn't expect me to play defense, does he?"

"Maybe a little, but nothing too serious. None of us really know how to play anyway."

Nate walked over and set Zach on the floor. Before he could straighten, the boy kicked the ball and chased after it, smacking it again. "Whoa, he's fast." Laughing, Nate took off after him. As Nate caught up with the ball, Zach giggled and kicked it. "Oh, that's the way it is, huh? Better watch out, I'm gonna get it."

Being careful not to bump or trip him, he raced beside the little guy down the long hall. Nate sped up to reach the ball before Zach. He turned, lightly hitting it back toward the living room. Squealing with laughter, Zach tore after it and knocked it into the big room.

Nate moseyed along behind him. The toddler reached the ball, turned around, and kicked it to him. They kicked it back and forth for a few minutes before Zach did an about-face and headed over to his white toy box in the corner.

As the child dug through the box, Dub nodded toward his office. "Let's escape while he's busy. Otherwise, you're liable to be sittin' on the floor, playing with his toy guitar while he plays his drum."

Nate followed him into the office and shut the door. "So he's a musician too?"

"I think he might be. He loves music and has good rhythm. He starts wiggling every time he hears a tune, and he keeps a good beat when Chance plays the guitar." Dub sat down behind the big oak desk that had been the main piece of furniture in the room for as long as Nate could remember.

The old brown leather chairs had been replaced with new brown ones since he'd left. There were some current family photos on the bookshelf along with several older ones — including one of him, Chance, and Will. Sue had taken it the day Nate stopped by to see them before he headed off to basic training.

Dub followed his gaze, swiveling his chair around. "You were skinnier then."

Nate laughed and relaxed. "Yes, sir, I was. I thought you worked me hard, but I didn't know how easy I had it until I hit basic."

"The army can turn wimps into men." Dub swung back around toward him. "And you weren't a wimp. We heard you got hurt. Any lasting trouble from it?"

"My leg gets a little stiff and sore occasionally, but that's about it. It wasn't bad." Though worse than he'd told his parents. He'd spent over a week in the base hospital, then more time on limited duty.

"You had a lot of people praying for you, including all of us."

"I appreciate that, sir. I know those prayers and the Lord got me through. I did a lot of praying myself." Still did. He absently brushed his finger over the scar on his arm.

"So you're still walking the straight and narrow? Didn't get messed up with drugs or booze?"

"Never have done any drugs. And the one time I got drunk and hungover was enough for me."

"Was that when you and Chance chased my bull all over the pasture in Dad's old pickup?"

Nate felt warmth creep up his neck. He'd hoped Dub hadn't learned about that escapade. "Yes, sir. Our junior year in high school. When did Chance tell you about it?"

"About six months ago." A smile crinkled the corners of the older man's eyes. "But I sorted it out at the time. The tracks pretty much told the tale, along with the fact that Chance was sicker than a dog the next morning. I spotted him a couple of days later trying to make peace with that bull. Ol' Brutus wasn't having anything to do with him, so I knew my suspicions were right."

"You never said anything about it." Nate was surprised Dub hadn't fired him. Or at least chewed him and Chance up one side and down the other.

"I kept my eye on you to make certain you'd learned your lesson. Besides, I figured it was partly my fault."

"How?"

"I'd done something similar in my youth. My cousin and I got to telling tales one night and spilled that one to the boys. It might not have been where Chance got the idea, but I'm sure it influenced him some."

"I couldn't exactly say. We were pretty drunk by the time Brutus lumbered into sight. About all I remember clearly is that we had the radio on, and we decided that he came to listen to the music." He thought he might have been the one to suggest chasing the poor bull, but that probably wasn't the smartest thing to say during a job interview.

Dub's expression sobered. "It took me awhile after Viet Nam to get comfortable with things. With people." The day before Nate left for the army, Dub had talked to him for a couple of hours about what it was like to be in a war. Dub had flown a Huey helicopter, carrying supplies and troops into combat, carrying the wounded and, too

45

often, body bags back out.

"I know I'll have some adjustments, though I've been back in the States for three months."

"So was I. It wasn't enough time to get my head on straight."

Nate understood what he meant. Sometimes he wondered if he'd ever get out of the tense, high-alert combat mode. Or if the nightmares would go away. They'd started about a month ago, but sometimes it seemed as if they'd haunted him forever. He probably should have mentioned them during his psych evaluation before he got out, but he was afraid that might delay his discharge. He hoped they'd go away once he settled in as a civilian. "You managed it, though."

"It took a long time." Dub's eyes narrowed. "Some men never get there."

"I think I'll do better when I get a place of my own. I love my folks, but I can't relax at home, not the way I used to. If a cabinet door slams, I fly about two feet off the couch. I've been there two days, and Mom is practically tiptoeing around the kitchen, trying not to bang the pans or close a drawer too hard. I told her not to worry about it, that I'll get used to it." He knew from experience that it wouldn't happen quickly.

"She's a mom, so she worries and does her best not to upset you."

Nate nodded. "And that's hard on her. She's had enough stress with Dad already. I'd really appreciate the job, sir. It may take me some time to get my expertise back, and I expect you may do some things differently now, but I'm a quick learner."

"You always were." Dub leaned back slightly in his desk chair. "You might miss the cow the first few times you try to rope one, but I don't think you'll fall off the horse in the process."

"I hope not. The men never would let me live that down."

Dub grinned and spun a pen around on his desk. "Chance and Will would be the worst." His smile faded as he slanted a glance at Nate. "What about Jenna? Are you still in love with her?"

Nate's first impulse was to tell him that it wasn't any of his business. But it was. Dub loved his children, especially his daughter. He wondered if her father regretted encouraging her to marry Jimmy Don. And despite their differences years ago regarding her, Dub was his friend. He owed him the truth. "Maybe. I'll always love her as a friend, but I honestly don't know if I'm still in love with her."

He looked down at his hands for a minute then straightened and met the rancher's gaze directly. "I'll never be rich or able to give a woman a big house and expensive things. But I'm responsible and a hard worker. If the Lord ever blesses me with a wife, I'll do everything possible to provide a good home for her. And she'll never have to worry about me being unfaithful. I'm not that boy you scared off ten years ago, Dub. And Jenna isn't the starry-eyed homecoming queen. We've fought our battles and survived. We've earned the right to find our own way."

Dub frowned and practically growled. "Jimmy Don almost destroyed that girl. She only crawled out of that pit about six months ago, and it won't take much to knock her back in. I won't let you hurt her."

"Hurting her is the last thing in the world I want to do." Nate leaned forward. "But I do want to see if God has something for us without worrying about you breathing down my neck or firing me if I ask her out." He slumped back in the chair. "We're gettin' way ahead of ourselves. She may not be the least bit interested in me. And I'm sure not ready to haul her to the preacher's in the next week or two."

"You don't have the job yet, either." A

faint smile flickered across Dub's face.

Nate shrugged and grinned. "True."

The rancher ran through the requirements of the job. As Jenna had said, generally three days a week, sometimes more. People didn't work eight hours a day on a ranch. As on a farm, the workday was pretty much from sunup to sundown, occasionally longer. He agreed that Nate could have more time off to bring in the cotton during harvest and again at planting time if he needed it. He named a wage that was more than fair — even generous to Nate's way of thinking, since he'd been away from ranching for so long — especially since housing was included. They discussed a few more details, then stood and shook hands.

"Can you start Monday?"

"Yes, sir."

"We'll ease you into things," Dub said with a teasing grin. "We start the roundup on Monday."

Nate laughed. "That's not exactly easing into it."

"But it'll be fun."

"Yes, it will." Excitement swept through him as the tune to "Back in the Saddle Again" ran through his mind. He would be one sore hombre all next week, but he looked forward to spending the time on horseback and working cattle.

"You can move in anytime. Nadine left the living room furniture. She said it wouldn't go with her new house, but if you don't want it, we can put it in storage somewhere."

"I'm glad to have it. I think the folks will let me take the bedroom set in my room, but that's about it. Guess I'll have to go shopping. I've never set up a house before."

"You might as well plan on eating dinner and supper here, at least the days you're working on the ranch. Will is here most of the time, and Chance eats here whenever he can. Ramona still thinks she's feeding a bunkhouse full of cowboys, so there is always more than enough food. She'll welcome someone else to spoil."

Nate wondered if Dub thought about how much he would see Jenna if he ate with them. "I appreciate it. I haven't had much practice at cooking, other than heating up rations while on patrol."

They walked toward the door, but before they reached it, Dub rested his hand on Nate's shoulder. "Be careful with my little girl. You hurt her, and you'll answer to me," he added gruffly.

"And Chance and Will too. As my dad used to say, I'm not cruisin' for a bruisin'.

I'll be careful. For her sake and mine."

Dub's grip remained firmly on his shoulder. "She's a partner in the ranch now."

"So she said."

"More than one man has made a play for her, noses in the air, sniffin' money for the taking."

"Then they didn't know much about ranching, did they?" Nate grinned and reached for the door handle. "It's about as much of a gamble as farming. Walkin' in high cotton one year and dirt poor the next."

3

Nate stuck a pillow behind him and leaned back against the oak headboard of his bed, cordless phone in one hand and a ticket to the homecoming game in the other. Chance had given it to him the previous evening after he talked to Dub. His friend had bought it in hopes that he would be home in time for the festivities. Chance had also quietly, if not subtly, suggested that he invite Jenna to go with him, since everybody could see fireworks between them clear across the room. Their seats were right next to each other anyway. Nate hadn't bothered to ask his friend how that happened. Obviously, Chance had taken note of his feelings for Jenna years ago too.

Now, all he had to do was work up the courage to call her. They'd often done things together around the ranch when they were younger, but he'd never officially asked her out on a date. He knew she was glad he was home. The hug she had given him proved that. She'd held him extra tight, but had she felt something more than just welcoming an old friend? Had he really seen interest in her eyes, not only when he stopped to help her on the road, but several times during that evening when he caught her watching him? Or did he want it so much that he was imagining things?

Funny how a man could charge into battle without hesitation, but calling a pretty, sweet woman made him as nervous as a porcupine in a balloon factory. "Lord, I need some help here. Help me to be calm and not make a fool of myself."

Taking a deep breath, he dialed the ranch. When Jenna answered, he breathed a silent sigh of relief. Hard as it was to talk to her, it would have been ten times more difficult if Dub had been the one to pick up the phone.

"Have you got a minute?"

"Sure. I'm entering some expenses on the computer. I can use a break. What's up?"

"I was wondering if you'd like to go to the homecoming game."

"We're all going together and meeting Chance in town. You know the folks. They haven't missed a game in almost forty years." Her voice trailed off as if she were distracted. When she spoke again, he pictured her holding the phone away from her mouth. Something, or somebody, was making an awful racket. "Zach, don't beat on the desk with your drumsticks. Hit the chair cushion. That's a good boy. Thank you." She took a breath and turned her attention back to him. "You could come with us. It might be cozy, but we can fit five in Mom's Lincoln."

Cozy sounded good. Being alone with her would be better. "That might work. But I was hoping I could take you." He cleared his throat. "By myself."

There was a long pause, and he heard her swallow. "Like a date?" Her voice was a little wobbly.

Great. Now he'd gone and shaken her up. "You can call it something else if you want to. But, yeah, I'm thinking of it as a date. One that's about twelve years past due."

"Twelve?" Now she sounded surprised, and maybe a little breathless.

Was that good or bad?

"Well, fourteen to be exact, but we would've had to go on horseback since I didn't have my license when I was fifteen."

"We went riding together a lot, even then. But I never got the impression that you considered it a date."

"Reality and wishes were completely different things." Nate grimaced and stifled a groan. *Lame.*

When she didn't respond, Nate tried to think of something to say, but his brain had turned to mush. She finally spoke, her voice soft and a little wistful. "I've always thought you only wanted to be friends. I assumed you weren't attracted to me."

"It went from friendship to the biggest crush ever the day Sunflower threw me in the water tank and you waded in to keep me company."

"Oh, I remember that!" She didn't sound nearly as nervous now. "I was so scared you were hurt, but you sat up and grinned like it was something that happened every day."

Nate chuckled and relaxed a little. "I was hurting too much to move."

"Well, you didn't show it. I thought you were tough."

"Embarrassed is more accurate."

"Well, that too. Your face turned awfully red."

"Is that why you joined me in the tank and got all wet? You felt sorry for me?"

He heard her chair creak. "Hang on a minute, I need to see where Zach went. I can't keep up with that kid." Her breathing quickened a little, and he guessed she was walking across the room. "He's headed toward the kitchen. Oh, good. Ramona spotted him. She waved at me, so she'll watch him." He heard the door shut, and then the chair creaked again. "It was a hot day, and cooling off seemed like a good idea. Sure, I felt bad for you, but I was impressed too. You did a pretty good flip. Or maybe a somersault. I'm not up on diving terms."

Nate laughed. "Was I graceful?"

"Not exactly, but what amazed me the most was the way you handled it. Just laughed it off. A lot of guys would have gotten mad and cussed a blue streak. But then, I've never heard you cuss, and I don't think I've ever seen you lose your temper. You've always been easygoing."

Not anymore. But he hoped and prayed that was something the Lord could fix. He didn't like being so uptight. "I have my moments. But I managed to keep my cool around you."

"Too cool. Why didn't you ever ask me out, Nate? I would have gone in a second."

Nate's heart tripped all over itself. "I was afraid it would ruin our friendship. Besides, somebody always beat me to it. If you remember, you had guys lined up at the door. Until you started going with Jimmy

Don, you changed boyfriends like I changed socks."

"Only if you wore your socks for a week or two."

He was relieved to hear a smile in her voice. "Well, I did try to save Mom work and wore them until the horses started complaining about the stink."

She laughed, and Nate's breathing settled back to almost normal. "So how about it? Will you go to the game with me?"

Jenna listened to the gentle encouragement in his voice and closed her eyes. Long before Jimmy Don finally left her for good, she had slowly and painfully built a wall around her heart. Or as her father put it — a fence so tall and with so many strands of barbed wire that nothing could get past it. But her daddy was wrong. The barbs might keep people out, but the fence wasn't solid. Between all those strands of hurt and anger, light glistened through, slivers of hope and longing that beckoned in her loneliness.

She wanted to spend time with him, to enjoy his company and get reacquainted. But to actually go on a date? As in a couple? With everyone in town and half the people who'd ever lived there witnessing it? The thought terrified her. "I . . . uh . . . I don't know if it's a good idea, Nate," she said softly.

"I don't want to push you into anything you aren't ready for. If you don't want to consider it a date, then we won't. We'll think of it as two old friends hanging out together and going to the game. If you want us to ride with your folks and Will, that's okay. Did Chance tell you that your seat is next to mine?"

"No, he didn't mention it." Was her brother trying to set them up? She hesitated for a few seconds. Maybe she was putting more importance on this than it deserved, and she was rattled for no reason.

"Okay, I can do friends hanging out together." She took a deep breath, excitement and nervousness practically making her head spin. It had seemed as if she were destined for a life alone, though not for lack of interested guys. She hadn't been able to work up the courage to do more than chat with a few of them at church or occasionally at the cattle auction. But this was Nate. "We don't have to ride with the folks. I want to go with you. It's just that . . ." She took another breath to steady her nerves and whispered, "I'm scared."

"You've been hurt real bad, sugar. I reckon anybody would be afraid after what you've been through. To be honest, I'm a little scared too. I don't have a lot of experience when it comes to women."

"I'm not buying it. A handsome hunk like you probably has a girl in every port."

Nate laughed. "That only works for navy guys. At army bases, the men outnumber the women by about a zillion to one."

"Lousy odds."

"Yeah. But I never met anybody all that interesting anyway."

Was it selfish for her to be glad about that? "Are you going to the parade and pep rally tomorrow?"

"I've been thinking about it."

"Ride in with Will and me. Having one of the Wolves' All-Region wide receivers at the pep rally will give the team and the fans a boost." It would also give her a little time to be with him but not alone with him. She hadn't been out to coffee with a man besides Jimmy or the guys in her family in ten years. She didn't know how to act. "You'll probably see more old friends. I've heard there are a lot of folks coming into town tomorrow."

"You talked me into it."

Jenna grinned because she certainly hadn't talked very hard. "We'll pick you up about 3:30 so we can get a good parking spot.

There should be plenty of time to grab something to eat after the parade and before the pep rally starts. Now, I'd better go rescue Ramona from Zach. I think he got into the pans and is using them for cymbals. See you tomorrow."

"I'll be ready."

When she hung up the cordless phone, Jenna laid it on the desk and leaned her head against the high back of the leather chair. "Lord, please don't let me be making a mistake. You know I don't want to get hurt again, but I don't want to hurt Nate, either. Please give me wisdom. Help me relax and enjoy having him around." The volume of noise from the kitchen intensified, propelling her out of the chair.

A little zip of excitement raced through her as she hurried toward the door. Suddenly life looked a whole lot brighter.

Turning over, Nate glanced at the clock: 3:00 a.m. He'd managed a little over an hour's sleep since 1:00. Better yet, he hadn't had a nightmare. As usual, it had taken him a long time to fall asleep, but tonight it was mostly because he'd been thinking about Jenna. Daydreaming a bit. Praying some. He was surprised by the strength of what he felt for her. Attraction, sure. Who

60

wouldn't be attracted to that pretty lady? But he wanted to wrap his arms around her, hold her close, and promise that no one would ever hurt her again.

Unfortunately, that was a guarantee he couldn't make. Not even about himself.

Click.

Nate shot out of bed and reached toward the nightstand for the gun that wasn't there. Instead, he grabbed the baseball bat leaning against the headboard. A shadow swept along the wall. Bending low, he crept across the room and lifted one corner of the beige curtain. He quickly scanned the yard, then slowly searched the darkness again. Was that someone crouching by the barn? Ducking beneath the window, he eased back the curtain, looked from that angle, and slowly released his breath. Just a roll of chicken wire.

He sank back against the wall, trying to calm his racing heart. The shadow drifted across the room again, and he spun toward the window.

A barn owl on his nightly patrol.

Down the hall the toilet flushed, and a minute later the bathroom door opened with a little squeak. *Mom.* She'd told him that she had started using the guest bath at night so she wouldn't wake up his dad. He should have remembered that.

Nate walked quietly back to the bed and sat down, propping the bat up against the headboard. Wiping the sweat from his forehead with shaking fingers, he whispered the mantra one of his buddies had shared with him. "I'm safe. Nobody's going to hurt me. I'm safe." Then he added the best reassurances that he knew. "God is with me. He'll protect me. God is with me. He'll protect me." Lying down, he kept whispering the prayer over and over until he finally drifted off to sleep.

His torment temporarily held at bay, he managed another two hours of fitful rest.

At breakfast, his father grinned as he watched Nate put away his second plate of pancakes. His pale blue eyes glinted with amusement. "The way you're chowin' down, you'd think the army never fed you."

"We had plenty to eat most of the time." Nate smiled at his mother. She didn't bother to color her hair, but she didn't need to. The gray mixed in with the short brown curls looked good. "But nobody makes pancakes the way you do. You'll have to teach me how to cook these, or I'll be showing up here for breakfast after I move."

Her happiness practically bubbled out of

her, putting a sparkle in her hazel eyes. "You can come for breakfast anytime. Though I suppose that might be a little hard on the days you work at the ranch."

"Probably wouldn't be the best use of my time. And I don't want you thinking you always have to cook for me like this. But I'll let you spoil me for another couple of days."

"Are you going to start moving to the ranch today?" Tom sipped his coffee. His color was better, not as pale as he'd been a few days earlier. His hair had turned mostly gray while Nate had been gone, but he supposed most sixty-year-old men had gray hair.

"I thought I'd take some of my gear over to the house early this afternoon. I'll have to go shopping to outfit the place, but I need to check it out first."

"I can fix you up with some things." Chris waved her fork in the general direction of the oak cabinets. "If secondhand is okay."

"I'm not picky. I appreciate anything you want to get rid of. I have some money put away, so I can afford to furnish the house. But I don't want to spend a lot. I figured I'd hit Goodwill first and see what I could find." He reached across the round oak table that had belonged to his great-grandparents and squeezed his mom's hand. "I promise, Mom, it won't embarrass you to come visit. At least not too much," he added with a grin.

Smiling, she playfully slapped at his hand.

Nate dodged with a laugh. "Can't shop today. I'm going to the parade and pep rally with Will and Jenna."

"Good! You'll probably see quite a few people you know. I heard at the beauty shop yesterday that the hotel is all booked up." His mom offered him one more pancake. When he shook his head, she plopped it on her plate and poured syrup over it. "I'm glad Jenna is going too. When she came home, she hid out at the ranch for ages. Didn't even go to church. She finally started getting involved in things about six months ago."

Under the pretense of gathering up a bit of syrup, Nate pushed the last bite of pancake around on his plate and said casually, "She's going to the game with me tomorrow night." He caught a surprised glance fly between his parents.

His mother stared at him, her expression hopeful. "A date?"

"Just a couple of old friends hanging out together."

"Oh." She stuffed a bite of pancake into her mouth with a frown. "Everybody is go-

64

ing to think it's a date."

"Hey, Mom, don't talk with your mouth full."

She wrinkled her nose at him and finished chewing. "Well, official date or not, you need to get her a mum. You don't want her to be the only woman in the stadium without one."

Tom snorted. "I doubt everybody will have one."

"Of course they will, especially if they go with a man. The alumni in some other places may not wear mums, but they do in Callahan Crossing. It's a slap in the face if a woman's beau — or friend — doesn't give her one."

Nate had wondered if it was still a tradition. The custom wasn't popular everywhere, but for as long as he could remember, in Texas, guys gave their dates a large chrysanthemum corsage for homecoming. It had been very important when he was in high school. If his mom was right, it still was.

He sat back in the chair, full of food and enjoying being with his parents. He might be jittery and tense most of the time, but unlike some of his buddies, he wasn't having too much trouble being around his family or friends. So far he had managed to enjoy them and not feel himself pulling away. Having a house of his own would help. As much as he loved them, he didn't think he could handle living with his folks all the time.

"I'd like to get her one, but I don't know what she'll think. She didn't want to consider it a date." The instant the words were out of his mouth, he wished he could grab them back. As expected, his mother pounced on that thought quicker than a roadrunner on a rattler.

"But you did." Chris beamed at her husband. "Didn't I tell you he was sweet on that girl?"

"Yes, dear. Twelve years ago." He lifted one eyebrow, nodding slightly to Nate. "And eleven and ten . . ."

"We're just friends, Mom. But I don't want her to feel left out."

"Right." She rolled her eyes. "Well, either way, you'd better hustle to town and order it. It's not something they can whip up in five minutes. They might not have any left as it is."

"I'll help you with the tractor first." Nate looked across the table at his father.

Tom shook his head. "Better run on into town. We can wait until you get back. It shouldn't take long. I need to pay a few bills and catch up on a little book work."

"You should be at the flower shop when they open. They're terribly busy this time of year."

"I'll do the dishes first." When his mother started to protest, Nate shook his head. "No argument. I have plenty of time. You go gather the eggs and feed your chickens, and I'll clean up in here."

"You're scared one of those chickens will peck you." Chris scooted back from the table.

"You got that right. They never have liked me." And he was afraid that if one decided to take offense at his presence, his mother would be frying chicken for supper.

4

At one minute to 9:00, Nate pulled up in front of Buds and Blooms as someone inside flipped on the neon "Open" sign in the window. He glanced down the empty street, relieved there wasn't a line of people waiting to dash through the door.

When he went inside, the young clerk smiled at him, her blonde ponytail bouncing as she walked behind the counter. Either she was part of the high school on-the-job-training program or she'd recently graduated. "Good morning. Are you here to pick up an order?"

"No, but I'd like to order a mum."

"I'm sorry, but the cutoff to order mums was Monday. We've been swamped."

Nate frowned, squelching an irritated retort. "Is there another place in town I can get one?"

"The high school choir is doing some as a fund-raiser, but I think their cutoff was last week sometime."

A woman carrying a big vase of yellow roses stepped from the back workroom, the flowers hiding her face. Nate figured she'd come out to give the clerk some support. When she set the vase on a side table, he recognized her. "Good morning, Mrs. Snyder."

"Nate! Welcome home." She rushed around the counter to give him a big hug. "Are you home for a nice long visit?"

"No, ma'am. My tour was up, so I decided to get out. I'll be working at the Callahan Ranch and helping the folks out on the farm."

"Oh, my goodness, your parents must be as happy as pigs in a peach orchard."

"Yes, ma'am."

"They're so proud of you. We all are. How's your dad?"

"He says he's getting better every day. They're planning to go to the game."

She laughed and picked up an order pad. "It would take more than neck surgery to keep that ol' quarterback cooped up in his house at homecoming."

"Yes, ma'am."

"Now, what kind of mum do you want? Real or silk?"

Frowning, the younger woman stared at

Mrs. Snyder. "But, you said —"

The florist interrupted her. "We'll make an exception for Nate. You probably haven't met him." She glanced back at him. "This is Marcy Phillips. Marcy, this is Nate Langley, Callahan Crossing's very own Iraq war hero."

Marcy's eyes widened. "You're the guy who won the Silver Star? The one who rescued those wounded men?"

"Yes, ma'am." Embarrassed, Nate shrugged. "But I didn't do anything special. Anybody on the team would have done the same thing." He turned his attention to Mrs. Snyder. He was probably being rude to the girl, but he didn't want to talk about that day. Ever. Nor did he like the hero worship that suddenly lit her face. He wasn't a hero. Just a regular guy who had done his job. And he hadn't done it all that well, either. If his leg hadn't given out on him and he'd been able to get Lt. Myers across the street, the man might not have lost his arm. "So which is better, real or fake?"

"Most girls — and women — prefer the silk ones. They don't make you sneeze, and a girl can keep them forever if she wants to. We have single, double, and triple. We have some samples over here. Marcy, will you put those roses in the cooler for me? Then you can go back and work on the orders. I'll keep an eye on the front for now."

Marcy nodded, cast a longing glance at Nate accompanied by a wistful sigh, then picked up the roses and carried them to the cooler.

The florist led Nate around a tiered stand full of multicolored bouquets toward the back wall. Out of the corner of his eye, he noted Marcy glance his way once more before she went into the back room.

He turned his attention to the big homecoming display hanging on the wall. He'd forgotten how much froufrou stuff went on a mum. Or maybe they'd simply gotten a lot bigger since he was in high school. Besides one to three huge white chrysanthemums on a stiff sparkling gold base, there were dozens of fancy white, purple, and gold ribbons hanging down, decorated with all sorts of things. A couple of them even had a small teddy bear nestled in the middle of the flower.

He rubbed the back of his neck. "They look bigger and fancier than they used to. They must weigh a ton." Jenna was on the short side. The ribbons would probably drag on the ground.

"The triple ones are very heavy. Usually only the seniors — as in high school, not ladies your grandmother's age — like those. We sometimes wire them onto a special harness." A sparkle lit Mrs. Snyder's eyes. "So who's your girl?"

"She's not really my girl, just an old friend." Not his girl — yet.

"Okay." She dragged the word out as if she didn't believe him. "Then if you'll tell me her name, I can probably tell you what kind of flower she likes." When Nate hesitated, she laughed. "Hon, everybody is going to see you together at the game, so it can't be a big secret."

He hoped his tan hid the blush warming his cheeks. "Jenna Colby."

"Well, hot dog! It's about time somebody convinced that young lady to go on a date."

"It's not a date. We're just going to the game together."

"But you're buying her a mum."

"It doesn't seem right for her not to have one."

Marcy popped her head around the door frame, obviously about to say something. Mrs. Snyder frowned and shook her head, her lacquered silver and black puffy curls not moving a whisper. The girl ducked back inside the workroom.

"Excellent point. I think Jenna would prefer a single one. But we'll put lots of ribbons and trinkets on it. And a teddy bear. We weren't doing teddy bears when you two were in high school." She pointed to some of the ribbons. "We'll do one with her name and the year she graduated. She and my Becki Sue were in the same class, so that's easy to remember." She scribbled on the pad. "Another for you, with your graduation year. You were a year ahead of her, weren't you? Same year as her brother Chance?" Nate nodded. "Another because she was homecoming queen. And one with your football number, which was?"

"Ten." Texas high school football teams didn't necessarily follow NFL rules when it came to assigning jersey numbers to the different positions.

"And anything else I think of." She grinned at Nate. "Sometimes inspiration hits in the middle of putting one together. I'll add some footballs and megaphone trinkets because she was a cheerleader. The school banned bells for the high school girls. Since they often wear them to school on Friday, the bells were too disruptive. But we could put some on Jenna's if you want."

Nate thought they would probably get annoying. "No, let's skip them. And she's only five-foot-three, so don't make the ribbons too long. Can't have her tripping on them."

"Got it." She made a note on the pad, then rested her hand on his upper back. "I'd like to add some little American flags. If you're like my husband, you probably don't want to talk about war, but I'm sure you're proud to have served your country."

"Yes, ma'am. A few small flags would be fine."

"I'll add some braided ribbon garlands too. We have some already made. That'll give it a little more pizzazz."

"Pizzazz." Nate nodded, smiling at her. "I like that."

"Okay. Let's go ring this up. I don't think we can have it done before noon tomorrow."

"That will be fine." He followed her to the cash register, noting the price list on the wall. Doing a quick mental calculation, he figured it was going to cost over one hundred dollars, maybe a lot over depending on how many doodads she added. But he didn't care what it cost to have something special made for Jenna.

"That will be eighty-five dollars, including the tax."

Skimming the price list again, he said, "You must be running a special."

Back in the workroom, Marcy suddenly had a fit of coughing.

"Yes, we are." Mrs. Snyder's serene expression belied the gleam in her eyes.

Nate handed her four twenties and a five. He ought to insist she charge him the full price, but doing something nice for him was making her happy. "You're sure that's the right amount?"

"Positive. Oh, I forgot to ask if you want a garter to wear on your arm." She pointed to some small mums with short ribbons hanging on the wall nearby. "They're all the rage with the high school guys."

"Then it's a good thing I'm not still in high school. I'd feel a little weird wearing one of those." As crowded as the stadium would be, he also thought the flower would be squished flat before halftime. "Thanks, but I'll pass."

"Fine with me. Enjoy the game, and tell Jenna hello for me."

"Yes, ma'am. I will." Nate glanced at his watch: 9:15. He had plenty of time to do the things he needed to before Jenna and Will picked him up. He didn't think the parade would be a problem. But he was worried about the pep rally, specifically the bonfire. He'd prayed all the way to town that it wouldn't cause another nightmare. Or worse, trigger a flashback. He hadn't had any yet, but he knew people sometimes did. After he got hurt, he'd developed an over-

75

whelming fear of fire, which was another reason he hadn't reenlisted. He couldn't risk possibly putting others in danger because he was a coward.

As Nate left the shop, the little bell on the door tinkled. Marcy came out front where she could see through the window and watched him walk to his pickup. "The newspaper said he rescued those guys even though he was wounded."

"That's right." Mrs. Snyder joined her. She watched him quickly scan his surroundings and check the back of the dark blue truck before he climbed in. She blinked back a tear. "I found another article online that gave more detail. He was injured when a man blew himself up in the building they were searching."

Marcy shuddered, and Mrs. Snyder put an arm around her shoulders. "Though he was hurt in the blast, Nate got one man to safety and went back for the other one. That's when his arm got burned, but that didn't stop him. He carried the second soldier out of the burning building, but when he reached the middle of the street, his injured leg gave way. He shielded the man from gunfire with his own body for over twenty minutes. And he took out one of the al-Qaida that was firing at them, even though he was lying in the street."

"It's a miracle he survived," Marcy whispered.

"Yes, it is."

"That's why you gave him the discount?"

"Partly. I'm thankful he made it home safe and sound. I'd do it for any of our men and women serving over there. It's a small way of saying thanks."

"So should we call Mr. Callahan and tell him he doesn't have to buy one for his daughter? It's next on the order sheet."

"No, go ahead and make it. I'm sure Nate wants to surprise Jenna. And Dub can afford it." She laughed as Nate drove away. "Knowing him, he'll have Sue wear both of them."

"Nate seemed a little uncomfortable about the whole thing. Like maybe buying the mum was a bigger deal than he wanted it to be. Do you think he'll chicken out and not give it to her?"

"No. You didn't see his eyes when he talked about her." She squeezed Marcy's shoulder, then released her and stepped away. "Romance is in the air, even if they don't want to admit it."

"I guess we can't tell anybody about him getting her the mum, huh?"

"That's right. We have to keep Nate's

secret like we're keeping quiet about every other man and boy who has ordered one." Mrs. Snyder's eyes sparkled merrily as she reached for the phone. "But I can tell my Roger that Nate's back and home to stay."

By noon, the whole town was buzzing with the news.

5

As they pulled up to Main Street, Will pointed toward the red-brick Callahan Crossing National Bank with a grin. "Looks like folks found out that you're home."

Nate studied the electronic reader board in the bank parking lot. Underneath the date and current temperature of seventy-seven degrees was a general greeting to the returning alumni. Below that, in capital letters three times the size of the others, two lines declared: WELCOME HOME SGT. NATE LANGLEY.

The welcome and the acknowledgment touched him, making his throat tighten.

They turned left onto Main, and Jenna let out a little squeak. She leaned up from the backseat of the pickup, her hand wiggling beside his face as she pointed from one side of the street to the other. "Look at that! There are signs everywhere."

"Erry-where," Zach repeated from his car

seat next to her.

Nate stared in amazement as Will slowly drove down the street. Practically every store downtown had a sign welcoming him home. On the north side of the street, City Drug and Ben's Auto Parts held similar greetings on the display boards that hung over the sidewalk. A large handwritten poster framed by a couple of old American flags in the window of Maisie's Antiques and Emporium not only greeted him but declared that he was a hometown hero.

Across the street, Brower Realty and Pickering's Insurance shared their feelings on the advertising space that stretched above the windows of their adjoining offices. Next door, the guys at Hunter's Sporting Goods had put up an even bigger sign than Maisie's, one that about filled one window.

"Looks like Maisie and Bob have a little competition going on," said Will.

"Friendly competition," added Jenna. "Mom and Dad saw them together at the Steak House the other night lookin' pretty cozy."

"Chance said he'd heard they were dating." Will turned into the empty lot between Hunter's and the Movie Place. There was still space for a few more vehicles.

Nate smiled at the thought of Bob Hunter,

a big bear of a man, dating tiny dynamo Maisie Sparks. They'd both be about sixty by now, and each had been alone for several years. He figured they'd be good for each other.

He glanced down the street, spotting his name on the big advertising board at the used car dealership, right above the week's hot buy — a 2002 Chevy pickup "with all the bells and whistles." Across the street from the car lot, a couple of guys at the hardware store were hanging another banner above the "Go Wolves!" sign that draped across the high false front of the old building. This one, too, was for him.

Nate was deeply moved by all the expressions of support and caring, but he was also embarrassed by all the fuss. "I hope they've done this for all the returning soldiers."

"They have," Will assured him, nodding to his mother and father as they pulled in beside them. They planned to take Zach home later so that Jenna could stay for the bonfire. "It's the town's way of telling y'all how proud we are of you and how thankful we are that y'all came home safe and sound."

Nate could agree with the safe part. But he wasn't so sure about being sound. His body was fine, but sometimes he worried about his mind. *Give it time,* he thought. *I'll settle down in a few weeks. Get back to normal.* Whatever normal was.

"It's almost time for the parade to start," said Jenna. "Shall we set up the lawn chairs?"

Laughing, Will glanced at Nate and opened the truck door. "What she's really asking is if we'll take care of the lawn chairs while she fusses with little britches."

"Chair," called Zach.

Nate glanced over the seat back as he climbed out of the truck. The kid was already squirming, wanting out. "Hang on, buddy. Give your mama time to unfasten you."

Jenna grinned as she got out of the truck. "Waiting isn't in his vocabulary."

Nate shut his door and chuckled as she leaned back in to release the straps holding Zach in the car seat. "It probably won't be for a long time."

She looked pretty, but to him she'd be attractive no matter what she wore. Decked out in purple jeans and a matching Western shirt with gold embroidered flowers, she once again wore the school colors. Her white tennis shoes didn't go with the outfit, but maybe she couldn't find any purple or gold boots. He looked closer at her dangling earrings. Gold megaphones. Where in the world had she found those?

She always had believed in dressing for the occasion. And she'd had the money to do it. Probably even more so now. Given the bucks Jimmy Don made in football, he figured she received some nice alimony payments. He was surprisingly relieved to note that she had put on a normal, everyday straw cowboy hat, instead of something that likely came from Neiman Marcus.

He'd done his part by wearing a purple T-shirt with Callahan Crossing Wolves printed on it along with a picture of the school mascot. Thankfully, the grocery store hadn't sold out yet when he stopped by there that morning. The old one he'd found in his dresser was faded and a size too small. It tickled him that Zach had on a new one exactly like his.

He walked around to the bed of the truck and took the two lawn chairs Will handed him. By the time Jenna and Zach joined them and her parents, they had the chairs and a small cooler lined up along the back side of the sidewalk in front of the pickups.

Though the little boy now wore a straw cowboy hat, he had on sturdy leather shoes. Given the way the kid ran around, he'd probably trip all over the place in boots —

if they made them that small.

When Jenna set Zach on the ground, he raced toward Dub. "Papa!"

Beaming, the tough rancher picked up his grandson and gave him a big hug. "Hi, Zach. Are you ready for the parade?"

He nodded, brushing Dub's chin with the brim of his hat. "My see parade."

Nate said hello to Sue and grinned at Dub. "So how long has it been since he's seen you?"

Dub laughed and shifted Zach so he could look around. "Since they left the house."

Zach wiggled, and Dub set him down on the ground. "You stay right here with us, understand?"

"Yeah." Zach wandered over to Jenna. "Nana."

"Okay." Jenna opened the bag beside her chair and pulled out a banana. She peeled it partway down and broke off about an inch-long piece. "Don't cram it all in at once."

Zach nodded, reaching for the banana, and took a bite. After he chewed and swallowed, he looked over at Nate. "Nana?"

"I'm still full from lunch, but thanks for offering." Nate winked at Zach and received a grin in return. He noted that Will and his mother left an empty seat beside Jenna. Sue told Dub to take the seat next to her and save the one on the end of the row for Chance. That made three members of the Callahan clan who were in favor of them getting together. When Dub didn't glare at him as he sat down, Nate relaxed.

"He's good at sharing for his age." Nate watched Zach shove the rest of the banana piece into his mouth, then swipe his hand on the side of his jeans. Did all kids wipe their hands that way or only little boys? Or grown men, he thought ruefully, aware that he still sometimes did the same thing.

"With food." Jenna held out another piece of fruit to her son, but he was distracted by some older boys chasing each other around the nearby cars. "And he's getting better with toys." She tipped her head, studying Nate's face. "So how did you know that? I don't remember you having much to do with little kids."

Nate kept his eye on Zach as he edged past him to watch the other boys. "I made friends with some Iraqi children in the neighborhoods we usually patrolled and at an orphanage. They taught me how to play soccer, and I made them laugh."

"You told jokes in Arabic?"

"No, but they laughed at my Arabic, though I wasn't intentionally trying to be funny. Mainly they were amused because I was so uncoordinated trying to hit the ball off my knee and head. I did fine with my feet, but it took awhile to get the rest of it down."

"Maybe longer than you really needed?" She gave Zach the rest of the banana when he wandered back to her.

"A little bit. The kids at the orphanage had it pretty rough, so it gave me a good feeling to make them laugh. I helped where I could. Repaired a few things, scrounged some things for them. Several of us went there as often as we could."

Chance joined them, having walked down from his office three blocks north of Main Street. He took the seat beside Dub, then leaned forward to say hello to the rest of the family and Nate. Zach ran over and gave him a slightly messy hug.

Nate pointed to a couple of the "welcome home" signs. "Looks like you started something."

"Wasn't me. I'm not sure who spotted you, but around mid-morning, they started going up all over town before I finished the one at my office. You'll have to come by and see my work of art," he added with a grin.

"It's a surprise, but they're nice. It feels real good to know people care."

A couple of blocks away, the high school band struck up a John Philip Sousa march. Zach's eyes grew wide, and he darted across the sidewalk. Nate and Jenna leaped out of their chairs to catch him, but he stopped at the curb and leaned over to look down the street. "Moo-sic."

"You're a good boy for stopping where you did," said Jenna. "But you need to stay back here with us. We'll see everything as it goes by."

Frowning, Zack shook his head. "See parade."

Nate knelt down beside him. "Come back to our chairs, and I'll put you on my shoulders. Then you can see better. Okay?"

Zach thought about it for a few seconds, then nodded. He spun around and raced to the chairs. Nate followed, tossing his hat on the chair seat, and swung the little boy up on his shoulders. Holding him securely, he stepped around behind Will. "Can you see the band?"

Zach's whole body wiggled in excitement. "Band. Moo-sic." His heels alternately tapped against Nate's chest, keeping time to the music.

"Zach, are you marching?" Nate grinned down at Jenna when she looked up at them. Her expression softened with tenderness, and his heart did a Texas two-step. Then sadness flickered across her face, and he frowned, mouthing, "What?" She shook her head and quickly turned back to watch the approaching parade.

Less than half a block away, the band began the school fight song — an original piece written by a student some twenty years earlier — and everybody on both sides of the street stood up and cheered. "Go Wolves," hollered Will, waving both fists in the air. Chance clapped and yelled, "Stomp the Tigers." Nate joined in with a loud whistle, and Zach added a "yea" of his own.

Suddenly, Nate was overwhelmed at being home — not merely on U.S. soil but being in Texas, where football was king, and in Callahan Crossing, where practically everyone turned out to support the school. He glanced around and across the street. Probably more than half of the men raising a ruckus — from twentysomethings up to a couple of old-timers leaning on canes — had played football for CC High. And if they hadn't, they'd likely been involved in some other sport or school activity, as had the women.

This love of family and community was more than a tradition. It was the heart of the town. This same spirit was found in thousands of communities all across Texas, and in some form or another in towns and cities all across the United States. This freedom — to live, work, play, worship, and celebrate life — was what he had fought for, what he'd risked dying for. What others *had* died for.

He had longed to be home with the people he loved, in the place he cherished, living the life he dreamed about. Then why did he feel out of place? Why couldn't he relax and truly enjoy it instead of automatically scanning the crowd, looking for danger?

Lord, help me. I don't want to be like this.

"Horsey!"

Zach's excited cry — and a thump on the head by two little hands — brought Nate back to the action as the sheriff's mounted posse came into view. "Wow, that's a bunch of horses."

"There's Deputy Renfro, Zach," said Jenna. "Remember him from church?"

"Uh-huh."

She glanced up at Nate. "Dalton makes it a point to get to know all the kids, even the little ones."

The deputy sheriff spotted Zach and waved. When he focused on Nate, he grinned and gave him a relaxed salute. They had gone through school together. Nate wasn't as close to him as he was to Chance and Will, but he considered him a good friend. Dalton glanced at Jenna, then back at Nate and Zach, his expression turning speculative.

Several of the other riders saw Nate and called out greetings as they rode by. Most knew that he and Jenna had been friends for a long time, so they didn't appear to think anything about him being with her family.

Still, standing up with Zach made them easier to spot. It might not be smart to be quite so obvious. "Let's sit down, bud. I think you can see just as good there, now." He lifted the boy from his shoulders and carefully set him on the ground beside Will.

Will put his arms around Zach and gave him a hug as Nate slipped past and sat down. "Are you having fun?"

Zach nodded, then pointed to a float coming into view. A skirt of purple and gold crepe paper flowers hung from the bed of the large, flat-bed trailer and almost touched the ground. Fake goalposts sat at each end, with the football team in their uniforms standing in the middle, waving at the crowd. Nate recognized Pinky from the grocery store. He'd exchanged the pink wig and tie-dyed shirt for a linebacker's jersey.

"Touchdown!" yelled Zach, throwing his hands up in the air like a referee.

Pinky waved at him and grinned at Jenna, who waved back. "Yeah, little guy! We're gonna make lots of touchdowns tomorrow night."

Zach did his referee imitation again, making Nate laugh. "Who taught him that?"

"Who do you think?" Will asked with a smug expression. "We've been watching the Dallas Cowboys on TV."

Nate turned to Jenna. "Does he know which one is Jimmy Don?"

She shook her head. "He doesn't remember him, so we don't mention it. When he's older, I'll tell him. But right now, he wouldn't understand."

"You mean he never sees Jimmy?" he asked quietly.

"We haven't seen him since the day he walked out on us." She kept her face forward, watching as the float with the cheerleaders came into view. Like the first one, it was covered in paper flowers and held a fake cage with a gigantic stuffed tiger inside. "He doesn't want anything to do with either of us."

Anger swept through him. "How can he turn his back on his son?"

91

"He's too wrapped up in himself to care about anyone else. I hear he's already left wife number two. Thankfully, they didn't have any children. He provided a very generous trust fund for Zach and a huge lump sum settlement for me. We only communicate through our lawyers." She finally looked at him. "He's never asked about Zach. Not once."

Nate had never liked Jimmy Don, but he hadn't realized he was such a selfish jerk. Focusing on the pom-poms the cheerleaders were waving as they led a cheer, he fought to control his anger. Now, he understood that fleeting sadness he'd seen in her face when she watched him and Zach. Sorrow because the kid's own father didn't care enough about him to share in his life.

Finally, he reached over and curled his hand around hers as it rested on the chair arm. "I really wish I'd asked you out all those years ago."

She blinked and slipped her fingers through his. "I wish you had too." Her gaze drifted past him, settling on her son. "But I don't completely regret marrying Jimmy Don. I wouldn't have Zach if I hadn't."

They watched the little boy bounce and wiggle to the Latin music coming from the Spanish Club float, then shared a smile.

"He's a sweetheart, all right."

Just like his mama, thought Nate.

6

Two hours later, full of barbecued brisket and potato salad, Jenna helped her mom clear off a picnic table at the city park while the men rearranged the lawn chairs in the slowly moving shade of an elm tree. For the second time, Nate placed his chair with the back against the trunk of the big tree. She caught her parents exchanging one of their meaningful glances.

"So what was that look about?" Jenna quietly asked her mother as they dumped the paper plates and napkins, along with the plastic utensils and empty containers, into the garbage can.

"Part memory and part understanding," said Sue, watching Zach carry a toy dump truck over to some bare dirt beneath the tree. "Protecting his back is the kind of thing a man does when he's been in a war. It used to get tricky when we'd go out to eat with other vets. All the guys wanted to face the door or a window, with their backs against the wall. I suppose it's a common trait for most anyone who has been in a dangerous situation."

"Dad still does that sometimes."

"Yes, but now it doesn't bother him too much if he can't." Sue rested her hand on Jenna's shoulder. "It's going to take Nate time to get used to civilian life, honey. He'll never be the same as he was before."

"We all change, Mom. Some more than others. But life would be pretty dull if we didn't." Nate's laughter drew her gaze and made her smile. "He's having a good time. I'm glad he came with us."

"Me too."

Walking back to rejoin the others, Jenna noted that once again her family had managed for her and Nate to sit side by side. She kept her eye on Zach as he pushed around his dump truck with the Callahan Construction logo neatly painted on the door. About once a minute, he would stop and add two or three pebbles to the load. When it was almost full, he drove it over next to a tree root and lifted the trailer, dumping the rocks out.

Nate chuckled. "Has he been watching Chance work?"

"We were out at his building site last week.

95

Chance gave him a whole set of construction equipment for his first birthday, though he was a little small to play with most of it. There are still a few pieces that he doesn't quite have down, like the crane."

"He was doing okay with it the other night," said Chance. "We had a good time hauling stuff around the living room."

"You're giving that boy a split personality, like you," said Will. "Half the time he won't know whether he's wranglin' a horse or a bulldozer."

Chance grinned. "You sayin' I'm weird?"

"Yep." Will grinned back.

"Careful, bro, or I'll take you down and sit on you."

"Yeah? You and who else?"

Nate glanced at Jenna. "They haven't changed a bit."

"Still mostly talk and not much action."

"Reckon that's good. Otherwise they'd be bruised and bloodied all the time."

Jenna relaxed, enjoying the cool shade, light breeze, and her brothers' banter. Soon the talk turned to the upcoming roundup, but she only halfway paid attention. She knew how her dad ran things. The discussion was mostly for Nate's benefit, to bring him up to speed on the few changes they'd made over the years.

Not all that long ago, she wouldn't have been sitting there. After one disastrous visit to town soon after she returned home, she hadn't set foot off the ranch for almost six months. She wondered if the folks who'd been so cruel in their criticisms and gossip that day had any idea how much they had wounded her. Some probably did, but didn't care. There had always been a few people who resented the Callahans and their success. Others were too caught up in the aura of the hometown-boy-who-made-it-big to look past Jimmy Don's football success and see his failures as a person.

Thankfully, God was faithful. Along with her loving and patient family, the Lord had comforted her, loved her, and brought her out of the depths of her despair. There were still remnants of pain, buried so deep that she didn't know if even the Lord could ever root them out. But for the most part, they stayed hidden and rarely bothered her anymore.

For months, she had wrestled with the worry that the gossips might have been right — that the failure of her marriage was really her fault and not Jimmy's. God had slowly given her clarity and understanding. Yes, she had made mistakes. Done things — or not done them — that had contributed to their unhappiness. She had learned from those errors and wouldn't make the same ones again. New ones, probably, but hopefully not the old ones.

When all was said and done, most of the blame lay squarely on her ex-husband's shoulders. In hindsight, she could see that he had always been self-centered, but fame and fortune had magnified it until his selfishness had become astounding. She knew that she still hadn't quite forgiven him, but she was working on it. Every day she asked God to help her, to wipe away another layer of the bitterness that cloaked her heart. Someday, it would be completely gone.

"Swing, Mama." Zach stood in front of her, resting his grubby little hands on her jeans. He pointed toward the big set of swings down the hill.

"Okay. Let's put your hat on. It's sunny down there."

He waited impatiently for her to secure the hat on his head, then took off.

"Hey, wait for me." Jenna scrambled out of her chair and jogged a few steps to catch up with him.

"Now I understand why you have on running shoes." Nate fell in step beside her. "Is it okay if I tag along? I'm tired of sitting."

"Sure. You can help push him if I get

tired." They strolled along in comfortable silence, letting Zach run a short distance ahead of them. He stopped by the little kid's swing, made similar to a child's car seat to hold him securely. Jenna lifted him up to the swing, and he poked his feet and legs through the openings.

"Mama, push."

"In a minute. Let me fasten you in." She clipped the safety belt around his middle, then stepped behind him and gave the swing a gentle shove. "Here we go."

Zach laughed and pounded on the molded plastic bar in front of him. "Swing!"

Jenna pushed a little harder, and he giggled. "He'd be happy doing this all afternoon." When Nate didn't make a comment, she looked up. He scanned the park and the people in it, and his gaze narrowed, clearly assessing the situation. Shifting slightly, he stood with legs spread, arms at his side and fists clenched, watching a small but loud group of cowboys and their ladies about fifty yards away. "Looks like they've gone through a few six packs already," she said.

"More than a few."

"They're keeping to themselves. Other than being loud, they aren't bothering anybody."

"And they'd better not." He seemed to realize how tense he was. Uncurling his fists, he shook his arms a little, then tucked his thumbs in the pockets of his jeans. He turned toward Zach, but his gaze darted in the rowdies' direction every few minutes. Jenna had the feeling that if any of them decided to wander their way, they would regret it.

A short, slightly plump blonde and a stocky man walking down the hill drew her attention. Lindsey Moore had been a good friend since junior high, and a closer one since Jenna had moved back home. But she didn't know the man with her.

Lindsey waved. "Hi, y'all." When she reached them, she gave Nate a quick hug. "Welcome home."

"Thanks. You're lookin' pretty as ever."

She laughed, swishing the crinkly skirt of her apple green sundress with the tips of her fingers. "Wider than when you last saw me, but thanks for the compliment. This is my cousin Roger from Sweetwater. We're having a little family reunion this weekend."

Jenna raised one eyebrow. Lindsey came from a very large family. "How little?"

"There will only be seventy-five of us this year. Aunt Liz and her brood couldn't make it this time."

Lindsey introduced Nate and Jenna to her cousin, and they shook hands. "I was giving him a tour of town and spotted you. I couldn't pass up the chance to say hello. How long will you be home?"

"Probably till I'm old and gray." Nate's gaze slid to Jenna for a second before he smiled at Lindsey. "I didn't re-up, so I'm a free man."

"Well, thank you for your service. Roger enlisted in the navy last week."

"Good for you. I thought about the navy," said Nate, "but the one time I'd ridden a ferry boat — the only thing I've ever been on bigger than a ski boat — I got seasick. So I figured I'd better stick with good ol' terra firma."

"I worked on a fishing boat for a while out of Corpus Christi, so I think I'll be all right on the water," Roger said.

"Mama, swing!"

"Oops. I'm falling down on the job. Excuse me." Jenna walked back around behind the swing, giving it a push. Lindsey followed her.

"Lindsey tells me you won a Silver Star." Roger's voice held both awe and eagerness.

"I didn't do any more than anybody else would have done. I was in the right place at the right time. Where do you go for basic?"

"The Great Lakes Naval Training Center on the shore of Lake Michigan. It's halfway between Chicago and Milwaukee."

Nate continued to ask Roger questions about his upcoming training, deftly deflecting the conversation away from himself.

"He doesn't like to talk about it, does he?" murmured Lindsey.

"No. He's embarrassed by all the fuss."

"I saw you two, or I should say three, at the parade." Lindsey had her back to Nate and spoke softly so he wouldn't hear. "So what's the scoop?"

"You know we've all been friends forever. Hanging out with us is normal. Dad hired him to work part-time at the ranch. The rest of the time he'll be helping his folks on the farm. This afternoon, they've been going over the plans for the roundup."

"But he's down here with you. Not up in the shade with Chance and the rest of the family."

"He has a lot of pent-up energy. I don't think he's used to relaxing much. And he likes Zach."

"And you."

"We're only friends, Lin." Jenna caught Zach's hat when he tilted his head back to look up at her. The motion of the swing took him away, so she let him go without it for a

102

little while.

"Methinks the lady doth protest too much."

Maybe. Sometimes when Nate looked at her, her pulse went into overdrive. But Jenna wasn't about to admit it. "Are you going to the bonfire?"

"No. Some of the other relatives are coming in this evening, so I need to be social and help Mom feed them. I'll be at the game, though."

Jenna was relieved that her friend let the conversation shift to other things. She plopped Zach's hat back on his head and chatted with Lindsey for a few minutes about who they had seen in town for homecoming and who they'd heard was planning to be there. As usual, the alumni coming home would increase the population substantially through the weekend.

Lindsey checked her watch and turned to her cousin and Nate. "We'd better get going. The horde will descend on Mom and Dad's place soon."

"That pretty much describes it." Roger shook hands with Nate. "It was good to talk to you."

"You too. Take care."

"I will." Roger nodded, his expression serious as they walked away.

"Were you able to give him any good tips?" asked Jenna when Nate moved a little closer.

"Not many. I don't know much about the navy." The group that had been so boisterous earlier had quieted down, and Nate seemed to relax, turning his attention to Zach. "Somebody's drooping."

Jenna peeked around to look at her son's face. He rubbed his eyes. "Are you ready for a nap, honey?"

"Ye-ah." He sounded too tired to talk.

She lifted him from the swing, and he cuddled close, resting his head on her shoulder, knocking off his hat.

Nate picked it up. "Do you want me to carry him?"

"No, thanks. I want to enjoy the snuggle time."

Zach was almost asleep by the time they reached the family, and she was only a little short of breath. She wondered how long it would be before she couldn't carry him up that hill without huffing and puffing. Her mom had seen them coming and had already picked up Zach's toys and put them in the pickup. Dub held out his arms. "Come here, buddy. Let's get you home for a rest."

Zach raised his head and looked at Jenna.

"Mama, go?"

"I'm staying in town for a while with the guys, but I'll be home before bedtime tonight. You go with Papa and Grandma, okay?"

"Okay," he said sleepily. He let his grandfather lift him from Jenna's arms without a fuss. He'd be sound asleep before they pulled out of the park. As Dub turned away, Zach looked at Nate. "Bye-bye, Nate."

Jenna was surprised by how quickly Zach had taken to him.

Nate swallowed hard, his expression tender as he focused on the little boy. "Bye, Zach. I'll see you soon."

It appeared the handsome cowboy was pretty taken with Zach too.

Jimmy Don was an idiot, but maybe his neglect would make it easier for her son to love a stepfather — if he ever had one.

7

They spent the rest of the afternoon swapping amusing tales, throwing a Frisbee around, and going to the Dairy Queen for sundaes. As dusk began to fall, they drove to the football stadium where the pep rally and bonfire would be held at one end of the dirt parking lot. Will found a parking space at the end of the high school five blocks away. It meant a longer walk but less hassle when it was time to leave. Judging from the crowd streaming toward the stadium, about two hundred people had the same idea.

Nate shifted to high alert. His vision sharpened, rapidly assessing those around them. Was that jacket heavy enough to conceal a gun or a bomb? What was inside that backpack? Why was that guy acting nervous? Nate slowed his pace, keeping his eye on the man in the white shirt and dark slacks. Looking ahead, the man smiled shyly, his face turning red when a pretty blonde hurried up to him. Nate speeded up to rejoin Jenna and her brothers.

Boot heels clicked along the sidewalk. Flip-flops slapped the cement. A Harley motorcycle drove slowly down the street. Gravel crunched as they crossed the driveway that ran around behind the school. A faint squeak drew his attention to a woman pushing a cute little girl in a bright pink lightweight stroller. Were those cloth pig's ears sticking out of the stroller's canopy?

Jenna noticed his double take. "That's the Piglet stroller from Disney."

"As in Winnie the Pooh?"

She looked surprised. "You know about Winnie the Pooh?"

He leaned closer, breathing in the soft coconut scent of her shampoo. "I had a Pooh bear when I was little. Real little." He straightened. "But don't tell anybody."

"Don't tell anybody what?" asked Will.

Jenna glanced up at Nate and winked. "Nothing."

Nate wasn't ashamed of having a bear when he was a toddler, but he knew the Callahan boys, especially Will, would figure out a way to kid him about it. And he wasn't in the mood for teasing. Even if the fragrance of coconut and a bright pink stroller with pig's ears eased his tension slightly.

Until he caught a whiff of smoke from somebody's barbecue. His mouth went dry and sweat broke out on his forehead. How long before the football team tossed torches onto the huge stack of dried scrap wood? Years ago, he'd been one of those wielding a torch to light the bonfire. Now the thought of it made his heart pound. *Lord, help me through this. Don't let me lose it.*

They strolled between the cars in the parking lot until they reached the back half of it, which had been roped off to keep the vehicles at a safe distance. Jenna spotted a group of old friends from out of town and rushed over to give them hugs amid girlish squeals and laughter.

Nate stared at the thirty-foot-tall pile made mostly of old pallets with some wooden odds and ends tossed around the bottom and a weather-beaten chicken coop perched precariously at the top. The stench of diesel hung in the air.

Foreboding crawled along his skin.

He couldn't do this.

He took a deep, slow breath. He had to do this. For Jenna. For himself.

"Our outhouse was better than that chicken coop." Chance's words barely registered. After a long pause, he added, "Earth to Nate."

When his friend nudged him with an elbow, Nate jumped, barely catching himself before he drew back a fist. He shoved his hands in his pockets to hide their trembling.

Chance frowned, his eyes filled with concern. "You all right?"

"A little jumpy."

"Hey, man, we don't have to stay."

"No, it's okay." Nate took a deep breath, focusing on Jenna. The women were all talking and giggling at the same time. "I think we've been beamed back to high school." His voice was steady. Maybe nobody else would notice that he had a major case of the jitters.

"It's good to see her having fun and acting a little goofy. So do you think they had to steal that chicken coop or did someone donate it?"

Nate didn't look at it again. "Donated it. It's too big to carry off without somebody noticing."

"A few years ago, Mr. Brown told me that he spotted us swiping his outhouse."

Nate turned to Chance. "And he didn't come after us with his shotgun? I'm not buyin' it." The fear of the cantankerous old man chasing them off had added to the excitement the night Chance, Nate, and two other guys from the football team appropriated the rickety one-holer in the name of school spirit. Not that Mr. Brown or anybody else had used the outhouse in ages.

"He'd been waiting years for somebody to take it for the bonfire and was about to give up and tear it down. So he was happy as a pig in slop that we hauled it away for him. He even attended the pep rally that year but stayed in the shadows so we wouldn't see him. Said he and his friends had done the same thing when he was a senior." Chance's face broke into a wide grin. "Only the one they pilfered was still in use. They went back the next day and built the owner a new one."

Jenna rejoined them, bringing her friends with her. The Callahan men and Nate were older, but they were acquainted with all of them. In a town the size of Callahan Crossing, most students at least knew the names of all the other people in high school. Nate figured Will and Chance had dated almost all of Jenna's friends at one time or another. They exchanged greetings and visited a bit, catching up on the nutshell version of what each one was currently doing.

Nate noted that a couple of the single ladies were still adept at flirting, though he was surprised when they gave him as much of their attention as they did Chance and Will. It certainly hadn't been that way before he left Callahan Crossing. He tried to be friendly — not easy when he was tied in knots — but not give them any reason to think he might be interested in anything more than a casual group conversation.

When the band began to play, relief that the women's attention turned to the twirlers' routine and the cheerleaders' dance steps swirled with apprehension of what was to come. The first two songs were new ones, but the third was an old standby. Laughing, Jenna and her friends did a few of the more sedate dance moves they'd used to the tune when they were cheerleaders.

Afterward, everyone joined in rousing renditions of several cheers, the last one ending with a mighty shout to "Cage the Tigers!"

The school mascot removed the laughing wolf head on her black and gray costume and handed it to a skinny kid who was at least a foot taller than her. Nate wondered if the outfit had been cheaper in a smaller size.

He glanced at Will. "When did the growling mascot turn into a happy one?"

"A couple of years ago. The old costume wore out, and since a girl usually wears it, they — whoever that is — decided it would be better to project a cheerful image."

"To reflect the expected victories," added Chance dryly. At Nate's skeptical expression, he grinned and shrugged. "I'm simply repeating what the cheer advisor told the newspaper. She said it was called the Big Bad Wolf in the catalog. She seemed to think that would mollify some of the irritated cowboys and former members of the Wolf Pack."

"Did it help?"

"Naw. But we've gotten used to it. Allie has been such a good mascot that nobody complains anymore. Wait until you see her doing flips and cartwheels in that getup."

Allie, the vivacious gymnast-mascot-homecoming-committee-chairman, pulled a white card from a furry pocket. Picking up an electronic megaphone, she announced the award-winning floats from the parade. The freshman class took first prize, the seniors second, and the Spanish Club third.

She passed the megaphone to the head coach and tugged the wolf's head back on, her friend snapping it into place. When she and the cheerleaders moved well away from the woodpile, Nate breathed a little easier. He had a few minutes' reprieve.

The coach introduced each of the football players. Nate was surprised that no one was wearing his old number this time around.

The team captains thanked everyone for coming to the pep rally and promised to give them a good game on Friday night.

Then the senior football players filed over to the back of a truck and picked up the unlighted torches. They formed a circle around an open barrel nearby that held a small fire. At the captain's nod, they dipped the torches into the flame, lifting them up in the air when they ignited.

Nate tried to turn away, but the flickering flames mesmerized him. His mouth went dry. His heart pounded, and his palms grew damp and cold. A shiver swept through him, then another.

With a yell, the football players jogged to their appointed places surrounding the chicken coop's pyre. The team captain gave the count. "One, two, three!" Five torches flew through the air in a low toss, landing at integral points at the base of the pile.

Whoosh!

The dried wood, much of it soaked with diesel, ignited with a roar.

The crowd shouted their approval, and the Wolves' fight song blared in the background. Sparks and embers flew into the air. Smoke billowed upward toward the stars. Crackling. Popping. A steaming, whistling sizzle. Flames danced and leaped, devouring one board after another, shattering the fragile thread holding Nate in the present.

He took the stairs slowly, watching for IED trip wires, listening for any unusual sound. Not that he could hear anything over the shouts of the Iraqi man downstairs. The man talked too fast for interpretation until a phrase jumped out. *Allah be praised.* "Bomb!"

The building shook, the noise deafening. The blast threw Nate near the top of the stairwell, and he sprawled on the stairs. His head throbbed, and a wave of dizziness had him reaching for the wall to steady himself. Pain stabbed his leg. A large jagged chunk of metal protruded from his thigh. Jerking it out, he pulled the silk scarf from around his neck and tightly wrapped the wound, mentally blocking out the pain. Had to move.

Lying on the stairs, he peered around the corner to the second floor. One big room. Empty. Smoke poured up the stairway, making him cough. Over the ringing in his ears, he heard moans. "Brown!" No answer. "Lieutenant!"

"Here, Sarge." The lieutenant's voice was weak.

Bracing against the wall, Nate stood and

hopped down the stairs on his good leg. Paused at the last step. Checked the room. Clear. A crumbled wall splattered with blood and a lone shoe told the fate of the Iraqi man who'd led them into a trap. Broken furniture blazed, and flames slithered through the rubble. Private Brown lay by the door, one leg twisted and broken, his helmet blown out into the street. Head wound, possibly a bad one.

Lieutenant Myers sat against the remnants of another wall, struggling to tie a tourniquet above a gaping wound in his upper arm. Nate dropped to one knee beside him, catching his breath at the pain ripping through his leg, and quickly tied the cord around Myers's arm. Did the officer realize that the bones were crushed? Trying to avoid the smoke, he dipped low and dragged in a breath of air.

"Get Brown out of here," said the lieutenant, coughing. "I'll be behind you."

Nate carefully lifted the kid from Ohio and laid him across his shoulder. Myers was on his feet. Nate hid behind the doorframe, surveying the area. Across the street, a young Iraqi woman opened the door of her house, quickly looked around, and motioned for him to bring the wounded man inside.

Limping, Nate ran across the empty street

as best he could. Hot, sticky blood saturated the bandage and the leg of his fatigues, oozing into his boot. He laid Brown on the floor of the house. Stepped back to the doorway. Street clear. *Where's Myers?* Smoke poured from the damaged house. Flames leaped from the roof and one shattered window.

He started back across the street. Couldn't run. Leg dragging. *Can't stop.*

Shouts down the street. American.

Myers on the floor. Door and wall on fire. *Have to get him.* Go through the flames.

Roof collapsing. *Shield the lieutenant.* Searing pain. Smell of burning flesh. *Mine.* Flames everywhere. Gunfire outside.

I will not die in here.

8

"We need to move back. It's too hot." Jenna tugged on Nate's arm, but he didn't seem to hear her. He stared at the flames, his body rigid, his hands knotted into fists. He was breathing way too fast. Sweat rolled down his face. She tugged harder. "Nate, we have to move back."

First one person, then another jostled him as the crowd moved away from the fire. He looked at her, his eyes filled with sheer terror one second, blazing with fury the next.

She dropped her hands and took a step back. "What's wrong?"

Without a word, he spun around and pushed through the crowd, shoving people out of his way. When he got past them, he broke into a run.

Jenna met Will's startled gaze, then turned to Chance. "What in the world just happened?"

"I think the fire got to him." Chance

shouted to be heard above the cheer the pep squad was leading. "We'd better go after him."

It took a few minutes to work their way through the crowd. At the street, they spotted Nate running full out toward the other end of the high school. Not an easy task in boots. He slowed to a jog, then a walk.

Jenna mentally kicked herself. She should have considered the possibility that the bonfire might bring back bad memories. No one forced him to come with them, but Nate was like most of the men she knew, macho to the core. He would never have admitted that the fire might bother him.

When they caught up with him, he was leaning forward against Will's truck, his hands on the hood, back curved, head down. Jenna and Will hung back, letting Chance take the lead.

"Are you all right?" Chance stopped beside Nate but didn't touch him.

"Yeah." He straightened and turned around to face them. Enough light shone from the streetlight on the corner to see that his hands were shaking. "I think so." He glanced at Jenna. "I thought I could handle the fire, but guess I was wrong."

"It's okay." She smiled, trying to reassure him. "You didn't knock anybody down."

He frowned. "What do you mean?"

Oops. "You were in a big hurry to get out of there."

He rubbed the back of his neck and slumped against the pickup. "So I was a jerk."

"Don't worry about it," said Will. "It didn't seem to bother anybody for more than a minute. They probably figured you got a spark down your shirt. Or were getting even for all the people who bumped you as they moved back from the fire."

Confusion clouded Nate's face, and he shook his head. "I don't remember any of that."

"I think you were caught up in some bad memories," Jenna said gently. She pretended to yawn. "I don't know about y'all, but I'm ready to head home. I want to see my little guy before he falls asleep."

"Don't you mean before you fall asleep?" teased Will, playing along.

"Well, that too." She slipped her hand around Nate's upper arm. "Come on, cowboy. Let's hit the trail."

He straightened with a smile, though it looked strained. "Gettin' a little corny, aren't you?"

She gave him a cheeky grin and tucked

her hair behind her ear. "Being true to my roots."

They walked around to the passenger side of the truck. Nate paused and made a show of studying her ear.

"What are you doing?"

"Looking for corn silk."

"No silk. And my ears aren't long, green, and pointed, either."

"Are you sure?"

She made a face. Nate smiled, thankful that she was still speaking to him. He'd heard guys talk about flashbacks, but he'd never experienced one before. At least not one when he was awake. Dreams were another matter. Opening the back door, he waited as she tucked her tiny purse in the backseat pocket.

Ka-boom!

"Incoming!" Nate grabbed Jenna and dove for the pavement, holding her so he absorbed part of the impact. He instantly rolled, covering her body with his, shielding her.

"Nate!"

He flinched as Jenna's shout rang in his ear. Smoke lingered in the air, but he hadn't seen where the bomb landed.

"Stay down. There might be another rocket."

"Rocket? What are you talking about? Get off me." Jenna tugged her arms out from between them and shoved against his shoulders. Not that a pipsqueak like her could move him an inch.

"Stay still." His order, spoken in his most commanding sergeant's voice, quieted her for all of two seconds.

"Nate, let me up."

Nate tipped his head, searching the darkness. Where had it come from? He noted Chance standing about five feet away. Beyond him, since his line of sight was at ground level, were two other pairs of boots along with several tennis shoes and a pair of purple flip-flops.

"Uh, amigo, a car backfired." Chance spoke cautiously, as if he wasn't sure what Nate might do next.

There was no debris. No rocket-propelled grenade. Nothing had blown up. The smoke was from the bonfire. He was on Walnut Street in Callahan Crossing.

And he had thrown Jenna to the ground. In front of who knew how many people.

He pushed up on his hands, rolled off her, and sprang to his feet. "Jenna, I'm sorry." He held out his hand to help her up, but she ignored it. When she sat up, he reached down to take her arm, but she shifted away.

121

"Wait a minute." She ran her fingers over the back of her head.

"Did I hurt you?" Was she just stunned or had he given her a concussion? "Is your head okay?"

"I bumped it, but there's no knot." She twisted her arm around and tried to see her elbow in the dim light. "I scraped my arm."

Nate's gut twisted. "Can you stand up?"

She nodded, then winced. He squatted, putting his arm around her, and helped her up.

"I'm all right." With a wary glance in his direction, she moved a few steps away. "Just a little shaken."

So was he. Only "a little" was an understatement.

He stood close by in case she needed assistance climbing into the truck, but she carefully avoided touching him. Her message was clear. She didn't want anything to do with him.

His face flaming in embarrassment, Nate glanced around. His gaze landed on Charlie Smith, a cowboy about the same age as his father.

"I thought that was you, Nate." Charlie stepped over and held out his hand. Nate absently shook hands with him. "Looks like you got a good case of battle rattle."

"Something like that." He nodded a curt greeting to another couple and their kids, who watched him curiously. He wished they'd go find their car and leave him alone.

Charlie leaned closer. Nate smelled liquor on his breath and remembered his dad saying that when Charlie came home from Nam, he'd been a drunk. "You make friends with ol' Jack Daniels, son. A couple of shots of whiskey will calm those nerves right down."

"I'll keep that in mind, sir." As something not to do. "Good to see you." He sent Will a let's-get-out-of-here look and opened the front passenger door of the truck. Chance had already joined Jenna in the backseat.

"We'd better get goin'," said Will, climbing into the pickup. "Take it easy, Charlie."

"Tell your dad hello for me." The older cowboy spit tobacco juice onto the pavement, splattering his boots.

"I'll do that. See you Sunday at church."

"I'll be there."

Nate climbed in the pickup and shut the door as Will started the engine. "So he's still coming to church with a hangover?"

"Most every Sunday. But at least he comes." Will carefully backed out. People were beginning to stream away from the bonfire, but they would beat the crowd.

Nobody said a thing all the way back to Chance's office. When Will pulled up in front of the redbrick building, Nate had the pickup door open before he stopped. He couldn't bail out of there fast enough. "I'll go with Chance. Thanks for the ride, Will."

"Sure thing."

Jenna opened her door, almost bumping him, and hopped out. He stepped back, but when she looked up at him with a perplexed frown, he was tempted to put his arms around her and hold her close. He clasped his hands behind him and apologized again instead. "I'm so sorry," he said softly. "That backfire sounded like an RPG going off."

Her frown deepened. "What's that?"

"A rocket-propelled grenade. They blow things up. I hit the ground automatically."

"And took me with you." She didn't sound quite as upset as she had earlier.

"I was trying to protect you." He shrugged. "That was automatic too."

"Do you dive for the ground a lot?"

He shook his head. "Most of the time I just duck." That was true. He'd only hit the deck twice since he came back to the States. "But it's pretty ingrained when you're in a war zone. Takes awhile to shift gears."

"I'll keep that in mind."

And keep her distance. She didn't say it,

124

but Nate figured that was what she was thinking. He didn't blame her. She thought he was nuts. Anybody would who witnessed his crazy behavior. And he'd had an audience, he thought grimly, both at the bonfire and in the street.

Maybe he *was* loco. Or heading that way fast. He hadn't merely remembered what happened in Iraq; he'd relived it. The sights, sounds, smells, tastes — the fear and the pain — had been as real as the day the suicide bomber almost killed them. His reaction to the car backfiring had been much the same, only briefer.

As he watched Jenna and Will drive away, he tried to piece together what happened between the bonfire blazing to life and standing in front of Will's truck, breathing hard. He'd obviously run down the street. Going by what Jenna said, he'd shoved people out of the way. He could picture that well enough — plowing through the crowd, knocking people left and right. But he couldn't remember it.

And that scared him as much as the flashback.

9

"Ouch!" Sue paused in pinning Jenna's mum on her silky gold blouse and sucked the spot on her index finger that she had poked.

"Do you want me to try it? You've already jabbed yourself twice." Jenna watched a tiny drop of blood seep from the skin as her mom checked her finger.

"No, I'll get it. It's hard to see what I'm doing with this nice big flower." She smiled at Dub and touched the one she was wearing. "They're beautiful as usual."

Jenna's dad leaned against the kitchen counter. "But a pain to pin on." He looked down at his thumb. "There ought to be a better way of fastening those things. Whoever came up with the idea of wearing mums to homecoming, anyway?"

"An ingenious florist, no doubt." Jenna's mom went back to work, finally getting the second long corsage pin to go through both the material and the flower.

Jenna glanced at the clock. Nate was due to arrive any minute. If he came. She should have called him to confirm the time he was picking her up. Any excuse to subtly let him know she still wanted to go with him. For a while, she hadn't been so certain about that. Being thrown to the ground had been unnerving and painful. In retrospect, she realized he had tried to take the brunt of the fall on himself, but she had still landed hard. Her skinned elbow and a bruise on her shoulder proved it.

She'd had a long talk with her mother, who told her that Nate's response to the backfire wasn't unusual. She shared how Dub had reacted when a plane went over their motel the first night he was home from Viet Nam. He'd dived off the mattress, lifted the whole bed up, and slid under it, even though there wasn't room for him.

Her mom emphasized that Nate had been trying to protect her. That spoke highly of his character despite the threat being false. She was more concerned about how he had reacted to the fire. He had gone through a great deal during the war — probably much more emotional and physical distress and pain than any of them realized.

"If you don't want to go with him, I'll tell

him," said Dub quietly.

"No, Daddy. It's okay. I don't think anything like that will happen again."

"Don't be so sure."

Jenna smiled at her dad, hoping to put him at ease. "I'll be on the alert from now on. If I hear a boom, I'll jump out of the way."

"You goin' to jump every time our team makes a touchdown tonight, and they shoot off the cannon?" Dub crossed his arms.

"He'll expect that noise, so he won't react the same way."

"Maybe." Her father looked so disgruntled that she wondered if he knew something about Nate that she didn't.

"Dad, is there some other reason you don't want me to go out with him?"

Dub looked down at the floor, then sighed and raised his head. "I don't have anything personal against him. I don't want you hurt, baby."

"I know." She walked over and gave him as much of a hug as the big flower would allow. "And I love you for it. But I can't stay scared forever." Stretching up on tiptoe, she kissed him on the cheek. "Thank you for the mum. It's beautiful."

"Boo-ti-ful," called Zach, banging on the side of his booster seat with his sippy cup.

"Can't have my girls going to the game without one."

"Looks like Jenna's going to have two." Will strolled into the kitchen. "Nate's coming up the sidewalk, and he's carrying a big ol' flower box."

"Oh, good grief!" Sue grabbed Jenna by the arm and swung her around. Quicker than a barn swallow after a mosquito, she jerked out the pins she had worked so hard to fasten moments before and tossed the lovely creation at her husband. "Hide that somewhere."

He caught it, frowned at his wife and then at Will, who was trying hard not to laugh. "Now, hold on, woman. I spent good money to buy a flower for my daughter."

"So did that boy walking up to the porch. And you have a lot more of it than he does." Sue waved her hands, shooing him away. "Don't start with me, Dub Callahan. Go."

Dub shook his head and disappeared into the big pantry, muttering about bossy women. The doorbell rang, and Will started for the living room.

His mom shot around in front of him, blocking his path with a hand firmly planted in the middle of his chest. "Stay right where you are and let Jenna answer the door. Nate is her date, not yours."

Will laughed and draped his arms over his mother's shoulders. "I know that. Though Jenna keeps saying it isn't a date. Reckon she's trying to convince us or herself?"

"It isn't," muttered Jenna as she walked past them. Then why was she so nervous? It was only Nate. Gorgeous, slightly messed-up Nate. Vulnerable Nate. That stopped her. She pretended to check her hair in the hall tree mirror near the door as she processed the thought. After what happened last night, he probably wasn't feeling real sure of himself. The truth was, neither was she.

Sheesh, we're a pair. The doorbell rang again, and she hurried to answer it. She couldn't let the poor man think they'd already left. Throwing open the door, she pasted on a smile, which instantly turned into one of admiration at the sight of Nate in a purple Western shirt threaded with metallic silver stripes. *Oh, my.* "Sorry, we were in the kitchen, uh, watching Zach eat his snack."

"Takes all of you to supervise?"

"He's entertaining." She stepped back so he could come in. That wasn't a lie. Her kid was fun to watch. She never knew what he'd come up with.

Nate walked into the room, and she shut

the door. When Jenna turned around, she half expected to see her parents and brother peeking around the kitchen doorway. Thankfully, they'd restrained themselves from watching if not from listening. Absolutely no sound came from the kitchen.

Nate kept a small multicolored flowered gift bag hooked on one finger and handed her the long white box. "Mom said mums were still a tradition, and you'd be embarrassed if you didn't get one."

"Oh." So much for her *friend* wanting to give her something special.

He wrinkled his face. "She brought it up, but I was going to ask her about it."

"You didn't want me to be embarrassed too?" Jenna cringed when she heard the note of sarcasm in her voice. *Don't make a big deal out of this.*

"No." He stopped and looked away, took a big breath and blew it out in a poof. When he met her gaze, his eyes were intense and serious. "That was part of it, I guess. But I got it because I wanted to." He took a step closer. "I wanted to give you something nice and . . . well, to let everybody at the game know that you're with me." His voice grew softer. "That you mean a lot to me."

Okay, so it was a big deal. Much bigger than it should be. *Don't you dare cry, Jenna*

131

Callahan Colby. "Thank you."

She walked around one of the two red leather sofas and laid the box on the massive, square, dark brown leather and oak coffee table. Sliding off the top of the flower box, she set it aside and tried to ignore the rapid *ka-thump* of her heart. She hadn't had this many butterflies since her first date with Jimmy Don, which had also been to a homecoming game.

Don't go there. Don't think about him. She would not let him ruin tonight.

Nate followed her and set the gift bag on the table.

Carefully lifting the lavender tissue paper, she gasped. It was the biggest, tackiest, most beautiful mum she had ever seen. A white teddy bear wearing a cute little black cowboy hat and a purple T-shirt with the number ten — Nate's old number — was tucked right in the middle of the huge silk chrysanthemum. Two white ribbons, one with her name and the other with Nate's in gold letters, were prominently displayed among at least twenty purple and gold ones. Another white and gold one declared that it was homecoming and the year.

"Wow." Lifting it from the box, she held it out in front of her. Besides the regular ribbons, there were four fancy braided purple and gold garlands. Several of the smooth ones had things written on them in either sparkly gold or glittering purple letters — Homecoming Queen and the year, Cheerleader, All-Region WR with the two years Nate had been honored as one of the best wide receivers in the region, along with the years both had graduated. There were the usual megaphones and football trinkets with several tiny cowboy hats thrown in for good measure. But what tugged at her heart the most were the silver stars and tiny American flags sprinkled throughout.

Nate shifted his feet. "Mrs. Snyder and I talked about some of the stuff, but she added a lot more. She got a little carried away."

"It's fantastic. The best I've ever seen." Jenna laid it down carefully and edged around the table, giving him a quick hug. "Thank you."

"You really like it? It's not over the top?"

"Yes, I like it." She ducked her head for a second, then looked up into the worry coloring his eyes a cloudy blue and grinned. "And, yes, it's a little over the top, but that's part of what makes it so great. With these things, the more stuff the better. Maybe I'm silly, but it's going to be fun to impress the high school girls and my old friends, both with this whoppin' mum and my cool hunk of a date."

Nate finally grinned. He reached down and nudged the teddy bear in the stomach, tipped his head, and met her gaze. "I don't know about being cool or a hunk, but I like the date part."

Zach came barreling out of the kitchen. "Nate!"

Nate moved over so the little boy could make a beeline for him. "Hi, buddy." He scooped him up and gave him a playful hug. "What have you been up to?"

"Snack."

"Oh yeah? What did you have?"

"Wo-gurt raisins."

Nate glanced at Jenna and raised an eyebrow.

"Yogurt-covered raisins."

He looked back at Zach. "Are they good?"

The little guy nodded his head. Then he swiveled and looked over his shoulder at the flower and ribbons spread out on the table. His eyes grew wide. "Wow."

Nate laughed and hugged him again. "You sound like your mama."

"Nate brought this for me to wear to the football game."

Zach turned back to Nate. "You go game too?"

"Yep. I'm taking your mama. Is that okay with you?"

Zach looked at Jenna, then back at Nate, his expression thoughtful. "Yeah." He twisted around again, a tiny frown touching his brow. "Mama's bear?"

"Yes. But I brought you something too. It's in that sack on the table."

When Zach squirmed, Nate set him on the floor. He ran to the table and pushed aside the tissue paper in the bag, then pulled out a little white teddy bear identical to Jenna's, cowboy hat, T-shirt, and all. "Cowboy bear!" He hugged it, then looked up at Nate. "My bear?"

"That's right. That one's for you."

"It even has the number Nate wore when he played football." Jenna knelt beside Zach and pointed to the T-shirt. "Ten."

"Ten."

"Tell Nate thank you."

"Thank you. My show Papa." Zach raced around the table and met the rest of the family coming out of the kitchen.

"It was very thoughtful of you to bring something for Zach," said Jenna.

Nate shrugged one shoulder. "It was Mrs. Snyder's idea."

Will laughed as he joined them. "Oh, man, don't tell her that. Just say thanks." He shook his head. "I need to give you some lessons on how to impress women."

"How to fool them, you mean." Jenna playfully thumped him on the arm. "You're an expert at that."

"And at dodging serious relationships," added Sue as she walked around the coffee table. "Oh, isn't that lovely."

"Papa's boo-ti-ful. Mommy's 'ovely."

Nate glanced at Dub as Zach leaned back against his grandfather's chest. Holding the bear by both arms, he jiggled it around in a little dance.

Amusement lit the rancher's eyes. "No, he's not saying I'm beautiful. But the mum I gave Grandma is, isn't it?"

"Yeah." Zach looked puzzled, as if something wasn't quite right.

Dub started quietly talking to him about the teddy bear. The women moved over in front of the hall tree mirror while Sue pinned the flower on Jenna's blouse.

Nate had the feeling he'd missed something.

"You did good." Will watched his mother and sister with unabashed affection.

"Thanks." Seeing the glow on Jenna's face and the sparkle in her eyes helped Nate relax. He'd been afraid she wouldn't speak to him.

After a hug and kiss for Zach, along with the reminder to be a good boy for Ramona, Jenna was ready to go. Escorting her to his pickup, Nate thought of all those years he'd longed to take her to homecoming — to take her anywhere. Now if he could keep his cool and not do something stupid like throw her under the bleachers when the cannon went off, this might not be the last time.

10

On the way to town, they chatted about everyday things. Whether or not the opposing football team was good. The plans the Historical Society had for the museum. A bit about Jenna's work at the local mission serving the needy by providing them with clothing and food. Safe topics for two people who had been friends forever, yet were well aware that they were breaking new ground.

Nate parked where the high school attendant told him to, but he would have preferred something nearer the exit. Walking through the crowd to the entrance, he tried to tamp down the anxiety swirling inside. A suicide bomber would pick a gathering like this, a soft target where he could do the most damage. But this wasn't Iraq, he reminded himself — again. If al-Qaida wanted to attack, they would do something in a big city, not a small town like Callahan Crossing. It was a logical conclusion, but he knew firsthand that logic wasn't always paramount in the enemy's plans.

They settled in their seats, and the Callahan clan joined them a few minutes later. Nate's parents were three rows in front of them and a few seats over. He liked having them close enough to keep an eye on his dad and to see that they were having a good time.

The cheerleaders from the opposing team stretched a large handmade paper banner across the entry from the Tigers' locker room. The football players burst through it and ran onto the field amid cheers from the visitor's side of the stadium and a feisty tune by the Tigers' band.

The pom squad lined up on each side of the Wolves' entry, waving their pom-poms in the air and making a pathway for the team to run through. When the cheerleaders stretched the banner in front of the open gate, the hometown crowd surged to their feet, yelling, whistling, and clapping. The band blared the fight song, and the team smashed through the banner and raced into the stadium, the crowd's volume increasing.

A few minutes later, a Boy Scout color guard marched onto the field carrying the

United States and Texas flags. The stadium quieted down. The announcer's voice came over the speakers, "Ladies and gentlemen, please stand for our national anthem."

The few people who had taken their seats stood again. Any man who was wearing a hat or cap removed it and, along with the women, placed their right hands over their hearts. Except for Nate and Dub and some other veterans scattered throughout the audience. They stood at attention and saluted the flag in the formal military style while folks sang "The Star Spangled Banner." Dub had saluted for as long as Nate could remember.

When the song ended, someone behind Nate tapped him on the shoulder. He jumped slightly, then turned around.

Mrs. Cross, his high school chemistry teacher, looked down at him with barely a hint of a smile. "Give me a hug, young man."

"Yes, ma'am." Nate always thought her name fit her personality, but he leaned over the seat back and dutifully hugged the woman who had come close to flunking him. Of course, he had blown up part of the chemistry lab. He'd been daydreaming about Jenna and missed the portion of the lecture on which of the chemicals they were using could be combined and which couldn't.

"You're looking well."

"Thank you, ma'am."

Her husband, George, leaned down, taking advantage of a pause in the crowd noise. "You've been hanging around with Dub Callahan too long. Now that you're a civilian you're supposed to put your hand on your heart instead of saluting military style. Unless you join one of the service organizations."

Nate barely kept his irritation from showing. Who appointed him the flag code police? The jerk had razzed Dub at football games for years about the same thing. "No, sir, you're incorrect. Congress passed a law giving military personnel out of uniform and all veterans, whether or not they belong to a service organization, the right to salute the flag in the military manner if they want to. The choice is a personal one."

"Really?" His tone was arrogantly skeptical. "When was that?"

"The fall of 2008, sir." Nate turned back around, ignoring whatever Cross muttered. He was there to enjoy the game and his date. Not put up with know-it-alls-who-didn't.

Dub leaned forward, looking past Will and

Chance at Nate. "Did you make that up?"

"No, sir. It hasn't been highly publicized, which is a shame. It was passed by Congress and signed by the president."

Dub's face broke into a broad grin. "Guess I'll have to think of some other way to annoy George."

Nate didn't figure that would be too hard. Soon he was caught up in the excitement of the game and enjoying the company of his friends — one pretty lady in particular. If her smiles, cheers, and one-armed hugs when the Wolves made a touchdown — two in the first quarter — were a good indication, she enjoyed being with him too.

Although football had been an important part of his life when he was in school, he hadn't been to a game since he moved away. He hadn't realized until after he left Callahan Crossing that belonging had been a crucial part of the sport for him. He still watched games on television and had played football with the men in his company, but nothing came close to playing for the hometown team. Actually, he thought with a grin, nothing much compared with Texas high school football, period.

With thirty seconds left in the first half and the score tied, a big Wolves guard scooped up a fumble by the other team. He took off toward the goal line, forty yards away. Everyone in the stadium jumped to their feet. One side cheered him on. The other side screamed for the Tigers to catch him.

"Go, Tony, go!" The cheerleaders started a chant, shaking their purple and gold pom-poms high in the air. The drummers, waiting along with the rest of the band near the end of the field for the halftime show, picked up the rhythm. The Callahan Crossing supporters joined in, yelling, clapping, or stomping their feet.

Tony lumbered toward the goal line, his teammates blocking two Tigers who tried to stop him. Another player from the opposition made a valiant attempt, but the big linebacker wasn't to be denied the only touchdown that he might ever make. He crossed the goal line, dragging the Tiger along with him.

The crowd cheered wildly, keeping it up as the kicker dropped a perfectly placed point-after right between the goal posts. The buzzer went off to end the half, and Jenna clung to Nate's arm, jumping up and down. He barely noticed the boom of the cannon telling the few people in town who weren't at the game that their team had scored.

During halftime, the band played a couple

of tunes as they marched onto the field and formed a large crown. The homecoming princesses were escorted onto the field by their fathers. After an unusually short speech, the high school principal announced the homecoming queen and king, who was a running back on the football team. The principal placed a sparkling silver and rhinestone crown on the queen's head, and the chairman of the homecoming committee presented her with a big bouquet of red roses. The king received a big puffy purple velvet crown with shiny gold trim.

Nate nudged Chance and leaned closer to be heard over the applause. "That's not as cool as the one you got."

"Bet it weighs less, though."

The band played another song as the queen and her court were escorted off the field, and the king jogged back to join the team on the sidelines, holding the crown on his head with one hand.

When the Boy Scout color guard returned to the field, the band silently stood at attention. Head Coach Snyder, whose wife owned Buds and Blooms, jogged out, followed by the entire football team. They lined up in front of the band. The principal handed the microphone to the coach.

"Ladies and gentlemen, we're honored to

welcome home a real local hero tonight."

Nate's heart pounded in his chest. *No, Coach, no. Let it go.* His throat went dry, and his palms began to sweat.

"In high school, Nate Langley was a two-time all-region wide receiver for the Wolves," continued Coach Snyder. Nate's mom turned and looked up at him, her face shining with pride, tears in her eyes. "While he was in school, he helped out on the family farm and worked as a cowboy on the Callahan Ranch. After graduation, he went to work on a ranch near Marfa. From what I hear, he's as good at cowboyin' as he was at playing football."

Nate glanced at Dub. The rancher nodded.

"A week after 9/11, he joined the army and served in both Afghanistan and Iraq. During his recent tour in Iraq, Sergeant Langley saved the lives of two of his comrades after his team was attacked by a suicide bomber. Despite being wounded himself and barely able to walk, he carried one man to safety and went back into the burning building to rescue the other. On the way out, they were pinned down in the street by enemy fire for over twenty minutes."

Jenna reached over and took his hand,

145

squeezing it gently. Someone nearby sniffed, and Nate realized a hushed silence had settled over the stadium. Somehow his dad managed to turn and look up at him, pride and tears gleaming in his eyes.

"Returning fire, Nate shielded the lieutenant's body with his own until help arrived. For his bravery in risking his life to save these other men, Sergeant Langley was awarded the Silver Star for heroism."

The stadium erupted in thunderous applause. Coach Snyder let folks clap for a minute, then held up his hand, asking for silence. "Nate, the boys wanted to do something to tell you how much they respect and admire you. And how much they appreciate your service to our country and our town. We had a team meeting this afternoon and voted to retire the number you wore when you played for the Wolves. Conveniently, nobody's wearing number ten this season."

Those around them chuckled, and Jenna smiled. But not Nate. It was a great honor, but he had a good idea what the coach would say next. It filled him with dread.

"Nate, I know you're hiding up there somewhere. Would you please come down so we can present you with your old jersey?"

Jenna bumped his arm with her shoulder.

"Go on, cowboy. Make all these people feel good."

He couldn't go down on that field. It was wide open. He'd be a sitting duck. His mom looked up at him again, this time with a slight frown. She motioned toward the field.

"This isn't the time to be shy, amigo," muttered Chance.

Nate looked in his direction. Dub shifted forward, drawing his gaze. "God has your back, Nate," he said quietly.

Nate nodded, acknowledging his understanding and encouragement.

God will protect me. Silently repeating the phrase, he stood and worked his way out of the row. The people around him started clapping, the applause growing as he walked down the bleacher steps. By the time he reached the field, the people who had come to root for their teams were standing and clapping for him.

The hometown hero. Right. If he were a hero, he would have stayed in the army, not run home with his tail between his legs.

He shook hands with Coach Snyder and accepted the purple jersey with gold lettering. The coach stuck the microphone in front of his face. Nate turned to the boys behind him, some of whom might join the service in a year or two.

"Thank you." Overcome with emotion, he cleared his throat. "I can't tell you how much this means to me. As for winning that medal, anybody in my squad would have done the same thing. We were a team, working together to do our job and keep each other safe." He looked back at Coach Snyder. "I learned about teamwork right here on this field, playing with the Wolves. Those lessons served me well. Thank you, sir."

With tears welling up in his eyes, the tough, burly coach shook his hand again. "Welcome home."

The band played "Stars and Stripes Forever" as Nate walked toward the sidelines, which choked him up even more. The Boy Scouts had moved, taking a position a few yards from where he would exit. When he was in front of the American flag, he stopped, snapped to attention, turned sharply to his left, and saluted. Ending the salute, he turned back to the right with military precision and marched the few yards off the field, falling into a normal step when he reached the running track circling it.

The crowd roared.

Nate wiped a tear from his cheek before he started up the bleacher steps. He hadn't done it for show or to please the onlookers. When he'd approached that treasured cloth of red, white, and blue waving in the gentle breeze, gratefulness had overflowed in his heart and soul. Gratitude for the privilege of protecting his country. Appreciation for those who cared. And above all, thankfulness to almighty God that he'd made it home.

It took a while to reach his friends. At every step, people reached out to shake his hand, thank him, congratulate him. His folks beamed as he made his way past their row. His mom had confiscated his dad's handkerchief.

He finally collapsed in his seat, his legs wobbly and his hands shaking. Good thing they were only ten rows above the fifty yard line instead of in the nosebleed section. He'd never have made it.

Dub gave him a thumbs-up, and Will and Chance were grinning like they'd been the ones to get the honor.

Jenna slipped her arm around his and leaned close. "Way to go, cowboy."

"Did I make sense? I felt like I was babbling."

"You were perfect. Except you ruined my makeup." She had a mascara smear under one eye.

"You're still beautiful, even if a little smudged."

"And you're sweet. Which side?"

"Right one."

She dug a tissue out of her pocket and wiped the skin beneath her eye. "How's that?"

"Better. There's still a little streak, but nobody will notice unless they're this close." He dropped his voice a little deeper, a little quieter. "And I don't intend to let anybody else get this close."

The second half began, and she looked back at the field, apparently not bothered by his little display of possessiveness. In fact, given the tight hold she kept on his arm, she was feeling a little possessive herself.

Nate didn't participate in any touchdown hugs for the rest of the game. Neither team scored again, so Callahan Crossing High won. It was a tough defensive battle on both sides, thus nerve-racking for everyone.

Afterward, the Callahans and the Langleys decided to go by Irene's Boot Stop, a popular restaurant with great home-style cooking. Nate and Will had fried catfish and french fries and a piece of banana cream pie. The others only wanted dessert.

The place was crowded with locals and

returning alumni. Some had been Nate and Jenna's classmates, others had gone to school with their parents. People roamed from table to table before and after they finished eating. Almost everyone stopped by to shake Nate's hand. With Irene and a waitress keeping coffee cups and iced tea glasses full, it turned into a gabfest, with acquaintances catching up on careers, marriages, kids, and grandkids.

A man waved at the owner to get her attention. "Hey, Irene, tell my wife how you named this place."

Irene smiled and kept pouring coffee. The noise died down, though at least half of the folks knew the story. "Well, I always wanted a truck stop, but I couldn't afford enough land to build one. Eighteen wheelers take up a lot of space."

"And with your great cookin', there would be a bunch of them," hollered a lanky cowboy about the same age as Irene.

She winked at him and told the waitress to get him another piece of pie. "So I settled for a place with plenty of room inside where all you cowboys and cowgirls could park your boots and stay awhile. A pickup stop didn't have much of a ring to it. So I called it a boot stop."

"We're glad you didn't build out on the

highway," said Sue. "It's nicer to eat downtown."

Nate had a second piece of pie, peach this time, and listened to the conversations around him. His dad and Dub were discussing the proposed farm subsidy bill in Congress. Sue had drawn his mother into planning a women's thing at church, and Jenna was chattering away with a classmate who lived in New York.

He ate the last bite and set the plate and fork on the corner of the table where the waitress could get to it easily. Leaning against the back of the chair, he took a sip of decaf coffee and sighed in contentment.

That morning, he'd gone to Sweetwater and found a kitchen table and chairs at Goodwill. Plain and inexpensive, but not ugly. For now, that suited him. He'd picked up dishes and silverware, a few pots and pans, and some towels at Walmart to supplement the things his mom gave him.

Years earlier, his family and the other neighbors between the ranch and town had benefited when Dub had the television cable brought out. He knew that all the houses on the ranch were equipped with it. But he'd been surprised to learn that the basic cable TV and broadband Internet packages were included in the utilities that Dub paid.

Now, he sat there with his family and friends he'd known all his life. Honest, hard-working people who loved God and country as much as he did. It had been a good day.

The Callahans and his folks left about ten minutes ahead of them. He took his time driving home, going a little under the speed limit. But Jenna didn't seem to mind. When he stopped in front of the ranch house, the porch light blazed in the darkness and the lights in the living room were still on.

He walked around the pickup and opened Jenna's door. "Reckon your dad is watching out the window?"

She grinned and laid her hand in his as he helped her from the truck. "I wouldn't put it past him. But that would be better than when I was in high school. He used to sit out here on the porch, waiting for me to come home."

Nate laughed, resting his hand at the small of her back as they slowly walked to the porch. "Even in the winter?"

"He bought a heavy parka for that sole purpose."

"You're kidding."

"No, honestly, I'm not. I never had a good-night kiss on that porch."

Going up the steps, he slid his hand lightly around her waist. "Do you want one now?"

he asked softly.

"And risk Daddy barreling out the door? Better not." When she looked up at him, he thought that under other circumstances she might have said yes. Then uncertainty clouded her eyes, and he decided he was merely seeing what he wished for. "Thank you for tonight." She touched the mum. "And for this. I had a wonderful time."

"So did I." He caught her hands in his. If Dub was watching, he hoped Sue was hanging on to his arm to keep him inside. "Thank you for going with me. It meant a lot."

"To me too." She took a deep breath, releasing it slowly. "I'm not sure if you realize how big a step this was for me. But you made it easy."

"After last night, I was afraid you'd slam the door in my face." They'd avoided talking about the bonfire all night. Why did he have to bring it up now?

She led him to the far corner of the porch, out of the glare of the light and away from the living room windows. "I was upset for a while, but Mom and I had a long talk. She helped me understand some things."

"That I'm nuts?" He tried to say it in a light, joking manner, but instead it came out sounding as if he believed it. Sometimes he halfway did.

Frowning, Jenna searched his face. "She pointed out that you've been through a lot, probably much more than any of us know. Maybe even more than you realize. She said it's natural for you to be jumpy and react to loud noises like that. Daddy did that kind of thing too." She squeezed his hand. "After all, you were trying to protect me."

He grimaced. "From a phantom enemy."

"In that moment, to you the threat was real. And I was the one you thought of, the one you wanted to keep safe. That's important."

"Yeah, I did a great job of keeping you safe." Anger at his stupidity made his chest tight. He turned her arm, nodding at the scab on her elbow. "You probably have bruises too."

"Just one. And it's not bad. I've had a lot worse working cattle. Nate, don't worry about it. We're going to have some ups and downs. Every relationship does."

"I hope the rest of the downs aren't literal."

She laughed and curled her arm around his, drawing him beside her to lean against the porch railing. "That depends on how well you stay on your horse Monday."

"Maybe I should ride Penny." Relaxing

against the railing, he let his upper arm touch her shoulder. He could get real used to that kind of closeness.

"Daddy put her out to pasture a couple of years ago. Dumpling is still available."

Nate snorted. "Y'all would leave us behind in two minutes."

"True, but she doesn't have the energy to buck. Will sometimes uses her for moving cattle, but mostly for checking the fence in the back pastures. Plodding along is good for that, and it makes her feel useful."

"Can't have her gettin' depressed."

"And I think she would. Penny had trouble adjusting to retirement, though she was worn out. Her body isn't up to it anymore, but her heart is still willing."

"They're like people, aren't they? Some gentle, sweet, and hardworking. Others mean and ornery."

"And everything in between."

Nate noticed the curtain flutter. He leaned over and whispered, "I think your dad is looking for us."

"He'd have to open the window and stick his head out to see us over here. I'm not sure I put it past him. That settles it, I'm going to move into my grandparents' house."

"I thought it was the guesthouse."

"They never use it for company anymore. They wind up having people stay here. It's in great condition. I'll have to ask about it, but I don't think the folks will object. It's time Zach and I had a place of our own." She looked up at him, her expression filled with mischief. "And the front porch is on the opposite side, so nobody can see it from any of the other houses."

Nate chuckled and put his arm around her shoulders, drawing her closer. "I'm likin' the idea more by the minute. Now, I'd better skedaddle. My folks are probably waiting up too."

Jenna laughed softly. "We're too old to be living with our parents."

"Definitely." He gave her a little squeeze and stepped away. When she opened the front door, he waved at the Callahans waiting expectantly in the living room. Sue and Will relaxed on one of the sofas. Chance occupied a big matching chair. All three had their feet resting on the coffee table, which also served as an ottoman.

Dub stood by the fireplace, but Nate bet a dollar to a doughnut he'd been peeking out the window moments earlier. He winked at Jenna and walked to the pickup with a much lighter heart than when the evening began.

11

On Monday morning, Nate fixed himself a big breakfast of ham, eggs, hash brown potatoes, and toast. He'd been up since 3:30 anyway, partly due to the anticipation of starting the job but mainly because of another nightmare. Friday and Saturday nights had been good with plenty of rest and no bad dreams. He'd hoped they were gone for good, but the one last night had left him too tied in knots to close his eyes again.

Finished with breakfast, he put the dirty dishes in the dishwasher and hand washed the pans, leaving them in the big dish drainer to air dry. He poured himself one last cup of coffee and wandered out onto the back porch.

Then went right back in again for a denim jacket to ward off the early morning chill. Easing down on the top step, he stretched out his legs and sipped his coffee, enjoying the millions of stars twinkling in the clear sky, letting the peace and quiet seep into his soul.

"Lord, thanks for setting up this job for me and for giving me a place of my own. I appreciate the things Nadine left too." He'd called Virgil and Nadine on Sunday afternoon to thank them for leaving the washer and dryer as well as the living room furniture. The blue flowered upholstery on the couch, loveseat, and one chair didn't exactly suit his tastes, but they were comfortable and in good condition, so he wasn't about to complain. They'd also left a big dark blue leather recliner that he planned to put to good use in the evenings.

Chance had helped him move his bedroom furniture on Saturday. He'd thought his mom might feel a little sad to see it — and him — go, but she was excited about turning his old bedroom into a craft and sewing room. He figured if he ever moved back home again, he'd have to sleep in the barn with the tractors.

She'd searched through their house and came up with all sorts of things for him to use. Extra sheets and blankets for the bed, kitchen utensils, a cookbook, a hand mixer, lamps for the living room, and a box of odds and ends. Some were already coming in

159

handy. With others, only time would tell if they'd be of use or not.

"Help me to do a good job today, Father, to pull my weight and not cause anybody or any animal harm." Downing the last of the coffee, he went back into the kitchen and put the mug in the dishwasher.

Excitement spiraled through him as he wrapped the brown soft leather shotgun chaps slightly below his waist and buckled them. Reaching around to the back of his left leg, he connected the zipper on the chaps and zipped it from thigh to calf, drawing the leather close for a good fit. He repeated the process with the right leg. He'd had those leggings for over ten years, and he still felt proud every time he put them on, the same kind of pride that he'd felt in his army uniform. It took hard work to earn the right to wear either one.

Resting first one foot and then the other on a kitchen chair, he fastened the spurs around the heel of his boots. He spun the rowel on the last one and smiled. He'd better find something else to prop his feet on. No sense wearing out the chairs, even if they were secondhand. If his mama saw him doing that, she'd scold him from now to Sunday.

He settled his sweat- and dirt-stained

straw hat on his head, thinking about the last time he'd worn it. He'd been employed at the Little Ridge Ranch near Marfa in far West Texas. It had been about the same size as the Callahan Ranch. The work had been much the same, with slight variations that came along with different terrain and weather. He had enjoyed it, but it never felt like home. Not the way the Callahan Ranch did.

Picking up his canteen, gloves, cell phone, and truck keys, he sauntered out the back door, grinning at the bell-like tones from the jingle bobs dangling from his spurs. Some cowboys thought that little bit of music was frivolous. Maybe it was, but it always lifted Nate's spirits. Kept the horses alert too.

Virgil had left a gooseneck stock trailer in the barn. It was large enough to hold six horses and could be used for hauling cows if the need arose. Nate had hitched it to his pickup before breakfast. He probably wouldn't need it to carry his horse to the pasture. A roundup crew typically carried all the horses in one or two trailers. But he might be bringing some back home with him.

Since he wasn't working full-time, he didn't know if Dub would assign him a string of horses, but he hoped he would. His new home was like the other camp houses on the ranch, a modest three-bedroom, single-story, white wooden house with porches across the front and back. It came with a barn and corrals out back and two pastures, called traps. One trap looked to be about half a section and the other a full section, or 640 acres. One square mile. In this arid country and on a spread the size of the Callahan Ranch — which covered 93 square miles — that was considered a small pasture, the kind set aside to graze horses or wean calves.

He slid the cell phone into a cubbyhole in the dashboard and laid the other things in the passenger seat. Starting the ignition, he drove slowly around the house and pulled out on the dirt road, heading toward the main corrals near the ranch house. He flipped down the visor with two fingers and checked the mirror. Yep, he was grinning like a monkey with a great big banana.

Nate reached the corrals in the earliest light of dawn. The Callahans had pulled in right ahead of him in Dub's big rig. Other than Ace, who had come along to drive Dub's truck back, Nate was the first of the hired hands to show up.

He got out of the truck, stuffed his gloves

in a back pocket, and retrieved a halter and lead rope from the back of his pickup. When Jenna strolled up to a little jingle bob tune, he winked at her. "You look like a real workin' cowgirl."

"What? I thought this was a photo shoot for a magazine ad." She made a show of looking down at her denim jacket, faded coral Western shirt and blue jeans, well-worn shotguns and boots, then struck an exaggerated modeling pose. "I'll have you know these are the finest clothes money can buy. At least they were about five years ago."

Even in the early morning light, she could see the sparkle in Nate's eyes. He enjoyed working the roundup as much as she did, but she didn't think that was the only thing that made his eyes light up. His happiness — and obvious admiration — made her heart skip a beat.

He had always been handsome in his cowboy gear, as well as relaxed and confident. But with his army-honed physique, he looked the best she'd ever seen him. If they wound up working near each other, she'd have to focus a little harder to keep her mind on her business.

They walked over to join the others. After Nate greeted her parents, brothers, and Ace, he turned to Dub. "Is there a particular horse you want me to use today?"

"Take your pick. I still keep a good-sized remuda."

"And he won't part with any of them." Jenna slipped her arm around her dad's waist.

Dub rested his arm around her shoulders, giving her a gentle squeeze. "Selling cows and calves is business. Selling a horse is parting with a friend."

"I understand," said Nate. "I've never owned a horse, but I've made friends with plenty of them."

Dub nodded toward Nate's trailer and pickup. "I see you came prepared to take some home."

"If that suits you, sir."

"Suits me," said Will. He grinned at Nate and leaned against the front of his dad's white truck. "Less work for me and Ace."

"All my hands have a string of their own. Don't see any reason for you to be any different, even if you'll be spending some of your time at the farm." Dub glanced around at his family. "We try to rotate through the herd that's here at headquarters, but we all have our favorites. This evening Will can help you pick out the ones we aren't so attached to."

Chance tilted his head toward the corral.

"Do you think you can still stay in the saddle?"

"Unless you stick me with a wild bronc." Nate scanned the horses. "You've added some new ones since I was here."

Although he hadn't mentioned it, Jenna already knew the horse he wanted to ride — Winston, a golden buckskin quarter horse with dark brown mane and tail. He and Chance had trained the gelding from the time he was a colt, but Nate had primarily ridden him the last year he worked at the ranch. Winston had moped for months after Nate left. She couldn't wait to see the horse's reaction when he realized his old friend was back.

Chance pointed to a sorrel with a white blaze on her face. "Rosie gets a little stubborn sometimes. And that big bay peeking through the fence from the trap is a scaredy-cat in a canyon. We only use him in the open pastures. The others are fine."

Ollie Mathers and his wife, Ethel, arrived, pulling a trailer with two horses. They'd picked up Buster Jones on the way. Ollie and Ethel had lived and worked on the Callahan Ranch for fifteen years. Buster and his wife, Natalie, had been there for twenty. She taught senior English and had been as strict with the Callahan kids as she had been with everybody else.

Ethel was filling one of the roles of a ranch wife — driving the pickup and trailer back to headquarters after they reached the pasture. Then she would help Ramona keep an eye on Zach and fix dinner for the crew.

After a round of handshaking and greetings, the Callahans retrieved the halters and lead ropes they had looped around the fence posts the day before and headed for the corral gate. Nate followed, closing the gate behind them.

The horses looked up. Winston watched Chance for a minute, then focused on Nate. He nickered, his expression alert and his ears pricked in Nate's direction. The horse slowly started moving toward him, studying him intently.

Jenna nudged Chance and caught Will's eye. They paused to watch. So did her parents.

"Hi, Win," Nate said softly as he walked over to meet the big horse.

Winston answered with a happy, excited nicker. He nudged the brim of Nate's hat with his nose, almost knocking it off. Laughing, Nate rescued his hat, then patted the horse on the neck. "You remember me, don't you?"

The horse snorted, tipping his head as

Nate scratched behind his ear. Then he snuffled around Nate's shirt pocket until he lifted the flap and slurped out a sugar cube.

Chance laughed. "I should have known you'd have sugar."

"Paid off."

Jenna blinked back the moisture in her eyes, glad that Nate was too far away to notice her getting all sentimental. She could well imagine how much it meant to him for Winston to be so excited and happy.

While he slipped the halter over the horse's nose and buckled it behind his ears, Jenna turned her attention to her own mount. She chose a pretty brown quarter horse mare named Clementine, a gentle girl who had the strength and speed she'd need. There were several trotty cows in the pasture they were working today — cattle that were on the wild side and tended to trot off in the opposite direction whenever they noticed a horse and rider headed their way.

Leading Rosie, Chance opened the gate. "I expected Win would remember you. He's developed a lot of cow sense. He'll make your job easy today."

"I'm countin' on it." Nate followed Chance out of the corral, with the rest of the Callahans right behind him.

Saddling her horse in the quiet of dawn

had always been a special time for Jenna. She expected it was the same for all of them involved in the roundup. Peace and excitement made an odd mix of emotions, one she had never experienced anywhere else or any other time. She had missed this when she was married. Jimmy Don had no interest in the ranch and had detested horses. He'd never ridden one and adamantly declared that he never would.

How could she have been so stupid to think that they could have had a good life together? She glanced at Nate as she untied the lead rope from the fence. How could she have fallen in love with Jimmy in the first place? Especially with Nate around?

She could analyze the past all day, but the answer probably was pretty simple. Nate had kept his interest hidden, and Jimmy had pursued her. Big time. He'd made her think he loved her when all he really wanted was the prestige, at least in Callahan Crossing, of being the one who caught Dub Callahan's only daughter. It was the challenge and fame — limited though it was — that lured him. She'd often thought that the only reason he continued their relationship in college was because her father had been a strong supporter of the university and had good connections.

After they were married and he was drafted by the Dallas Cowboys, her father's influence was no longer important to Jimmy's success. Thus she was no longer important. Or as he had often pointed out, worthless.

Jenna shook her head, annoyed that she let those painful thoughts intrude on a good morning. Pastor Brad had taught her that the best remedy for feeling down was to praise the Lord. Stopping for a moment to admire the glorious pink and golden streaks lighting the sky, she sent a silent prayer heavenward. *Thank you for bringing Zach and me back here, Lord. For this ranch and a wonderful family who love and nurture us. Thank you that I'm not worthless in your eyes nor in my own. Not anymore.*

She led Clementine over to the trailer, waiting patiently while her dad and Will loaded their horses.

Chance and Rosie stopped beside her, waiting their turn. He looked up at the growing beauty of the rose and purple sunrise. "God is good."

"Yes, he is." She watched Nate coax Winston into Ollie's trailer. The trailer was the one thing the horse didn't like, but under Nate's guidance, he stepped in like a kid going to the amusement park.

"Should I send you and Nate to opposite sides of the pasture?"

Jenna looked up into her brother's twinkling eyes. "Who made you boss?"

"Well, I am older."

"So?" She spoke like a sassy little sister, but she enjoyed the banter.

"I could point out to Dad that you and Nate have a hard time keeping your eyes off each other. But I expect he's already noticed. And I get a kick out of watching you. Besides, you're both professional enough to work together without missing too many cows, right?"

"Right."

"Good. I think you'll make a good team." He leaned a little closer and lowered his voice. "And I'm not only talking about the roundup."

"Don't get pushy."

Chance shrugged. "I just want you to be happy."

"I am." *Sort of.*

"Yes, but I think you could be happier." He glanced at Nate, who was talking to Buster. "And I know he could be. He's hurting, sis."

"I know, but I'm not sure how to help him. Love him, I guess." Chance's eyebrows shot up, and Jenna quickly added, "As only good friends can."

"Works for now." Her brother put his arm around her shoulders and gave her a little hug.

After all the horses were secured in the trailers, everyone gathered around Dub and Sue. Nate slipped in beside Jenna.

"Any questions?" Her dad glanced around.

"Is Ramona frying chicken?" asked Buster with a grin.

"She was making a cobbler when we left, but chicken is on the menu."

"Then I'll have to work up an appetite."

Ollie bumped Buster's shoulder with his, making the older man's slight paunch jiggle. "Pressing the button on the TV remote works up your appetite."

Dub laughed with the others and waited a few seconds for additional questions. When there weren't any, he took off his hat and reached for his wife's hand. For as long as Jenna could remember, her father had prayed every morning during roundup.

The men removed their hats, and everyone respectfully bowed their heads. Jenna felt Nate's hand slip around hers. His touch was warm, comforting, and felt right. She added a silent prayer that God would bless her friend that day.

Her dad spoke quietly and reverently. "Heavenly Father, we thank you for a good day. This ranch belongs to you, Lord, as do all of us. We ask you to bless our efforts today and keep everyone and every animal safe and unharmed. In Jesus' name, amen."

When Nate gave her hand a little squeeze and met her gaze with sweet tenderness in his eyes, she wondered if the term *friend* even came close to what she felt for him.

12

On the circular sweep through the ten thousand acre pasture, Nate and Winston drove two cows and their calves out of the thick cedar brakes along a creek bed. The cows were old hands at this roundup business, but some of them still didn't like it. As a rule, the calves didn't like it at all. Maybe they still remembered the spring roundup, with the branding, shots, and all the other things the little critters were subjected to. Nate knew it all was necessary, but he figured it had to be traumatic. And he knew for a fact that some cattle had long memories.

Like the one Jenna was chasing full out through the mesquites, dodging the thorny limbs as best she could. That ol' lop-eared Hereford had been trotty since she was weaned years ago. Guiding his foursome around a clump of brush, he picked up the calf that hadn't been able to keep up with her mama and herded her into his little group. It was one of the rare times a panicked calf didn't bolt in the opposite direction.

He tried to keep Jenna in sight in case she ran into trouble. The cow broke into a small clearing with her about fifteen feet behind. She spun the loop in her rope twice — all she had room for in that small space — and let it fly, sailing it over Ol' Lop-ear's head pretty as you please. Clementine put on the brakes, but the cow went over the edge of a ravine seconds before she hit the end of the rope. Clem and Jenna skidded over the edge right behind her, dirt and small rocks flying in the air.

Fear sliced through Nate. He abandoned his cows and spurred Winston after Jenna, slowing before they reached the ravine. He couldn't risk going blindly over the edge. If she was lying at the bottom of the draw, they'd run right over her.

He reined in and spotted her and Clem bringing the cow to a screeching halt about twenty yards away. Breathing a sigh of relief, he relaxed and glanced over his shoulder to see where his cattle were. To his surprise, they'd stopped too. He looked back at Jenna, listened to her scold the cow for being a brat, and laughed.

Clementine backed up and turned around so Jenna could lead the troublemaker out of the draw. She muttered the whole way, occasionally glancing back at the animal, grumbling louder.

Nate tried to put on a serious expression since laughing right then might not be wise. He decided he wasn't entirely successful when she rode up an easier slope a little farther down, her frown deepening when she looked at him.

"Are you all right?"

"Yes." She glanced down at a long rip in her denim jacket. "No. Well, I am, but my jacket isn't." She glared at the cow now following her like a pet on a leash. "Ornery thing. Why couldn't you mosey over to Chance's section? Or Nate's?"

"Good thing she wasn't in my territory." Nate ran his gaze over her to check for damage. Other than the tear in her coat, she seemed all in one piece. At least he couldn't see any scratches or bruises. "I'd have missed her." He eased Winston closer and plucked a mesquite twig that was jammed into the brim of her straw hat. "That was mighty fine ridin'."

She sat there for a minute, then slowly grinned. "It was pretty good, wasn't it?"

"Better than that. You haven't lost your

touch. Or your grit."

Jenna reached for her canteen. "Speaking of grit . . ." She took a swig of water, swished it around in her mouth, leaned to the side, and spit it out. She wiped her mouth on her sleeve, and a mischievous expression spread across her face. "I'm real ladylike too."

"When it's appropriate, but you're also practical. I like that."

"Oh yeah?"

"Sure. It doesn't make any sense to sit there with a mouth full of dirt." He couldn't resist teasing her a little bit and ran a fingertip across her dusty cheek. "Even when you're covered with it."

She made a face. "Back to work, cowboy."

"Uh-oh, she's gettin' all uppity on me."

She tipped her head up, her nose pointed high in the air — and lost her balance.

Nate reached out to steady her, resting his hand along her side. All he had to do was lean a little bit to his right, and if she kept her head tipped up, and he angled just so . . . A light flared in her eyes, bringing him to his senses.

He pulled his hand back and straightened, easing Winston away from Clem. Putting distance between him and Jenna. He was not going to kiss her for the first time with both of them filthy and on horseback in the middle of a pasture where anybody in the roundup crew might spot them any second.

And with a calf bawling at the top of her lungs to attract attention. He noticed that Ol' Lop-ear had edged past Jenna and was now at the end of the rope, stretching in an effort to reunite with her calf. But the calf was too scared of Jenna and Nate to come any closer.

"Reckon I'd better get back to work."

"We both should." But instead of moving, she searched his eyes.

"I will kiss you, sweetheart. In the right time and place." He scanned the pasture, noting that his little bunch of cows were trying to slip away, and smiled sheepishly. "But this ain't it."

"I'll hold you to that, cowboy," she said softly.

"Yes, ma'am. A wise man always keeps his promise to the boss lady." He winked and trotted off to catch a cow and calf that had sneaked around a big prickly pear cactus and were making a beeline back to where they came from.

Nate quickly rounded them up along with the other two that had stopped to graze and herded them back to where Jenna was leading the cow with her calf trailing happily along behind. They headed toward the trap that held the cattle they brought in.

Dub liked them to move the cattle at a walk or slow trot whenever possible. It was much less stressful on them, which paid off in better condition and weight.

Nate fell in close enough to Jenna for conversation, though it probably wouldn't be long before he had to move to the outside of his little herd to keep them going the right way.

She looked over her shoulder to check on her cow and calf. "I thought I might see you at church yesterday."

"I'm ashamed to say I overslept. I'd intended to go, but I stayed up so late Saturday night working on the house that I slept right through the radio. I dreamed that I was still unpacking stuff and listening to the radio. In my dream I turned it off, but some guy kept talking. I turned the radio on and off a couple of times —"

"In your dream?"

He nodded. "But when it was turned off the guy was still talking. And people were laughing. It was weird and annoying. I dreamed that I threw the radio outside."

Jenna had an idea where this was going. "But the guy kept talking."

"Right. I finally woke up enough to realize

I was listening to Chuck Swindoll."

Jenna laughed. "So you got some good teaching anyway."

"Most of it subconsciously."

"Maybe that's the best way to understand things. I had a friend in college who learned French by listening to it while she slept. By the end of the year she could speak it fairly well. She couldn't read it very well, though, so she flunked the class."

"So it didn't do her much good."

"Actually, it did. She went to Paris that summer, met a French businessman, fell in love, and got married."

"There's nothing like living in another culture to learn about it and the people."

"Like you did in Iraq and Afghanistan."

"I tried to learn as much as I could. My tours were fifteen months each time, but there are things you can never understand unless you stay in a country for a decade or two."

He kept an eye on a cow who was thinking about making a break for it. All on his own, Winston moved over a little to keep her in line. Nate was impressed with how much the horse had learned since he'd been gone. He caught a glimpse of a cow and calf hiding in the mesquite trees. "Duty calls."

Guiding Winston to the right, he circled around behind them and drove them out to join the others. With the new additions, he had to stay off to the side to keep them moving, ending any chance of conversation.

When they reached the fence between the pasture and the trap, Jenna held the cattle in place while Nate leaned down and un-latched the gate, swinging it wide. Some of the gates on the ranch were made of barbed wire and posts that had to be lifted from a loop of wire and dragged open. But the ones leading into the traps consisted of a metal pipe frame and posts with wide mesh wire in between. They were made to open easily from horseback.

He and Jenna herded the cattle into the half-section pasture and away from the gate, holding them there because Buster and Ol-lie were bringing more in. The others soon followed with more cattle. When the animals were all in the trap and the gate shut, Dub motioned for everyone to join him. They went around the circle, with each person giving him a tally of how many cattle he or she had brought in on the various sweeps through the pasture.

Dub added them up and nodded. "We got them all: 110 cows plus their calves." He looked down the dirt road at a trail of dust in the distance. "Right in time too. Here comes dinner."

The group scattered along the fence line to unsaddle and tether their horses. Within minutes their saddles were lined up on the ground and saddle blankets hung over the top strand of barbed wire to dry out. When Ace arrived, they took hobbles from the back of the pickup and secured the horses. They each filled a feed bag and draped it over their mount's head so the horses could eat.

Then they took turns washing up at the open metal tank, catching fresh water as it swooshed from the pipe with each pump of the windmill.

After Ramona, Ethel, and Zach arrived, Jenna lifted her son from his car seat in the truck and adjusted his cowboy hat so it fit right. Ramona had dressed him in pull-up jeans and a blue T-shirt with a cute brown horse on the front. She set him on the ground and held out her hand.

"My ride horsey?" Zach curled his hand around her fingers and looked longingly at Clem.

"Not today, sweetie. The horses have been working hard, and they need dinner and a break. See all those cows in the pasture?" She pointed toward the cattle milling on the far side of the trap. When he focused on them, she continued, "We'll be rounding more cows up all week, but I promise I'll take you for a ride on Saturday, okay?"

"Okay." He glanced around to see what else was interesting. "Nate!"

At the sound of his name, Nate looked up and grinned. "Hey, Zach." He sauntered toward them. "How are you, buddy?"

"My good."

Zach held up his arms, and Nate picked him up. Then he glanced down at his clothes and frowned. "I'm awfully grubby to be holding a clean little boy."

"Don't worry about it. A little dirt won't hurt."

"Dirt won't 'urt," echoed Zach.

Nate grinned at Jenna. "I think there's a parrot loose around here."

"Parrot."

Jenna giggled. "He's repeating things left and right. I'm amazed that he's learning so many new words and putting them together in little sentences already. Doctor Cindy says he's off the top of the chart with his language skills."

"They actually have a chart for that?"

"Well, I'm not sure. I didn't see one, so she might have only been using the expression. Either way, she was impressed when we saw her last week at the grocery store. She said she hoped I'd started a college fund."

Zach looked at her, then Nate, his little face breaking into an impish smile. "My cute." Nate laughed and hugged him a little. "Oh yeah? Who says so?"

"Mommy." Zach sent her the sweetest smile and nodded his head decisively. "My cute."

"Well, your mom is right. Are you hungry too?"

"Uh-huh."

"Did Ramona bring anything good to eat?"

"Chicken."

"Yum. What else?"

"Obbler."

"Cobbler?" Nate glanced at Jenna.

His pride at catching on to Zach's kid-speak was adorable. Would a rugged, macho guy like him take that as a compliment? She might have to ask about that sometime.

Zach nodded. "Peach."

"Looks like they have dinner set up," said Nate. Ace had brought along a handful of folding lawn chairs. "We'd better get over there before Buster eats it all."

"Buster eat it all."

Nate grimaced comically. "Oops. Guess

we have to be careful what we say."

"That's a lesson we're all learning." They started toward the pickups, where everyone else was lining up. "Do you want me to take him?"

"I'll hold him while you get food for the two of you. How do you handle him eating without a table?"

"Good question. I think we'll share a plate this time. I can keep his food on one side and mine on the other." Maybe. Zach liked to feed himself these days.

She dished up some fried chicken, potato salad, and a big spoonful of fruit mixed with whipped cream. In the small spot left on the plate, she added some black-eyed peas with a little piece of bacon. Several times earlier in the year, she had helped Ramona and her mother pick the peas in the garden, shell them as they sat around the kitchen table or outside on the patio or porch, then prepare them for the freezer. They were so much better preserved that way than canned or dried. She took a fork for herself and a spoon for Zach.

"Zach's sippy cup is in his bag," said Ramona as she filled a plastic glass with iced tea for Jenna. "Nate, it's in the backseat."

"We'll find it." He opened the back door to the big pickup. "Can you show me where

184

it is, Zach?"

Zach pointed to the red zippered pocket on the end where she always put it. "Over there."

"He's somethin', isn't he?" Ramona said softly, watching the little boy and the big cowboy.

"Pretty smart kid."

The housekeeper set the pitcher in the back of the pickup and grinned. "I was talking about Nate."

Jenna watched him for a minute as he and her son checked to see if there was water in the cup. Her heart filled with tenderness and longing.

He turned right then and met her gaze, and she saw her heart's desire mirrored in his eyes.

"But there's no need to rush things," murmured Ramona. "Enjoy the courtship."

"Is that what this is?" Jenna asked softly, moving to the side of the pickup out of Buster's way. He was already coming back for seconds.

"You bet it is, honey. The nice, old-fashioned kind where love develops slow and easy."

Jenna looked at her old friend with a tiny frown. "Is love ever easy?"

"It is for me and Ace. Not that the ornery

ol' coot doesn't make me mad sometimes, and vice versa. But we've been squabblin' and lovin' for almost forty years now, and love wins out every time. The trick is finding a man with a kind heart, and that young fellow has one. But then you've known that all your life. Now go eat and feed that young'un."

Jenna found a comfy spot on the ground beneath a mesquite tree with her mom.

Nate waited until she was settled before he brought Zach over. "I think this guy is hungry. He's been gnawing on my arm."

Zach frowned, his expression puzzled as he looked up at Nate.

"I'm teasin'. Nothing is wrong. But I bet you're hungry."

"Uh-huh." The little boy nodded, and Nate set him down. "My eat chicken."

"Me too. And I'd better go get some before Buster dives into it again."

"Thanks for taking care of Zach."

"I enjoyed it. I'll see you later, pardner."

Zach looked up at him with a smile. "Pardner."

Nate held out his upraised hand. "High five."

Zach slapped his hand with his then turned his attention to the food.

Jenna absently handed her son some

chicken and watched Nate walk over to fill his plate. With spurs jingling, the high-heeled boots added a little swagger to his step. He said something that made the men laugh, then he gave Ramona a hug and thanked her and Ethel for all their hard work.

When he turned away from Ramona, she caught Jenna's gaze. Jenna nodded slightly, agreeing with her.

He was somethin', all right.

13

As Dub led the way, the rest of the crew kept the cattle moving and together, traveling through the gently rolling rangeland four miles to the pens without any major mishaps. Every so often a few of the more cantankerous cows would try to take off or a calf would get spooked and run, but someone would catch them and bring them back to the herd. None made enough of a ruckus to cause a stampede, which would have endangered both animals and people and made a long day even longer.

One of the main purposes of the fall roundup was to wean the calves. At the pens, with some of the cowboys on horseback and some on foot, they separated the calves from their mamas — not always an easy task. Nate was thankful that Dub had him stay mounted. After years of not riding, he was getting so stiff and sore that he didn't think he could have run after a calf if he had to.

They herded the cows into one pen, then divided the calves by putting the heifers in a second pen and the steers in a third. The calves were weighed and driven through a squeeze chute, which held each one in place for their vaccinations. Afterward, they were turned into a small pasture with plenty of good grass saved for that purpose. They'd been eating grass for some time, but they had also depended on their mother's milk for sustenance. The transition to only grass wouldn't be an easy one for the calves and the cows.

Or for anybody around them. The bawling from both cows and calves already forced the cowboys to shout, and they had only brought in the first part of the herd.

The vet tested each cow to see if she was pregnant, then the cowboys herded them into a pasture adjacent to the calves. Soon the cows and calves matched up on each side of the fence, pacing back and forth, crying for each other. The fence dividing them was the strongest on the ranch, otherwise the cows would have gone right through it.

The calves would be kept in the pasture for at least thirty to forty days to make sure they were healthy. The cows would remain in the bordering pasture for about five days, until they had grown accustomed to being away from their babies. Then they would be moved to other grazing areas on the ranch.

After all the cattle were worked, Ace and Ethel arrived to take everybody back to headquarters. As the crew loaded the horses in the trailers and climbed into the pickups with tired sighs and good-natured grumbling, Nate managed to stifle a groan. He was used to working hard and was in good shape, but riding a horse all day used muscles he'd forgotten about.

Buster leaned his head against the headrest on the backseat and closed his eyes as they pulled out onto the road. Nate thought he'd gone to sleep, but when they were away from the cattle noise, the middle-aged man asked, "How you holdin' up, son?"

"Better than I thought I would. But I expect I'll be mighty sore tomorrow."

"It'll take awhile to get used to it again," said Ollie. "I think Dub should buy us all hot tubs. He could chalk it up to business improvements."

Buster snorted. "I don't think the IRS would buy that deduction, even if it did mean more productive workers. I looked into one last year. Thought we might get it for Christmas, but it was too pricey for my blood. And the missus needed a new washer and dryer anyway. She'd been nursing that blamed washer along for over a year."

Nate relaxed and halfway listened to the conversation as it drifted to football and rodeo. He was worn out, but it was a good tired. He'd held his own and done his job. No slacking, no mistakes. Dub shouldn't have any complaints. And he'd get to do it all over again for the next four days. Glancing out the window at the fading light, he smiled.

When they arrived at the headquarters' corrals, Nate removed the saddle and other gear and laid it in the back of his pickup, then led Win around to the rear of his trailer. "Who should I pick to go home with us, boy?"

The horse looked at him and groaned, a little I-can't-wait-to-roll-in-the-dirt comment. It had been Winston's habit since they first started training him.

"I guess you don't care. You've always been the easygoing type."

"Except with Snoopy," said Jenna, leading Clem toward the corral after she'd removed the saddle. "He's the gray out there in the pasture. He's a good horse but still young enough to be a bit of a scamp. Win doesn't have any patience with him."

Nate loaded his horse in the trailer and followed Jenna to where she was putting out feed for Clem. The horse was already rolling in the dirt to absorb the day's sweat.

"Did you get some hay and oats to take home?"

"Virgil left some in the barn." He nudged his hat up on his forehead with his knuckle and smiled. *Home.* He liked the sound of that. "There should be enough to last through the week for six horses. I'll haul a load of hay and grain over on Saturday."

"Don't work too hard on Saturday. Sunday is Zach's birthday, so we're having a party later in the afternoon after he has a nap. We'd like you to come too."

"I'll be here. Is there anything special he wants?"

"He likes cars and trucks and anything he can push around. He likes balls too, but he has a bunch of those. Every time my brothers see a new one, they get it. But don't buy anything expensive. He tends to ignore the pricey stuff."

Nate decided he'd better run over to Sweetwater early Saturday morning and hit Walmart. He'd cruised through town enough since his return to see that there still wasn't any place to buy decent toys.

Will came out of the barn and helped him

pick out the rest of his string. After they loaded the first four horses in the trailer, Will rested his hands on the top rail of the corral. "Those four are seasoned veterans. They can do about anything you ask." He pointed to a pretty black mare. "Ebony is a rookie, but she's eager to learn. She's ready to play with the pros."

Nate watched the horse prance around the pen and chuckled at his friend's terminology. "You expect me to teach her to run the bases and catch fly balls?"

Will laughed and opened the gate. "Maybe not fly balls, but I wouldn't bet against grounders." He walked in and slipped the halter over the horse's head. Nate followed, unable to avoid limping slightly. He'd worked his injured leg hard today, and it was talking to him. "Ebony, this is Nate. You're going home with him."

The horse's ears twitched as she glanced at the horse trailer, then focused on Nate. He had the impression she wasn't thrilled with the idea.

"You've been training her?"

"Mostly, though Dad's worked with her some. I think she'll do okay, especially if you sweeten her up with your sugar trick."

"Winston ate all I had in my pocket." Nate talked quietly to the horse, letting her get used to his voice and his smell, sweat and all. He scratched her withers and promised to take good care of her. When he turned to lead her to the trailer, she followed without resistance, though he caught her glancing wistfully at Will. "You'll be all right, girl. Your friends are going with you. And you'll see Will pretty often."

He didn't know how much she understood, but she went into the trailer without a hassle. Before he closed the tailgate, he heard Winston greet her with a friendly blow of air, reassuring her that she wasn't being shipped off to Montana or some other remote place, like the other side of town. A couple of horses followed his lead, and Ebony relaxed a bit.

Dub walked up as he reached the pickup cab. "Good job today. You haven't forgotten how to work cattle."

"And I didn't even fall off my horse."

"Not where anybody could see you," teased Dub, slapping him lightly on the back.

Nate played along. "Has Winston been tellin' on me again? That horse can't keep his mouth shut. No more sugar cubes for him."

Dub laughed and took a step backward. "Stop by the house for supper if you want."

"Thanks, but I should get the horses home and take care of Win. I'll nuke something in the microwave." He knew the invitation was sincere, but he also knew Dub would like it better if the horse he had ridden all day was a higher priority than his stomach. Nate wasn't doing it to make points. He simply believed a man tended to his horse before himself.

"We'll be working in the hills and canyons tomorrow. Jazzy is the best one for that pasture."

"Yes, sir."

As Dub strolled away, Nate put one foot in the pickup but stopped when he spotted Jenna coming toward him. Easing back down to the ground, he took off his hat and wiped his forehead on his sleeve — no doubt adding to the dirt on his face. "Good thing there really isn't a photographer here. You're a mess, Miz Colby."

"Can't say as you're any cleaner, Mr. Langley."

"Well, you could, but you'd be stretchin' the truth an inch or two."

"More like a mile." She leaned against the side of the pickup. "Are you stopping by the house?"

"Not this time. Win says he's starvin', and I'm beat."

"But you enjoyed it?"

"Yep. Even if I am an old, out of shape, saddle-sore cowboy."

She raised one eyebrow. "You aren't old. If you were, that would make me old, which I'm not." She poked his bicep. "And you're not out of shape."

"Okay, I'll give you both of those points. But I am definitely, without a doubt, sore."

"Do you have some ibuprofen?"

"The economy-size bottle. And a tube of Aspercreme." Plus ice packs in the freezer and heat wraps to throw in the microwave. "I'll be used to it by the end of the week."

"Just in time to ride the cotton stripper."

"Only if we have a good frost. Dad's hoping that will wait at least a couple more weeks because the cotton isn't ready. He had to plow up his first planting. The lack of rain and the hot, dry, and windy weather in the spring burned it up. He'd waited to plant a couple of fields and replanted another one, but we need more warm weather to open up the bolls. We still have a lot of green ones."

"Glad to know this heat is good for something. I'm a little embarrassed to realize I don't know much about raising cotton."

"You shouldn't be. You've never grown any here on the ranch. And I'm positive you didn't have any in your backyard in Dallas."

"The neighbors would have had a walleyed fit. Well, one of them wouldn't have minded. He was the president of a big corporate farm and had a wacky sense of humor. But the others were adamant about strictly adhering to the landscaping requirements in the division covenants. Things like having a certain percentage of the grounds in lawn, weed-free, and always mowed, of course. The trees couldn't be higher than ten feet, and no plants that might creep into the neighbor's yard were allowed."

"I couldn't live in a place like that."

"I understood the reasoning behind those rules. But quite a few of us got riled up when the homeowner's association board thought we should only have certain kinds of yard art." She grinned and wiggled her eyebrows. "Some people rebelled."

"How?"

"The corporate farm president put pink flamingos in his front yard. On holidays, he would dress them up. Red hearts for Valentine's Day, green hats for St. Patrick's Day, reindeer antlers at Christmas. On May Day, he put up a small maypole and circled them around it with streamers going to each one. In the summer they waded in a kiddie pool

197

and stood at attention in front of an American flag on July Fourth. For Halloween, one flamingo was caught in a big spiderweb while the others stood by in horror."

"How does a fake flamingo look scared?"

"Well, you had to use your imagination."

"So what did you do to protest?"

"I bought an old ranch wagon and plopped it in a prominent place in the front yard, in view of the grumpy society lady across the street. Then I added a hitching post and draped some reins and coiled rope over it. They were acre lots, so it only took up a little of the yard. I had some other ideas, but Jimmy Don came home from a trip to Green Bay before I could do them."

"He didn't like your creativity?"

"By that point, he didn't like much of anything that I did. He was furious and smashed everything. I couldn't even save that beautiful old wagon." She sighed. "At first I thought it would be all right. We settled in a new, lovely house, and I made friends with some of the team wives, as well as a few women from church. It was the city, but I was determined to make a go of it. But Jimmy didn't like the same people I did."

Nate studied her face in the fading light. How could Jimmy Don have been so cruel to such a sweet woman? "He liked the fast life?"

She nodded and watched her family pile into her dad's pickup. Chance stood beside the open door. "You comin' with us, sis?"

She glanced up at Nate. "Will you drop me off at the house?"

"Sure."

"I'll go with Nate," she called to her brother. He grinned and climbed in the truck.

When Jenna started to walk around the front of the pickup to the passenger side, Nate followed her. She stopped and looked at him over her shoulder. "I can open my own door, cowboy."

"My mama taught me to be polite." Besides, helping her into the truck would give him an excuse to touch her. "You don't want me to get into trouble with Mom, do you?"

"Like she'd know." Jenna smiled and shook her head, continuing on her way with him right behind her.

He opened the door, and she put one foot on the running board, reaching up for the handhold at the top of the doorframe. Resting his hand on her back to steady her — even though they both knew she didn't need it — he stood protectively behind her as she hauled herself up into the high vehicle.

She settled in the seat, and her gaze met his. He figured she knew exactly why he'd insisted on being polite, but he didn't think she minded a bit. He went back to the driver's side and got in, starting up the engine without looking at her. If she wanted to continue with her story, he'd let her do it when she was ready.

"There were some good Christian men on the team who managed to have a pretty normal family life," she said quietly. "Even some of the non-Christian guys did. They weren't interested in the parties and late nights. But Jimmy Don thrived on it."

"He always was a party animal."

"He liked the fun and drinking, though he rarely got very drunk. It was the attention that he craved, from the regular fans, the fanatics, and especially the groupies."

"I suppose there were groupies everywhere they played."

"Yes, but some of the women followed them from town to town. Eva wasn't his first affair, but that's how they met. He said she kept chasing him, but I don't think he resisted temptation for very long. If at all."

Nate heard bitterness in her voice. "I can't understand how he could choose another woman over you."

She shrugged and tried to act as if it didn't bother her. "It was easy. Eva liked the party life and fit into his new world. I didn't. She made him feel more important than anyone or anything else, and evidently I didn't."

"You had a baby to take care of."

"He met her before I got pregnant. Their affair began long before I had Zach. I was so excited about having a baby that I didn't really see how much it bothered him. I wanted him to be as happy as I was. I thought having a child would draw us closer, but instead it drove us further apart. My psychiatrist said I projected my excitement onto him and couldn't see his true feelings."

"You went to a shrink?"

"I saw one in Dallas for a few months before Jimmy left us. After I moved back home, I decided that focusing on God, my family, and the ranch would do me more good than a doctor. I know there are good psychiatrists, but he wasn't one of them."

"So this guy said you caused Jimmy to be an idiot?" He clenched his fingers around the steering wheel, itching to punch out Jimmy and the psycho-doc.

"Not totally, but that I greatly contributed to his problems because of my attitude."

"That's garbage." Nate scowled at her. "I hope you don't believe him. Jimmy Don was always a self-centered jerk with an ego as big as Texas and Alaska combined."

Jenna laughed. "You got that right. No, I don't believe that. Not anymore. Talking with Pastor Brad helped me more than all the visits to the psychiatrist."

"So Grace Community has a new minister?" Had his mom mentioned that? He vaguely remembered her saying something about it, but obviously he hadn't been paying much attention.

"Yes. Pastor Higgins retired a couple of years ago. Pastor Brad is a good guy. He's in his early forties, married, and has a couple of teenagers. I think you'll like him. He served in Iraq as an army chaplain before he moved here."

"Then he's bound to be a good man. Those guys are a special breed. I look forward to meeting him." He stopped the truck and trailer in front of the ranch house.

"Ramona will be disappointed that you aren't eating with us."

Was Jenna disappointed? He couldn't tell. "She'll have plenty of opportunities to feed me supper, but it wouldn't be fair to make Winston wait for his chow and a good brushing."

"I do like a man who takes care of his horse."

"Just like your daddy taught me."

"It's good to see you took it to heart." She reached for the door handle. When he started to open his door, she rested her other hand on his arm. "Stay put, Nate," she said gently. "I know your leg is hurting." She got out of the truck and paused before she shut the door. "You go home and take advantage of that recliner. Do you have an ice thingy to put on your leg?"

"Several of them. Sounds like a good plan. You should kick back for the evening too."

"I will if I can persuade Zach to watch a video or something."

"Good luck with that. I'll see you bright and early in the morning."

"Take care." She shut the door and walked toward the house, her feet dragging a little.

He waited until she was safely inside, then headed home. It was nice having a woman besides his mom care about him.

Selfishly, he was glad that Jimmy Don hadn't seen what a good woman he had.

14

On Sunday, Jenna sat at an angle in the pew in Grace Community Church, chatting with Lindsey, who sat behind her. She was excited that her friend had been commissioned to paint a mural on the outside of Maisie's antiques store and wanted to hear all about it. Watching the door of the sanctuary without being completely obvious was an added bonus. The service would start soon, and Nate still hadn't arrived.

She was worried about him. He'd done fine on the roundup, but he'd looked exhausted Friday night. Maybe it was nothing more than him getting used to the work. After all, everybody was tired by Friday. But his fatigue seemed deeper than normal, as much a weariness of heart and mind, perhaps even soul, as it was physical.

"Where will you put a mural?" Jenna pictured the old building, which had been built around 1900 if not before. Her eyes widened as she focused on her grinning friend. "The only wall with enough room is the false front. You're going to paint it up there?"

"Yes, ma'am." Lindsey was practically bursting with excitement.

"But that's like working on the second story."

"Dad's going to set up a scaffold for me. He has several for his house-painting business and can spare one. I've worked on them before when I helped him, so it won't bother me."

"Do Maisie and the historical society have something particular in mind or are they letting you be creative?"

"Both. They want an 1880s–1890s laundry day theme. I'm thinking outdoors with a fire and an old wash pot, rinse tubs, a cow or two in the distance. The housewife, a couple of kids, and a dog running around, maybe grabbing some long johns hanging on the line. I'll do up a sketch and see what they think." Lindsey shifted her gaze toward the aisle, and her face lit up in a smile.

Jenna turned slightly as Dalton Renfro smiled back at Lindsey and nodded a greeting. But the deputy sheriff didn't take advantage of the empty space beside her friend. He spoke to someone at the front of the church, then retreated to the back pew by himself.

"You're going to have to plant yourself in the last row if you want that man to sit by you."

Lindsey sighed. "He sits back there in case he gets a call. He doesn't want to disturb everyone else. Believe me, I've thought about it. But with the five rows in front of him usually empty, it would be all too clear what I was up to. It probably wouldn't work anyway. He barely knows I'm alive."

"Don't be silly. I didn't see him smiling like that at anybody else. Don't give up."

Sadness filled Lindsey's eyes, and the corners of her mouth dipped in disappointment. "I'm ready to." She leaned forward, her voice barely above a whisper. "I've been in love with him since I was a junior in high school. Eleven years, and he's never shown any interest. I'm such a goof. It's stupid for me to think anything good is going to happen between us."

"He keeps pretty busy with his job." Though Jenna wasn't quite sure doing what. There wasn't a large criminal element in the county. Probably because Dalton and the rest of the sheriff's department kept a close watch on things.

"He had time to date Alyson Ford, Miss

I-Can-Do-Everything-Perfect County Extension agent." Lindsey made a face. "Sorry, that was uncalled for. She was nice enough and very good at her job. And everything else."

"She chose a job promotion and move to Dallas over him. I don't know how much he cared for her, but that had to be disappointing."

"So now he's gun-shy, which gives him another reason to have nothing to do with me."

Nate walked through the door, and Jenna's heart did a little flutter.

"Nate must be here."

Jenna's gaze slid back to Lindsey. "I'm that bad, huh?"

"You are." She rested her hand on the back of the pew. "And I think it's great. I'll stay up here and prattle about how bored I get at the bank until he looks at you."

Nate's parents came in after him, and Jenna's joy took a nosedive. She'd saved a seat for him, but with all the Callahans filling the rest of the row, there wasn't room for his folks. What loving son would abandon his mom and dad on his first day back in the church he had grown up in? Especially when they hadn't been in church for a while, either?

He looked at her and smiled, then glanced at the almost full pew and shrugged. She smiled back and nodded in understanding. He shook hands with several men.

As he passed them, Lindsey slid back, picking up the bulletin. Nate followed his parents into seats two rows up, right where Jenna had a good view of him. She'd noticed dark circles under his eyes, but his back was straight and his shoulders squared with the military bearing that seemed second nature these days. He still looked good in a navy blue Western shirt and new blue Wranglers.

As the worship team began to play guitars, piano, and drums and led out in a joyful wake-up, everyone-hurry-inside chorus, Jenna automatically sang the words. But her heart wasn't in it. She was busy watching two young women check out Nate and try to catch his eye. Where had they been, Mars? Surely the gossip mill had alerted every eligible female in the county that he was dating her. *Isn't he?*

He didn't appear to notice them, or at least he wasn't paying them any attention. Good. She missed the next verse and sang the wrong words for a full line, earning a glance and raised eyebrow from her mother. *Oh, bad.* Being jealous was wrong anytime, but on Sunday morning during church?

And being so transparent? *Very, very bad.*

What business did she have being jealous anyway? They'd only gone on one date. Yes, they cared for each other. They always had. But there was no special, hands-off-to-anybody-else commitment between them. She didn't even want one.

Silly woman. Of course she did. Jenna noticed the rest of the congregation beginning to sit down, so she quickly did the same. She'd been so lost in thought that she hadn't realized the song had ended. Good thing she'd quit singing somewhere along the way.

Will leaned closer, whispering in her ear. "You okay?"

"Fine, but my mind keeps wandering."

"Thinking about little britches' party?"

She nodded, then inwardly grimaced. Add lying to her morning's list of sins. *Father, forgive me.*

"With you in command, it'll be great." He patted her hand, then turned his attention to the song leader as the worship team began another song.

That's the problem, she thought. *I'm not in command of anything. Not my life. Not my emotions or feelings. Not even the party.* Her mom had done most of the organizing and preparation. She apparently hadn't considered that her daughter might like to plan the party or decide on the theme. Cowboys or race cars? Mom picked race cars — which was fine, but Jenna thought Zach would have liked Elmo more. Lately, he was big into the happy red muppet.

She hadn't said anything about it. When Sue debated between burgers or tacos, she should have suggested pizza, one of Zach's favorites. But she hadn't. Throwing parties was her mom's thing. She loved it and took great delight in putting together the celebration for her precious only grandchild.

So while Jenna had been miffed and inwardly pouted, she'd kept her silence, not wanting to diminish her mother's joy. Nor was that the only reason for not wanting to stir things up. She owed her parents. Though she didn't think they realized it, certain things were expected of her because she lived with them. At times she felt as if she was under their control and authority as much as she'd been in high school.

Yet they were wonderful to her and Zach in so many ways. After Jimmy left, her deep depression and despair had made it impossible to be on her own. She had needed her parents and her brothers to ramrod her life. It had taken all her effort to tend to Zach, leaving no energy or motivation to take care of herself. Her family and the Lord had saved her. She thanked God every day for their love, support, and protection. But now they were stifling her.

Or perhaps more truthfully, she was finally ready to make a go of it on her own. Hopefully, she wouldn't have to live her whole life alone, but she could if that's what God had in store.

She hadn't asked to move into her grandparents' house yet, but she had to talk to them about it. Maybe today after the party. For certain tomorrow.

They sang a couple of slow praise songs. This time she tried to focus on the music. Nate appeared to be doing the same, although Misty Dumont still seemed more interested in him than the church service. Jenna decided she couldn't fault her too much since she was watching her watch him. The cute brunette sat right across the aisle from Nate and in front of Jenna. The only way to ignore her was to close her eyes, which she finally did.

When Pastor Brad began preaching, she took notes. That helped keep her mind somewhat on the sermon, instead of totally focusing on the other woman's ridiculous attempts to get Nate to look at her. How many times could one person drop her bulletin or cough delicately or say "Amen!" when the minister made a point? Or no point at all, since Misty piped up once when he paused to look up a Scripture. That earned her some curious looks — including one from Nate. All that from someone who hadn't shouted amen the whole time she had attended Grace Community.

At the end of the service, Misty timed her exit perfectly to bump into Nate. After a fake flustered moment, she introduced herself, batting her eyelashes and holding out her hand. Nate politely shook her hand and told her his name. Misty loudly began to fawn over him, acting as if she hadn't known who he was all along, going on and on about him being a war hero.

Jenna didn't think that earned her any points, but she watched to see Nate's reaction anyway. His face turned red, and he tried to edge away.

Will nudged Jenna with his elbow. "Are you going to go rescue him or keep me trapped in this pew all afternoon?"

"Oh, sorry." She stepped into the aisle. "Do you think I should?"

"Better you than me. If I go over there, she might think I'm interested in asking her out again."

"What a good idea."

"No way." He lowered his voice so nobody else would hear him. "She's trollin' for a breadwinner and uses a short skirt for bait."

"She's always seemed nice." Until now. "Her skirt's not that short."

"It's Sunday." He let the implication sink in. "The only reason she comes to church is to find a man, and the pickin's are better here than in a bar."

"That's a harsh thing to say."

"I'm not being judgmental. She told me that herself."

"You're kidding." Jenna stared at her brother.

Will shook his head grimly. "Afraid not. Now, go rescue the poor guy."

Jenna looked back at Nate as Misty possessively grasped his arm, her lips forming a flirty pout. Anger flashed across his face, and he jerked free from her grasp. For a second, Jenna was too surprised to move. Then she decided Misty might be the one who needed rescuing.

Hurrying the few steps down the aisle, she heard Nate growl, "Back off, lady." Wide-eyed, Misty nodded and scooted between two rows of seats toward the other side of the sanctuary.

Jenna spoke quietly. "Hi, Nate."

He turned toward her, fury blazing in his

eyes. He took a deep breath, and his anger dimmed but didn't fade away completely. "Hi."

There was no sense in asking if he was okay. *Make small talk.* "We're moving the party to 4:00 instead of 3:00. That way Zach can have a good nap. If we can get him to take one at all."

"I suppose he's pretty excited." His voice sounded strained, and she could see his pulse pounding in the vein in his neck.

"That's an understatement." She turned toward the back of the church. Because of the crowd ahead of them, the going was slow. Her arm swung naturally between them, and she let the back of her hand brush his. When he curled his fingers around hers, almost crushing them, she knew she had to get him out of there.

"Let's go out the back way and down the hall to get Zach in the nursery. He's liable to make his getaway if nobody is watching him closely."

Nate nodded and let her lead him through an empty row and back down the outside aisle, which had already cleared out of people. They went through a side door and down the hall, dodging a group of elementary kids playing chase. The farther they went, the more Nate's grip eased. By the time they were close to the nursery, his hold had relaxed to normal. She glanced at him, and he nodded, releasing her hand.

"I'm okay now. I'm not going to slug anybody."

"As if you would." Jenna chuckled.

He shuddered, bringing her to a halt. She ushered him into the empty kindergarten room and shut the door. "Nate, what's going on?"

Closing his eyes, he slumped against the wall, his shoulders sagging. "I don't know. I should have been flattered by . . ." He looked at her. "What's her name?"

"Misty."

"Or maybe amused by Misty's attention. But she was too pushy. She wouldn't back off. Wouldn't take the hint that I'm not interested and wanted to be left alone. When she grabbed hold of my arm, I almost lost it."

"You wouldn't have hit her. I know you, Nate. You've never hit a woman in your life."

"Wrong."

"What?"

"She was trying to smash in my face with a piece of pipe."

"Oh, well, that's different." She moved closer. "But I don't believe for a second that you would have hit Misty."

He rubbed a hand over his face and sighed heavily. "I guess I still have a thread of decency left."

"More than a thread. You look terribly tired." Now she was annoyed but not at him. "Daddy shouldn't have worked you so hard your first week back."

"It wasn't the work." Nate pushed away from the wall and wandered around the elementary-school-sized desks to the windows, watching the churchgoers slowly disperse. "I enjoyed every minute of it, even when I was worn out. I haven't been sleeping much, so my nerves are on edge. It's been going on for a while, even before I came home."

"Can't you take something?"

"No! No pills." He sent her a sharp glance. "I've known too many guys who got hooked on them. And they mess with your mind."

"Not any more than total exhaustion will." She joined him by the window, mindful that she could only linger a couple more minutes before picking up Zach. "I've been down that road. Finally getting something to help me sleep probably kept me from a nervous breakdown."

"I can't do it, Jen. They had me doped up after I got hurt, and it was awful. The meds

216

made me hallucinate. I didn't know who or where I was."

"Pain medication is different from sleeping pills."

"Maybe it is, but I'm not going to risk it."

"What about something over the counter?"

"I've tried everything out there and nothing helps. But I'll get over it. I always do. Being on edge for a while has happened every time I returned from the war zone. It's just taking longer to go away this time." His lips lifted in a smile, but there was no joy reflected in his face or his eyes. "Shouldn't you pick up Zach?"

"Yes. It's not right to make the nursery volunteer wait."

He rested his hand on her shoulder as they walked to the door. "Please don't mention this to anybody. Especially not your dad. I don't want him to send me packing after a week on the job."

"I think he'd be more understanding than that, but I won't say anything to anyone."

Standing behind her, he slid his hand around her waist and stopped her before she opened the door. He rested his cheek against her hair, his breath warm against her temple. "I'm sorry you were hurt so bad, honey, but I'm thankful that you're part of my life again."

She closed her hand over his. "I am too."

Would she become a bigger part of his life? Could she?

Please, God, help me not to be afraid to love again.

15

Nate carried Zach, and Jenna hauled the diaper bag as they made their way to the church foyer. They could have sneaked out the back door, but he wanted to meet the pastor. He suspected that even if he hadn't, Jenna would have insisted on it. She thought highly of the minister.

Most of the folks were already outside, so they didn't have to wait in a line to speak to him. Jenna made the introductions, and Nate shook hands with Pastor Brad.

"I'm glad to finally meet you, Nate. I've heard a lot about you. All of it good," he added with a friendly smile.

"I've heard good things about you too, sir." Nate glanced at Jenna. "I understand you were a chaplain in Iraq."

"Finished my tour a couple of years ago. I was mostly in Baghdad."

"My unit spent some time in the city. Generally, things were getting better when I left than when I first arrived."

"That's good to hear." Despite the pastor's friendly smile, he studied Nate's face, searched his eyes. Could he see into his soul? Discern his torment?

Pastor Brad shifted his attention to Zach. "I hear today is your birthday."

Zach nodded. "Uh-huh."

"How old are you?"

"My two." Zach held up four fingers.

"Are you going to have a party?"

"Yeah, birf-day party. With 'loons."

"And cake?"

Zach looked at Jenna. When she nodded, he turned back to the minister. "Yeah. Cake." He grinned and shifted, resting his arm across Nate's shoulder.

As always, that little symbol of acceptance and affection warmed Nate's heart.

Pastor Brad noticed it too. He met Nate's gaze with a twinkle in his eyes. "I think you've made a friend."

"Yes, sir. Zach's my buddy."

"He's a good one to have." The merriment faded from the pastor's expression. "Come by and see me, Nate. I'd like more of a chance to talk."

I bet you would. The conversation might not start out about the war, but Nate figured it wouldn't be long before the astute

220

ex-chaplain brought it up. Talking about the war was the last thing Nate wanted to do. He wanted to forget it. Not rehash everything and revive more memories to haunt him.

"I'll try to make time, but between working at the ranch and the farm, I'm going to be pretty busy." The best thing he could do was keep his distance from the well-meaning preacher.

Pastor Brad held his gaze. "I hope you can make time. But if you can't stop by, give me a call. Anytime."

"I'll keep that in mind, sir." Nate nodded to let him know he understood the underlying message, that the minister was available night or day if he needed counseling. Not that he would take him up on it. He'd never talked about anything personal with a chaplain.

There had been times he'd discussed sermons or Scripture, but he'd never given anyone in the military a glimpse of what was going on in his mind. From what he'd seen, if there was any hint that a soldier was cracking under the stress, his career would be finished. He didn't figure it would be any different as a civilian. If people thought he was going wacko, they wouldn't want anything to do with him.

"I'd better get this little guy home so he can have lunch and rest. It was a good sermon." Jenna played with Zach's fingers as he wiggled his hand in front of her face.

The pastor glanced at Nate, then focused on Jenna. "Glad you think so." His expression held a hint of amusement, and Jenna's face turned pink.

"Well, that poor fussy baby was a little distracting."

Nate remembered a baby crying for a few minutes, but the mother had hustled out of the sanctuary before it caused much of a problem.

Pastor Brad grinned. "Among other things." He scanned the foyer and lowered his voice. "I heard more amens this morning than I've heard in a month."

"Like I said, it was a good sermon." Jenna laughed, and the minister joined in.

Nate knew they were talking about Misty, but he didn't particularly appreciate their humor. The woman had done everything except stand on her head and whistle "Yankee Doodle" to get his attention. Evidently, it had been apparent to everyone. He felt a flush creep up his neck. *Great.*

"Nice to meet you, Nate."

"You too, Pastor." He was relieved that his voice didn't betray his annoyance.

Nate carried Zach out to Jenna's pickup. He didn't bother to hide his irritation. "So was everyone watching Misty and me during church?"

She threw the diaper bag on the front passenger seat. "I expect a few people figured out what she was up to, but I doubt most people realized what was going on. For the most part, the folks around me weren't paying her any attention."

"But you were." Fastening Zach in the car seat, he waited for her answer. When she didn't say anything, he clicked the last strap in place and straightened, looking at her.

She made a face at him. "Caught me. As did Pastor Brad. I'll admit it. I spent almost the whole church service watching her make a play for you. And I didn't like it one bit."

That put a whole new wrinkle on things. Nate grinned and opened the driver's door. "Jealous?"

"Yes. And don't you dare gloat."

"Aw, come on. My girl is jealous, and I can't gloat? That's no fun."

"Am I your girl?" she asked softly, her expression thoughtful, maybe a little wistful. She looked so pretty in her turquoise dress that he was sorely tempted to lean down and kiss her.

"Honey, you're the only girl — or woman

— I've ever truly been interested in. The only one I've ever cared about." He decided to be completely honest. "The only one I've ever dated."

She blinked, then frowned. "But we've only had one date."

"That's right."

"You've never taken anyone else out?"

"Not really. I spent time with a woman in Marfa at a couple of church picnics and met her once for coffee at the cafe. She was visiting her cousin for the summer, then went back to Boston. I never heard from her."

"Did you write her?"

"Naw. She didn't suggest it, and I didn't ask for her address. We didn't have any special connection, only interesting conversation."

"You've been deprived."

"I'm bashful."

"A little bit in high school, maybe. But you shouldn't be now. Nate, every single woman from fifteen to forty in Callahan Crossing would turn cartwheels down Main Street for the chance to go out with you."

He tweaked a little curl that blew across her cheek. "You tryin' to get rid of me?"

"No, but I don't think you should underestimate yourself, either."

"Ma-ma!"

Jenna stuck her head into the pickup and looked over the front seat. "What's the matter, Zach?"

"Fruit snack."

"Okay." She leaned across the seat and dug through the diaper bag, coming up with a little package. After ripping it open, she handed it to her son. Straightening, she rested her hand on the truck door. "I really have to get him home."

"I'll see you around four. Jenna, just to be clear on this — I don't want to go out with anyone else." He hesitated a second. "And I hope you don't want to, either."

Her smile sent his heartbeat into overdrive. "I don't."

"Good." He helped her in the truck, waited until she was buckled up, then shut the door. He waved to Zach and chuckled when the little boy waved back, happily chewing on his snack.

Nate watched them drive away, his good mood restored. Glancing at his watch, he jogged over to his truck. His folks were expecting him for Sunday dinner, and he was late.

Jenna laughed as her big, tall brother bent down, swung a blue kid's-size plastic golf club at the large white plastic ball, and completely missed it. Zach stepped up and smacked the ball clear across the room. He raised his hands and a red golf club up in the air. "Yea!"

"Good job, buddy." Jenna clapped her hands. "Now, why don't you and Uncle Chance play golf a little later? You have other presents to open."

Chance pouted for a second, then ruffled her son's hair. "Go on, pardner, see what other good stuff you got."

Zach handed him the golf club, and Chance tucked both of them away in the little cart.

"This one is from Nate." Jenna picked up a colorful balloon-patterned bag. "There's a card too." With Zach standing beside her, she pulled the card out of the bag and handed it to him. "What a cool card. It has cars on it." He opened it and music began to play, punctuated with an occasional "Vroom, vroom." The little boy studied it seriously as he closed and opened it a couple of times. Then he began dancing around to the music.

After a couple of minutes, he set it on the coffee table and peered into the sack. Pushing aside the blue speckled tissue paper, he pulled out a clear plastic package with two cars, what appeared to be launchers of some kind, and a post with countdown lights similar to what was used in car racing.

Jenna pointed to one of the toys. "Cool, Zach. Race cars." He grinned and tugged on one corner of the thick plastic, but it was sealed tight. "Why don't you take it over to Nate and let him open it. You need some grown-up help with this one."

Zach obediently carried it over to Nate, who was sitting on the red leather couch. Her little guy stood at her big guy's knee, watching intently as Nate tried to figure out how to get into the thing. He pulled his pocket knife out of his pocket. "This may take awhile, buddy. All the pieces are fastened in. Why don't you open something else while I work on this?"

Zach frowned and thought about it for a minute, then nodded and went back to Jenna.

"This bag is from Grandma and Papa." Jenna put the big bag on the floor. The first thing Zach pulled out was a green plaid cowboy shirt. "Oh, that's nice."

Zach's gaze drifted to Nate. He glanced in the bag — more clothes — and headed back to check on the race car unwrapping progress.

Jenna pulled out a little blue Western shirt with pearl snaps. "Zach, look at this cute shirt that Grandma and Papa got you."

Zach stopped, turned, pointed his index finger at the shirt, and nodded once. "Yeah." Short and sweet. He spun around and went straight to Nate while all the grown-ups laughed.

"He's definitely more interested in those cars than clothes," said her mom with a grin.

"But he'll like wearing them." She took out a couple pairs of jeans. "He knows when he looks snazzy." In the bottom of the bag, Jenna spied a bright red furry toy. So her mom hadn't missed his love for the red muppet. "Zach, you'd better come check this out. There's something really cool still in the bag."

Zach watched Nate struggle with a plastic strap holding one of the cars in place.

"Not there yet, bud."

The little boy went back to his mom and peeked in the bag. "Elmo!" He tugged on it, tipping over the bag. When he got it out and hugged it, the toy started talking.

Zach jumped and held it out away from him. Elmo's mouth moved when he said hello and his head turned from side to side. Zach's forehead wrinkled in concentration, then he grinned and looked at his grandma. "Wow."

"You like that?" asked Sue.

"Uh-huh."

"Papa picked it out."

Jenna stared at her dad. "Really?"

"I notice what interests my grandson. And the rest of my family too."

Jenna grinned at him. "And here I thought you paid more attention to the livestock than us."

Her dad winked at her. "Don't count on it."

She instructed Zach to set the toy on the coffee table so everybody could see and hear it. He obeyed, listening as Elmo sang a tune. He giggled when the toy crossed its legs.

Will stared at it. "How does it do that?"

"You're jealous because that red thing is more agile than you are." Chance ducked when his brother threw a pillow at him.

Nate set the toy cars and the rest of the race equipment on the coffee table. Zach went around the table to check them out. He pushed a button on the start tower and it blasted out "Start your engines." Lights flashed — red, yellow, green.

Nate glanced at Jenna. "Oops. I didn't know it would be so loud. Maybe you should play with the cars."

Zach picked up a car. "Nate help."

Nate helped him gather up the two cars

and launchers. They moved over to a spot with plenty of room and sat down on the hardwood floor. Nate fastened each car into a launcher and lined them up side by side. Then he showed him how to make them go. Zach tried pushing the lever with two fingers, then three, but he couldn't make it work. So Nate helped him, launching his own car simultaneously. The cars raced across the floor and partway down the hall. Giggling, Zach ran after them and brought them back.

They raced the cars over and over for the next twenty minutes, sometimes using the ramps in the set and sometimes not. Zach tried hitting the lever with his fist, but that didn't work. So Nate kept helping him. He laughed almost as much as Zach and never lost patience with the little boy. They finally moved so they could sit back against the wall.

Jenna watched them for a long time and noticed her dad doing the same, a smile lighting his still handsome but weathered face. As if sensing her appraisal, he turned his head and met her gaze. When he nodded his approval, she almost hopped up and did a happy dance.

"Is it time for me to start grilling the burgers?" asked Will. "I'm hungry."

"Me too." Chance rose from his chair. "I'll help."

Her brothers headed for the patio to fire up the grill, and Jenna and her mom started for the kitchen to get everything else ready. Zach stood by Nate instead of sitting down as he'd done all the other times. She paused to see if he was getting too tired and might need to do something quieter for a while.

He rested his hand on Nate's shoulder. "Push with my toe."

"Good idea." Together they put the cars in the starting blocks. Zach stood and hung on to Nate's arm for balance. Watching as Zach positioned his foot on the lever and pushed, Nate launched his car at the same time. They zipped across the room side by side. "Hey, that worked great." Nate held up his open palm. "High five."

Zach slapped his palm, then ran to get the cars.

"Did you suggest that?" Jenna decided her son still had enough energy to play for a while longer.

"Nope. He thought of it all by himself." Nate smiled up at her, beaming like a proud papa.

Jenna's throat clogged with emotion. She might be scared of love, but that didn't seem to matter to her heart. She was falling fast.

The rest of the afternoon and evening passed quickly, with delicious food, lots of good-natured teasing, and laughter. Zach blew out his two candles with her help. He swiped his finger in the blue icing on the race car cake — which now seemed perfect given the way he'd spent much of the afternoon — before she could cut him a piece.

When Nate decided he needed to go home, Jenna walked out to the pickup with him. It was dark, but she purposefully didn't turn on the porch light. The half moon illuminated the yard well enough to see. Still, she was thankful that Nate had parked with the driver's side away from the porch. She wouldn't put it past her dad to flip on the light.

Nate waited to open the truck door, settling his hands at her waist instead. "I had a good time. Thanks for inviting me."

"Zach would have been disappointed if you weren't here." She moved a little closer. "I would have been too."

"He's quite the kid." His hands tightened slightly, drawing her nearer.

"He thinks the world of you, Nate." She slid her hands up his chest, resting them on his shoulders. Her heart pounded so hard she was sure he could hear it. "So do I," she whispered.

He lowered his head slowly, giving her plenty of time to stop him before he feathered a kiss across her lips. She moved her hands around his neck, and he pulled her against him, kissing her tenderly. His touch was gentle and so sweet that her eyes misted.

When he finally, but all too soon, raised his head and eased his hold, she brushed aside a tear that had slipped down her cheek.

"Hey, what's this?" he asked quietly, his voice filled with concern. "What did I do?"

"Nothing bad." She swiped the other eye with her fingertips and smiled up at him. "For my first almost-on-the-front-porch good-night kiss, that was really somethin'."

He grinned and lightly caressed her cheek. "It *was* pretty good."

"Just pretty good?" Wide-eyed, she tried to see his expression more clearly in the silvery light. He had to be kidding. Nobody had ever kissed her like that. *Because nobody has ever cared for you the way he does.* Her mouth went dry.

"Well, I thought it was great, but I don't have anything to compare it to."

That got her attention. She drew in a deep breath. "Nothing?"

Chuckling, he released her and rubbed

the back of his neck. "I think I'm digging myself into a hole here." He shifted and leaned against the pickup, crossing his arms. "Put two and two together, sweetheart."

So she did. He said he'd never dated anyone but her. So that meant . . . "You've never kissed anybody else?"

"Give the lady a gold star."

"Really? That was your first kiss?"

Nate groaned. "Jenna, don't rub it in."

"Sorry. I didn't mean that in a bad way."

"No?" He sounded irritated. And probably embarrassed.

"No." She trailed her fingertips along his jaw as she backed away, making a sassy, girlish twirl before she reached the front of the pickup. "I'm thinking if the first one was that great, I have a lot to look forward to."

His laughter followed her up the walk and onto the porch. She decided to wait on the steps in the moonlight and wave at him as he drove away. Maybe it would give her flushed cheeks enough time to return to normal.

16

Nate settled into a good routine, working with his dad a couple of days a week. They repaired a tractor and made sure the cotton stripper was in top shape. They cleaned out the barn, expanded the fenced area around the chicken coop, and added new shelves in the pantry.

The rest of the time he was at the ranch, occasionally working on Saturday too. Sunday was the only day off he could count on, but that would have been normal if he'd been full time either place.

He often ate with the Callahans at noon, unless he was in a pasture on horseback and too far away for an easy ride back. They extended a standing invitation for supper, which he sometimes accepted. He tried not to infringe on the family's time too much, but it wasn't easy to bid Jenna and Zach an early good night.

That might change before long. Her folks

had agreed to let her move into her grandparents' house, but Dub had insisted all the single pane windows be replaced with good insulated double pane ones first. The old windows were fine if someone was only staying there for a few days, but with winter coming on, he didn't want his grandson and daughter living in a cold house fighting drafts.

They would all probably still eat with the family most of the time, but he looked forward to spending some longer evenings at Jenna's place. It was the season to take advantage of quiet times snug and warm inside on cold days, or enjoying a light breeze drifting through an open window on warm ones.

The first few days after the roundup had been spent herding the cows away from the pasture next to the calves and back to other parts of the ranch. Some of the calves weren't thrilled with the idea of losing sight of their mamas, but the cows had resigned themselves to the inevitable and were ready to move on.

Now the work on the ranch was more low key and solitary. Riding fences to check for breaks or weak stretches, sometimes on horseback, sometimes in the pickup, was on the agenda. If he found a problem, he fixed it.

Checking the windmills was also on his list. When he came across a squeaky one, he climbed up the forty or fifty foot tower to oil the head. A lot of cowboys didn't like the chore, but he enjoyed the view from way up there. And the adrenaline rush. With everything locked down so nothing would turn, he often took his sandwich up with him and ate lunch perched at the top.

After functioning on adrenaline surges much of the time in Iraq, he needed a charge now and then. Racing a horse full speed across an open stretch was almost as good as climbing the windmill, and more fun. The horses loved it too.

Other days, he rode the pastures, counting the cattle and checking for any that might be missing, injured, or sick. Dub liked all the pastures checked every day, dividing them up between himself, Will, and the hired hands. In the flatter, open areas they could use pickups, but the more rugged terrain required a horse and rider.

He and his dad were getting along well. They always had, but working together with his father treating him as an equal was a new and gratifying experience. Just as things had changed some on the ranch, farming techniques had evolved too. His dad was a good teacher, and Nate was a quick study, so there weren't any major problems.

The warm weather continued for a couple of weeks until a blue norther blew in late Saturday afternoon and dropped the temperature into the twenties. The timing couldn't have been better. By then most of the green bolls were open, and the fields were filled with white, fluffy cotton. The freeze killed the leaves on the cotton plants, making them ready to strip without having to use chemicals.

Sunday remained cold and clear. Nate and his dad hauled the long module builder to the field during the afternoon and parked it in the turn row.

On Monday morning, they waited for the dew to burn off and for the cotton to dry out completely before starting the harvest. Any dampness could cause fungus to grow in the cotton, which ruined it.

When they decided the field was ready, Tom drove the huge cotton stripper, leading their little procession. Nate followed on a John Deere tractor, pulling the boll buggy, a big portable basket used to carry the cotton away from the stripper. His mom took the pickup, parking it near the module builder and the tractor used to pull it.

Nate drove along behind his dad, keeping

an eye on the stripper so he'd be in the right place when the basket was full. He timed how long it took to fill the first load, which told him how long he'd have to drive to the module builder, dump the cotton, and get back to the stripper.

He pulled up alongside his dad, who stopped the stripper. Nate pulled forward a little to line up the baskets. Father and son exchanged a grin as Tom operated the controls to lift the stripper basket way up and at an angle, tipping it almost upside down to pour the contents into the boll buggy.

Through the cab windows, Nate read his father's lips. "Ain't this fun?"

Nate nodded and gave him a thumbs-up. When the stripper basket was empty, his dad maneuvered it back into place and put the machine in gear, continuing down the rows. Nate pulled away, circling around toward the turn row.

He heard his dad call his mom over the walkie-talkie, "Sugar, your boy is bringing you the first load."

"I'm ready." She laughed and gave a little whoop. "This is like old times."

And Nate was glad all over again that he'd come home.

His mother had abandoned the warm

pickup and sat on the high seat of the module builder. She had it cranked up and ready to start packing down the cotton.

He stopped beside her and slid open the tractor cab window. She had on a heavy blue coat, multicolored crocheted hat, and leather work gloves, but it was still nippy out. "Are you cold?"

"I'm fine."

"If you need to switch jobs, let me know."

"Will do."

He pulled up a little farther and tilted the basket up and over, dumping the cotton in the long, narrow rectangular container. As he drove away he had the window still open, and he heard the light *squishy-crunch* above the sound of the motor as the big bar began moving up and down, compacting the cotton.

They followed the same routine until mid-morning, when his mom insisted they take a break. Even when he'd worked on the ranch out West, he'd come home for harvest. He'd also made it once while he was in the service. For as far back as he could remember, the work had never stopped until noon. But his dad hadn't been recovering from surgery then.

Nate and his mom hopped in the pickup and drove over to see how his dad was far-ing. To their relief, he appeared to be holding up well. They stretched their legs and walked around a little, ate some muffins and drank a little coffee, then got back to work.

At noon they shut down the machinery in the field and drove back to the house. His mom had spaghetti and meatballs ready to warm up in the microwave. Nate threw together the green salad and set it and the salad dressings on the table, while his dad poured the iced tea.

They chatted a little but mostly concentrated on eating. Chris insisted that her husband take at least a thirty minute rest after the meal. When Tom didn't complain and went willingly to his recliner, she and Nate exchanged a worried glance.

"Is he overdoing it?" Nate cleared the dishes off the table while she put the leftovers in containers.

"Probably. But you know he'll never admit it. If he falls asleep, let's stretch it to an hour. Any longer and he'll be mad as a bobcat in a mud puddle."

"Can't waste the daylight." Nate frowned as he put a plate in the dishwasher. During harvest every minute counted, especially when there was another cold front up north that might come their way and bring rain. Some farmers kept stripping into the night, but they ran the risk of the cotton getting wet from the dew. "Maybe we should hire someone to fill in for him. I've got the money."

"He'd never hear of it." She paused on the way to the refrigerator and dropped her voice to a whisper. "That would be harder on him than getting worn out physically. For now, the best thing we can do is make sure he takes enough breaks and actually rests."

Nate peeked into the living room. His dad was sound asleep. "Doesn't look like we'll have to push him on that."

"You need a little siesta too." His mom put the food in the fridge and came back to stand beside him. "Dub is working you too hard."

In a flare of irritation, he glanced sharply at his mother. "I don't work any harder than anybody else."

"You look tired," she snapped. "Worse now than when you first came home."

He tried to lighten the mood — and distract her. "That's not what the ladies think." He winked at her. "From what I hear every single woman in Callahan Crossing would turn cartwheels down Main Street to get a date with me." He'd paraphrased a bit, but the gist of it was the same.

His mother laughed. "Wouldn't that be a sight? I doubt two-thirds of them can do cartwheels. Who told you that?"

"Jenna."

"I thought you were dating *her*."

"I am."

"Does she want to keep seeing you?"

"Yes." He draped his arm across her shoulders. "It's kind of convoluted, so I won't go into the details." Mild disappointment flashed across her face, making him grin. "Suffice it to say that unlike another woman I know, Jenna was trying to flatter me."

"She has a funny way of doing it." Glancing at the clock, she nodded toward the living room. "I'm going to take a little nap. You can do whatever you want."

He gently squeezed her shoulders again and whispered, "I don't mind a siesta."

She made a face. "But you don't like me telling you to do it."

Nate lifted his arm from around her shoulders and shrugged. "Sorry, Mom."

"Well, get used to it, son. You may be all grown up, but that doesn't mean I'll quit looking after you."

"You'll probably be reminding me to wear a coat when I'm seventy."

"That's right."

Nate pretended exaggerated consternation and pointed her toward her recliner. She wasn't fooled a bit. He stretched out on the couch, propping his ankles on the armrest and letting his boots hang over the end. His mom was right. He looked bad. Who wouldn't if he'd run out of reserves? He seldom managed more than two hours of sleep a night.

The previous Thursday, he hadn't slept at all. He'd made a run to Abilene that day to get a part for the cotton stripper. On the way back, some guy in a blue souped-up Chevy had been tailgating him on the highway. The man could have easily passed, but he stayed right on his tail. Nate lost his temper and slammed on the brakes. The Chevy missed his pickup by inches. The other driver sped around Nate then slowed way down. When Nate tried to pass him, he shifted over in the left lane to block him. On Nate's next attempt, the man moved left again, and Nate floored the pickup around him on the right shoulder, spewing gravel all over the other car.

Nate was doing over ninety on a straight stretch of road when he finally cooled down enough to pay attention to his speed. Thankfully, the other guy had enough sense not to chase him. Or maybe his car was more noise than substance. Either way, it was a blessing he didn't show up again or he would have wound up in the hospital one way or another.

Nate had rehashed the episode all night long, bouncing between feeling guilty about how he'd acted — certainly not Christ-like — and imagining various detailed scenarios for getting even. He hadn't been able to turn off his mind or control his thoughts.

But today he could. He closed his eyes and pictured Jenna's sweet smile.

Mid-morning the next day as Nate pulled up to the module builder to dump another load, Jenna and Zach drove into the field, stopping nearby but out of the way. He parked the tractor and boll buggy and walked over to see them.

She rolled the window down on the pickup. "Good morning. Don't let us interrupt your work. I thought Zach might like to see all the machinery."

"Good morning." Nate rested his hand on the pickup door. "You're not interrupting. We're ready for a break anyway." His mom shut her machine down, and his dad stopped about ten rows away. When Jenna lowered the back window, he ducked his head so he could see Zach on the opposite side. "Hi, buddy."

"Hi." Zach pointed at the module builder. "What's that?"

"It's a module builder. It presses all the cotton together into a big block."

The little boy pointed to the tractors. "Two tractors."

"That's right. And that big basket trailer is called a boll buggy."

"Boll buggy. What it do?"

"That's what I use to bring the cotton over here." He spotted some bags of groceries behind the front seat. "You've been to town already?"

"No. We're on the way. Those are some things for the mission. Whenever Mom's bridge club meets at our house, they always bring donations."

"That's cool. I'll have to stop by there and check it out. Not that I need a handout but to see what you have. In case I run into someone who might need something. And what you need. I can always pick up some extra groceries to help out."

"Donations are always welcomed. We take everything from clothes to food to some furniture. I can always use help stocking the shelves or hauling furniture inside. People drop things off behind the building."

"Next time you need some muscle, call me."

Jenna grinned. "Okay." Her gaze shifted to his mom as she walked up. "Good morning, Chris."

"Good morning." She waved at Zach. "We're going to have some coffee and doughnuts. Will you join us?"

"Sure. I never pass up doughnuts."

Nate stepped back. "I'll get Zach."

"Thanks."

Nate walked around to the other side of the truck and took the little guy out of the car seat. He listened to the women talk as they walked to his folks' pickup and smiled to hear them discussing cotton and cattle prices. Typical farm and ranch women.

He fished Zach's sippy cup out of the diaper bag, then carried him over to join the adults. When Jenna noticed the little covered cup of water in his hand, her expression softened with appreciation.

Nate mentally patted himself on the back. He'd brought it because he didn't think the kid could drink coffee, but it didn't hurt to earn a few points with the boy's mama. Given the approval shining in his own mother's eyes, he'd made a few points there too.

Jenna broke off a little piece of cake

doughnut and gave it to Zach, who crammed it in his mouth. When he grinned, she gently reminded him, "Chew with your mouth closed, please."

Nate set the sippy cup on the pickup hood and helped himself to a chocolate-covered treat. When Zach eyed it, he looked at Jenna. "Is it okay if he has some of this?"

"A tiny bite." She touched her son's hand to get his attention. "You let Nate put it in your mouth. I don't want a big mess."

"I'm going to let you sit up here on the hood, but you have to stay real still, okay?" When Zach nodded, Nate eased him down onto the hood, standing in front of him in case he lost his balance. He broke off a small piece of the doughnut, making sure there was some chocolate icing on it. "Open wide."

The little boy complied, and he popped the doughnut morsel into his mouth. Zach's eyes sparkled as he chewed.

"Pretty good, huh?" Nate ate most of it and drank a little coffee. Jenna gave Zach a few more bites of her doughnut before Nate slipped him the last little bit of his.

Zach kept trying to turn around to look at the cotton stripper. "What's that?"

Nate set his coffee cup out of the way and picked him up so he could see it better.

"That's a cotton stripper. It scoops up all that fluffy white cotton so we don't have to go along and do it by hand."

"I don't see how anybody could have picked all this without machinery," said Jenna. "It would take forever."

"Not as long as that." Nate's dad smiled and drank a sip of coffee. "We always hired good hands that worked for us every year. Some lived around here and some were migrant workers, mostly from Mexico. Some legal, some not."

Jenna bent down and inspected an open boll. "Those sharp points on the base look like they would cut your hand."

"They can if you aren't careful. That's called a burr. It's what's left of the seed pod after it opens. In places where they actually pick the cotton — pluck it from the burr — people suffered a lot when they did it by hand, even though the cotton practically fell out of it. In West Texas, it's too windy to grow that type of cotton, so we use a variety that clings to the boll. The stripper pulls off the whole thing."

He gazed out across the farm, a hint of nostalgia on his countenance. "Sometimes we had thirty workers out there, bent over the rows, filling the long white canvas sacks as fast as they could. They got paid by the pound, not by the hour. When I was ten, Daddy started letting me drive the tractor and pull the trailer out to the field. But he spent the day out there too. He had to weigh the full sacks. I couldn't do it because they often weighed about a hundred pounds. A good worker would pull 250 to 275 pounds in a long day."

"How did you weigh them?"

Nate thought Jenna was interested in the history, but he had a feeling she knew she was nurturing his father's soul by asking him to share his memories. She had a knack for seeing the need in people's hearts. He wondered if she saw into his. Part of him wanted her to. But another part of him was terrified of what she would discover.

"We had a scale rigged up on some braces at the end of the trailer. Daddy would lift that big heavy sack up and over the hook on the scale, letting it hang free. Part of the scale slid down with the weight of the cotton. Whatever number it stopped on told us how much had been picked.

"Then my dad would empty the bag in the trailer, and I'd climb up in there and stomp it down so we could put more in. The general idea is the same as the module builder, only it packs the cotton a whole lot tighter than a kid or even a grown man could. It has a big bar that presses on the cotton. We used our feet. School closed down for a week or two in the fall so the kids could help in the fields. Of course, for the town kids it was another vacation."

"I grew up on a farm too," said Nate's mom. "But it was smaller than this one. I got to tromp cotton as well. It was fun to jump up and down on it. My mother was a nurse and often worked the three-to-eleven shift at the hospital. When my brother and I were too young to stay home by ourselves, we'd go to the gin with Daddy in the evening. We'd sit in the gin office doing our homework. If there were a lot of trailers ahead of us, we'd have a long wait. I fell asleep curled up on the chairs more times than I can remember."

Nate's dad picked up the story. "Sometimes there would be a dozen or more trailers lined up in the evening. Trailers only held a single bale, and many farmers only had one —"

"Like my dad," said Chris.

"So they had to make sure the load was ginned, and the trailer freed up to use again the next morning. When we switched to mechanical strippers, we had to buy bigger trailers."

There was a note of pride in his dad's

voice that came from following in a long line of Langley footsteps. Nate's great-grandparents had homesteaded the farm in 1908, and every generation since had lived there and raised cotton — or attempted to — through good times and bad. It was a good legacy to have, to continue.

"How did they get it out of the trailer?" Jenna helped Zach down off the pickup so he could walk around. "Stay close."

"With suction." Nate's dad grinned. "Picture a big metal tube attached to a giant vacuum cleaner. A man would climb into the trailer and guide the tube around it until all the cotton was sucked up into the gin. It was noisy. You couldn't hear anybody if they tried to talk. And it was dangerous. A man could get hurt real bad if he slipped. Then the cotton would go through all kinds of brushes, separators, dryers, and eventually wind up in a bale that weighed five to six hundred pounds.

"The modules make it easier these days. They're picked up by a big truck and stored on the lot at the gin until they're processed. The newest strippers have a small module builder included. It compresses the cotton, forms it into a big roll, wraps it to protect it from the weather, and spits it out in the field. It can be hauled to the gin when it's convenient. Most of the gins are adding the machines to handle that kind of module as well as the big ones. The new stripper is expensive, but it's the only equipment you need. Plus it only takes one man to do the job that requires three now. It's the way of the future."

Nate didn't know how soon the future would come to them. Not this year. They'd need several good crops to make purchasing a new stripper feasible.

His dad turned to him. "Why don't you take Zach on the stripper and show him how it works. I'll meet you with the boll buggy, and we can switch out. He can ride back here in the tractor with you."

Nate noticed a spark of apprehension in Jenna's eyes. "It's safe. We'll be enclosed in the cab on the stripper and then in one on the tractor. I can run them both with him on my lap." Without thinking about his parents' presence, he caught her hand. "I'll keep him safe, sweetheart."

"I know you will. And he'll love it. Go ahead. But you know my dad and brothers will rib us both about trying to turn him into a farmer instead of a cowboy."

"No reason he can't be both." Nate caught up with Zach, who was gingerly touching the fluffy cotton in a boll down the row. He knelt down beside him. "Do you want to go ride in the cotton stripper with me?"

Zach raised his head and stared at the big machine, his expression serious and thoughtful. "Yeah," he said finally.

Nate picked him up and walked over to the stripper, climbing inside and settling Zach on his lap. "You have to stay right here and don't touch anything unless I tell you that you can, okay?"

The little boy nodded, clearly fascinated by all the gauges, buttons, levers, and knobs.

"It's going to be noisy, kind of like your papa's tractor."

"Okay." He sounded a little nervous.

Nate started the engine and felt Zach's fingers grip his shirt sleeve. "Are you all right, son?"

The term was commonly used in Texas when a man talked to a younger male or even one his own age. It shouldn't have caused the sharp stab of longing in Nate's heart or the sudden lump in his throat.

As he maneuvered the controls and set the stripper in motion, he barely noticed Zach nod his head. A few minutes later, the little boy stretched his neck to see the front of the stripper, then twisted around to watch the cotton shoot into the basket and laughed in delight.

Please, Jesus, I want him to be my son.

17

Jenna moved into her grandparents' house later in the week, so she'd only taken Zach to the farm once more to watch Nate and his parents work in the field. But that hadn't stopped her son from asking about the cotton stripper and the boll buggy half a dozen times a day. Or from pestering his grandfather in his sweet little way — "Papa, we go tractor?" — until her dad broke down and took him for a ride.

During the transition to the new house, they'd eaten with her folks as usual. It didn't appear that the tradition would change much anytime soon, unless Zach's tiptoeing into the terrible twos became a full-blown assault. He did pretty well most of the time but had a couple of meltdowns when it was time for them to go home.

Jenna worried that she was damaging her son emotionally by taking him out of his familiar and secure environment. Had moving to a house of their own been a mistake? Her mom had reassured her that his behavior was typical for his age, and that he wasn't nearly as bad as she or her brothers had been.

Within a week, he'd pretty well adjusted to sleeping in a different place. He seemed to realize that much of their previous routine was the same. She spent time at the ranch house working on the books and keeping the Callahan Ranch website up to date. Zach had gone to day care on the mornings she worked at the mission as usual. She could keep him with her without any trouble, but he loved playing with his friends, most of whom were a year or two older than he was. Being the only little kid at the ranch, he needed more opportunities than Sunday school to be with other children.

A few minutes before noon on Thursday, they moseyed down the road to join the family for dinner. Noting Nate's truck parked out front, she walked a little faster. Zach spotted it too, and broke into a run. Nate had been riding pasture on a far corner of the ranch since Monday, so they hadn't seen him.

Jogging after Zach, she caught up with him at the porch steps. He held on to the lower railing beside the steps and walked up all by himself, something she still marveled at. She was proud of his accomplishments, but her baby was growing up too fast.

When they walked through the front door, she noticed Chance sprawled out on the couch, dozing. She touched Zach on the shoulder, stopping him, and knelt down. "Be real quiet," she whispered. "Uncle Chance is asleep."

Zach studied his uncle before he walked very quietly behind the red leather sofa, halting at the end where Chance's head rested on a Navajo patterned pillow propped against the arm. Her folks stepped out of the kitchen and stopped. When Jenna started to go after Zach, her mom grinned and shook her head. They waited to see what he would do.

Zach eased around the end of the couch until his face was right in front of Chance's. He breathed on him for a full minute. Chance's lip twitched, but he didn't open his eyes. Zach leaned a little closer, resting his forearms on the sofa cushion. "What you doin'?"

Chance kept his eyes closed. "I'm sleeping."

"No, you talking."

Chance laughed and hauled him up on

his chest in a hug. "Hi, squirt. I can't fool you, can I?"

Zach shook his head. He wiggled around until he was sitting up. "You drive bulldozer?"

"I did. I moved a whole bunch of dirt around this morning. You'll have to come out to the job site and check it out. We're building a new house."

"You go to work?" Zach climbed down with a little help.

Chance held on to him until his feet were firmly on the floor, then he sat up. "After dinner. Maybe your mom will bring you out there so you can see it."

Zach turned to Jenna. "You go to work?"

"How about we do that tomorrow morning?" She looked at her brother. "If you'll still be using the dozer then."

"I will."

The little boy swung around to face Chance. "Okay, I go to work too."

"Tomorrow."

Zach considered it, almost pouted, then nodded. " 'Morrow."

Will and Nate strolled in from the patio, and Jenna's heartbeat speeded up. She'd missed him. His gaze met hers, and warmth filled his eyes. Seconds later, tension tightened his face. Had he and Will been discussing something that upset him?

Chance stood and stretched while Jenna's mom related how Zach had awakened him. As the others laughed, Nate attempted a half-hearted smile. Something wasn't right.

"Sis, I keep tellin' you that Chance is a bad influence on Zach." Will slanted a glance at his brother. "Not only is he lazy, sleeping away half the morning, but he wants to turn him into a contractor instead of a cowboy. He's filling that child's head with thoughts of driving bulldozers, backhoes, and cement trucks."

"Hey, it's not my machinery the kid's been jabberin' about all week. No, sir." Chance sidled away from the coffee table and moved into an open area facing Will and Nate. "That boy is excited about cotton strippers and tractors and boll buggies. If you're going to blame somebody for corrupting him, blame Nate." Chance grinned at Nate.

He didn't smile back. A hard glint flashed through his silver eyes before they darkened to a thunderous blue.

But Chance didn't notice. No one seemed to but Jenna. A spark of mother's intuition — or a nudge from the Lord — prompted her to scoot around and pick up Zach. She moved behind one of the sofas. "So what's for dinner?"

Either no one heard her or they chose to ignore such a dumb question. Anyone who'd ever eaten Ramona's spaghetti knew that's what they were having. The distinctive aroma filled the whole house.

Chance shook his head. "Luring him over to your place with rides on the cotton stripper or taking him on the tractor and towing the boll buggy. Showin' him how to squish all that purty fluffy cotton into a big hard lump. It's sad, just sad."

"Knock it off, Chance." Nate flexed his fingers, but he kept his hands at his sides. He shifted his legs, one foot slightly in front of the other. His jaw tightened and his face grew flushed.

Jenna decided her whole family had suddenly become obtuse. "Chance, let it go," she said softly.

Both her brothers sent her a questioning glance, but when they were in tease mode, they were hard to stop.

"Yes, sir. It's a downright shame that you're trying to turn that boy into a sodbuster." Chance started forward, extending his hand as if he might pat Nate on the shoulder to emphasize his point. "A tractor wrangler. A pumpkin rol—"

In a fluid movement, Nate pushed Chance's arm aside, caught him mid-step with one leg, and swept his feet out from under him. One second her brother was standing up laughing; the next he was flat on his back on the floor. With a snarl, Nate dropped to one knee, looming above Chance.

"Nate!" Jenna furiously tried to think of a way to stop him, but how? What would he do? Ramona and Ace came running from the kitchen, halting in the dining room.

He drew his hand back to his shoulder, his fingers closing almost into a fist aimed at her brother's face.

"Hey!" Will lunged, grabbing him from behind, and caught hold of his arm.

Nate dipped his shoulder and rolled Will over it, throwing him on the other side of Chance. Will's head bounced against the hardwood floor with a loud thud.

"Nate, stop!" Jenna held Zach close. But he twisted around, watching the fight with wide, frightened eyes, and began to wail.

Still kneeling over Chance, Nate straightened and drew his hand and arm back again.

Dub moved around behind his boys. "Nate, stand down." His voice was strong, calm, and filled with a note of authority that Jenna had never heard before.

Nate blinked and hesitated.

When Will started to get up, ready to renew the fight, her father nudged his shoulder with the toe of his boot and ordered quietly, "Don't move, son. Both of you stay where you are."

Will slumped back to the floor.

"Stand down, Nate," her father repeated. His stance appeared nonthreatening, but Jenna knew he would pounce on Nate if he had to.

Nate scowled at Will and Chance. Then he glanced down at the way he was positioned on the floor, and confusion clouded his eyes.

Zach quit screaming and clung to Jenna, inhaling on a silent shudder. She cuddled him against her shoulder and rubbed his back. "It's okay, honey," she whispered. "Everything is all right now."

How she wished that were true, but it wasn't. Tears streamed down her face and her heart ached — for her frightened little boy, for her brothers and a lifetime of trust and friendship that may have been destroyed, for herself and her fear of the man she loved. But most of all, she ached for Nate — for the wounds to his heart and soul, for the inner torment that he endured even now, for the experiences that brought him such pain. *Lord Jesus, heal him, comfort him. Help us to do what's right.*

Nate turned his head, staring at his still-clenched hand. The blood drained from his face as the implication of the situation became clear. He slowly uncurled his fingers and lowered his hand and arm. As he focused on Will and Chance again, sorrow filled his face. They slowly leaned up on their elbows and warily watched him. He looked at her dad, and Dub held out his hand to help him up.

Nate shook his head and pushed himself to a standing position. It seemed to take all the energy he had. Pale, his shoulders drooping, he began to tremble.

"Nate, come sit down," her father said gently. His kindness surprised Jenna. Hauling Nate out of there and giving him a good tongue-lashing, if not a plain old thrashing, was more his style. Normally, Dub didn't tolerate any kind of threat to his family.

Instead, Nate took a step backward, turned, and met Jenna's gaze. She gasped at the bleak emptiness in his eyes, the despair in his soul. Still clinging to her, Zach sniffed and took a shuddering breath. Tears filled Nate's eyes, spilling down his cheeks.

"I'm sorry," he whispered. Stumbling slightly, he hurried toward the front door.

"Nate, wait." Jenna started after him, but

her mother caught her arm, halting her.

"Let him go, honey. He needs time to get his bearings."

He jerked the door open and bolted outside, letting the screen door slam shut behind him.

Jenna watched through the open doorway as he ran unsteadily to his pickup. She tried to tug free, but her mother held tight. "No, Mom. He shouldn't be alone. He's distraught." They didn't know how that felt, what it might cause him to do. A memory burned through her mind.

She stared at the bottle of sleeping pills. Dumped them into her hand. Curled her fingers around them. Picked up the glass of water with her other hand. She wanted so desperately to end the heartache of Jimmy's rejection and abandonment. To ease the pain of her worthlessness. A baby's cry broke through her despair. Stopped her. Zach needed her. She had to live for him.

A wave of panic swept through her. "What if he tries . . . tries to hurt himself?"

"Better him than you." Rubbing the back of his head, Will let his dad help him up. "He's been eatin' loco weed with his Wheaties. We should call the sheriff."

"Nobody is going to call the sheriff." Dub gripped Will's shoulder. "Understand me?"

Will nodded reluctantly, then frowned at Jenna. "But you stay away from him."

Chance hauled himself to his feet. "I agree." He sighed heavily. "It's my fault. I should have kept my big mouth shut. I noticed he was annoyed, but I thought I could tease him out of it."

"You and Nate have joked with each other all your lives," said her mom. "You had no reason to think he wouldn't go along with it like he always does."

Chance walked over to the window and shook his head as Nate spun his wheels, then roared down the road. "I should have picked up on how upset he was." He studied Will, who eased down in the big red chair and impatiently let their mother inspect the lump on his head. She murmured that he needed ice and went to the kitchen. "He didn't seem real happy when y'all walked in. Were you on his case about something?"

Will glanced at Dub and hesitated. "He was supposed to mend a stretch of fence down by Muddy Creek this morning. I drove past there on my way to check the cattle in Red Ridge and spotted him asleep in the pickup. He's been lookin' worn out lately, so I let him sleep. I figured he'd rest a little and then get it done.

"When I came back by, he was gone. That

was fine since it was time to head home to eat. Part of the broken section had been fixed, but the rest hadn't been touched. I figured he'd go back and finish it this afternoon. When we were outside, I mentioned it, and he looked at me like I was one taco short of a combo plate. He said he didn't need to go back; he'd fixed the whole thing.

"I told him that he was mistaken, there was still some left to do. He was emphatic that he'd done the job before he rested." A worried frown creased his forehead. "I think he really believed he'd fixed that fence."

Sue walked back in and handed Will one of the flat cold compresses they kept on hand in the freezer. She and Dub exchanged a glance as he sank down on one end of the couch.

"When he ran away from the bonfire, he didn't remember pushing his way through the crowd." Jenna cradled Zach against her shoulder, gently rocking back and forth. He was almost asleep.

Her mom sat down right next to her dad. She looked at Chance and patted the cushion beside her, then motioned for Jenna to sit across from them on the other couch. After they were all seated, she said, "Nate has the classic signs of post-traumatic stress disorder."

"How do you know?" When Zach stirred, Jenna rubbed his back. He settled down and snuggled closer to her neck.

"I had it when I came home from Viet Nam." Dub focused on his hands and absently picked at a fingernail. "According to a psychologist with the Veterans Administration, I still have it. For most people, it never goes away completely."

Chance leaned forward to see him better, resting his forearms on his thighs. "What do you mean, Dad? How does it affect you?"

"Now, it's mostly the memories that occasionally bother me. You know how I get emotional sometimes when I see something about the current war on television, or sometimes when you boys get me to talkin' about how things were in Nam."

Jenna and her brothers nodded. Sometimes he was fine when he was telling war stories. Other times, he'd suddenly choke up, even shed a few tears and cut it short. She thought of the times her brothers had tuned into a war movie on television, and her dad left the room.

"The last year or so, I've been more forgetful. I blamed it on gettin' old, but the doctor said it's a common symptom that's showing up a lot these days in Viet Nam vets. He said memory problems are affecting the current vets much sooner."

"When your dad came home from the war, he was a lot like Nate. Jumpy, always on alert, had trouble sleeping." Sue reached for her husband's hand, resting it on her thigh. "Nate is probably having nightmares, reliving incidents in his dreams or possibly dreaming about something that he feared the most. Dub kicked me out of bed once."

Will lowered the ice pack. "What was that about?"

"We figured out later that I was dreaming my helicopter was shot down. I was fighting off the Viet Cong." He smiled wryly at Sue. "Hit your mom with a blade kick right in the rear end. She flew out of bed and hit the wall."

"I wasn't hurt, but it served as a good warning. The next time he started mumbling in his sleep, I bailed out of bed pronto. Good thing too, because I'd no more than stood up when his fist hit my pillow. It happened so often that I kept an extra blanket at the foot of the bed. When he started moving around and mumbling, I'd grab the blanket and my pillow and go sleep on the couch for a while.

"Then one night before I left the room, I understood what he was saying. He was giving a mayday call. So I stayed in the room until the dream was over and he woke up. After I told him what I'd heard, he remembered part of the dream."

"It was the last time I ever had that nightmare. I've had different ones occasionally over the years, but none where your mom had to run for her life. We both slept better after that. But I had other problems — a need for adrenaline rushes for one thing. So I drove fast and took up bull riding."

"That ended when Dynamite stomped on his leg and broke it."

"Later, I began having trouble with my temper. Rage that came out of nowhere for no reason."

"You haven't done that in a long time," said Will.

"Not as much. When it does happen, I can control it better. But it really affected me when y'all were growing up. It was hard on all of you."

No one said anything. For several years the whole family had walked on eggshells, never knowing what would set him off or when. He'd never hit any of them, but he'd thrown Will and Chance to the ground a couple of times.

Jenna swallowed hard. Like Nate had done

a few minutes before.

"God has helped me a lot these last fifteen years. Healed a lot of wounds I didn't know I had. Most people weren't aware of PTSD in those days. I've read lately that there were some folks studying it back then, trying to figure out what was going on. But I don't think many vets knew about the research and possible treatments."

"We didn't know what it was," said her mom. "We just knew the war had changed him. We muddled through on our own, with love and God's help."

"Some people didn't make a recovery. That's why there are so many Viet Nam vets who are drunks, drug addicts, homeless, or have spent time in jail. The divorce rate is a lot higher for vets who served in a war zone than it is for civilians, as is the suicide rate. I'm one of the blessed ones. God has been gracious to me, as has your mother."

"Let me go put Zach down," Jenna said softly. She stood carefully so she wouldn't wake her little boy and carried him into his old room. They'd left a bed and plenty of toys there for him to use on the days when she was at the ranch house. She got him settled and prayed over him, asking God to wipe away the memories of what had happened earlier. "Please, God, don't let him be afraid of Nate."

When she rejoined her family, she studied her dad's face, then her mother's. "How do we help Nate?"

"You should go see him." Her mother checked her watch. "Give him about another hour."

"No," Will said ardently. "He's dangerous."

"Mom, Will's right." Chance glanced at Jenna and frowned, probably because she was glaring at both of them. "I'll go talk to him."

"No. He needs Jenna. The rage has passed for now."

"How do you know?" Will jumped to his feet, then flinched. "We can't be sure of that."

"Jenna should go talk to him." Her father pointed at Will and motioned for him to sit back down. "Stick that ice back on your head. It'll take the lump down and cool you off." Grumbling, Will obeyed. Dub turned to Chance. "You go with your sister but stay in the pickup. You'll be close if there's a problem. Right now Nate needs to know that he hasn't destroyed his chance at the one thing he wants most in this world — Jenna's love."

18

Nate sat in back of his house, tears pouring down his face. The drive from the Callahans was a blur of dust, heartache, and terror.

He vaguely remembered throwing Chance to the floor, then Will jumping him. Tossing him aside had been easy. But what had triggered the rage? Nothing Chance could have done deserved that kind of response. But that's all it took lately — nothing. He assumed he'd been ready to hit Chance, otherwise Will would have stayed out of it. And if he'd been about to deliver the same kind of blow the first time as he was the second, he would have crushed his windpipe.

He could have killed his best friend.

And Jenna and little Zach would have witnessed it. It was bad enough that they had seen what they had.

"What kind of monster am I?" His chest

ached, and a wave of dizziness hit him, adding to the pounding headache he'd had all week. Leaning against the headrest, he swiped at the tears that wouldn't quit.

Disjointed scenes from the war flickered through his mind like an old movie reel. Taking fire, returning it. Laughing with a kid, running with a wounded child. Hiding behind a rock in Afghanistan, diving into the sand in Iraq. A rocket attack in the mountains of Afghanistan, pinned down by the firefight. His buddy hit and dying. Another man wounded. Back in Iraq, the truck ahead of them hit an IED. A rocket took out the Humvee behind them.

Yelling at the top of his lungs, he beat his fists against the dashboard. "Make it stop, Lord. Please, make it stop!"

Sobbing, he slumped forward and gripped the steering wheel with both hands, resting his forehead on them. Lost in pain, he cried out to God for help, for peace — for forgiveness. He believed fighting to protect his country was right and necessary. He'd never harmed anyone who wasn't trying to harm him or someone else, but he still felt guilty for the lives he had taken. And for the men he hadn't been able to save.

Nate didn't know how long he sat there. Minutes? Hours? His tears spent, he slowly straightened. His hands still shook, though he didn't know if it was from nerves or the cold. He'd left his jacket at the Callahans. When he pulled the keys from the ignition, they slipped from his fingers. He left them on the floorboard. He was too tired to care.

Opening the console, he stared at the holstered .22, the pistol he kept with him for snakes. And intruders. But not crazy drivers. At least he hadn't pulled it on anyone yet. Better not leave it in the pickup or take it with him when he was on the road. That proved he had a little sense left, didn't it? He picked up the gun and managed to hold on to it.

Opening the door, he slid out of the truck and walked slowly toward the house. He tried to go faster, but his feet and legs wouldn't cooperate. *So tired.* Winston stood next to the pasture fence, watching him intently, his ears pricked forward. He nickered softly, sounding concerned.

"I'm okay, boy," he called. What a whopper, but maybe lying to a horse didn't count. Probably didn't matter anyway. Not after the things he'd already done today.

Nate went inside, pausing at the sink to get a drink of water. When he set the glass on the counter, he noticed the thermometer outside the window. Sixty degrees. No way should he be as chilled as he was. Was this what it felt like to die? Not physically. His heart didn't feel as if it was going to stop pumping. But emotionally, psychologically. Did a man go cold inside when he'd lost all hope? When he'd destroyed his dreams?

Jenna's stricken face hovered in his mind. And Zach . . . Nate closed his eyes and leaned his hands against the counter, picturing that precious child clinging to his mother, his breath coming in raspy shudders. How he must have scared that poor little kid. And wounded him. Wounded them both.

He went into the living room and laid the gun on the coffee table. Using the bootjack in the corner, he pulled off his boots. One fell over, but he left it lying there in the way.

Pulling the big cream-colored afghan off the back of the couch, he wrapped it around himself. His mother had crocheted it for him one year for Christmas when he worked out in Marfa. Normally, he would have stretched out in the recliner. This time, he lay down on the couch on his side, curling up in as tight a ball as he could.

Things began to come back to him. Chance had been razzing him about being a farmer. It was an old running joke between them. His friend would call him a sodbuster, a plow chaser, or pumpkin roller. He'd retaliate by calling Chance a goat roper, saddle warmer, or leather pounder. They each had a long list of friendly taunts, always done in fun and ending in a laugh. Until today.

He'd been troubled by what Will had told him. Angry with himself because he hadn't finished the job he'd been assigned and rattled because he thought he had. He didn't remember stopping in the middle of it or putting his tools away and throwing the roll of barbed wire in the back of the pickup. He'd awakened from his nap, checked his watch, and headed to the ranch house for dinner.

But already being upset was no reason for him to explode the way he had. There was no logical explanation for it.

His stomach growled, reminding him that he hadn't eaten any of Ramona's famous spaghetti. And he'd never have another opportunity.

He'd blown it, pure and simple.

Nobody would trust him again. How could they? Dub would show up any minute, ordering him to pack his saddle and get off the ranch, threatening to shoot him if he tried to see Jenna. Not that she'd ever speak to him. He'd really scared her this time.

Scared himself.

What are you going to do about it?

"I don't know." Now he was answering himself. That couldn't be good. Could it? Unless it was the Lord nudging him. He had asked God for help. He slowly uncurled and sat up. Warm now, he threw off the afghan. Wallowing in self-pity wouldn't solve anything.

He'd lost Jenna and Zach and his job. No question about that. Will would probably punch him the next time he saw him. Nate hoped he would. He deserved it. But what if he couldn't stand there and let him? What if his instincts and training overrode his intentions? Better to avoid him.

Chance might be a little more forgiving. Unless he realized what Nate had intended to do to him. He didn't think his friend knew much about martial arts, but Dub did. Before Nate had gone into the service, the former helicopter pilot had suggested he get more training than the standard military fare. Dub had also understood that it would take a military order to penetrate the rage when Jenna's cries and Zach's shrieks couldn't. He realized now that he'd heard her and Zach, but his mind had blocked the sounds, disconnecting them with what was happening.

"I'm a danger to other people." His gaze fell on the gun. He needed to get rid of it before he hurt somebody. Or himself. No, he wouldn't go there. "I will not think about suicide. No matter how much you tempt me, Satan, that is not an option. God is my strength and my shield. Jesus is my Lord and my protector. The Bible says to resist the devil and he will flee. So get out of here!"

He heard a vehicle pull up out front. His first impulse was to take the gun out of the holster. Instead, he ran across the room, ducked beneath the window, and stood on the other side of it, keeping his back against the wall. Nudging the edge of the cream-colored curtain out of the way, he released his pent-up breath. Chance. And Jenna was with him. She climbed out of the pickup, but her brother rolled his window down and stayed put.

Hope leapt in Nate's heart, but he quickly buried it. She'd come to tell him to keep away from her and Zach. Even if she didn't, he had to tell her he didn't want to see her anymore. He'd hurt her, and he couldn't risk doing that again.

She knocked on the door. "Nate, let me in."

"Go away, Jenna." He watched her through the window.

"No. I want to talk to you." She stepped to her left and shaded her eyes with her hands, trying to see inside between the open curtains.

He'd heard that stubborn tone often enough to know she wouldn't give up. Opening the wooden door, he looked at her through the screen. His hands were shaking again. He gripped the doorknob with one hand and stuck the other in his pocket. "So talk."

"We want to help you, Nate."

"We?"

"All of us." She shrugged. "Well, Will wants to knock your block off, but he'll come around."

"Not if he's smart. Go home, honey. Stay away from me."

"No."

Nate closed his eyes and dragged in a breath. Couldn't the woman see that she was tearing his heart out? "Don't you understand, Jenna? It's not safe to be around me. Tell Dub I'll be out of here as soon as I can load up my stuff."

"Where will you go?"

Good question. He couldn't put his folks in jeopardy. Or anyone else. "I don't know."

"You don't need to go anywhere." Before he could think to lock the screen door, she opened it and stepped inside. Sliding her arms around his waist, she rested the side of her face against his chest and held him tight. "You need to stay right here."

Tears burned his eyes and throat. His mind screamed for him to get away from her, but his heart overruled his common sense. He needed her like he needed air to breathe. And she forgave him. She hadn't said the words, but he felt it in her touch. He embraced her, holding her close. She was his lifeline. And Jesus was his anchor. With their help, maybe there was hope after all. "I don't want to hurt you."

"I know."

"But I might, no matter how hard I try not to." Not physically. Somehow he knew he'd never hit her. "I don't want to break your heart."

She eased back and framed his face with her hands. "If you leave, that will break my heart. You're going through a rough patch —"

"Honey, I'm losing my mind."

She lowered her hands, resting them on his chest, and smiled gently. "But you haven't lost it yet. I don't think crazy people know they have a problem."

"I guess there's some sense to that. I think I have PTSD."

To his surprise, she nodded. "Post-traumatic stress disorder. That's what Mom and Dad said."

"How do they know?"

"Daddy had it after Viet Nam. Actually, he says he still has it according to the VA. They can help you, Nate. From what they said after you left, he's been through some of the same things you're going through."

"Did I hurt Will?"

"He has a lump on the back of his head from hitting the floor. But he was griping more about Mom making him put ice on it than he was complaining about his headache."

He figured Chance wasn't hurt, or he wouldn't be sitting out front.

"And Zach?"

"He was really frightened, but he's asleep. Mom is keeping an eye on him too."

"I'm so, so sorry for scaring him." He couldn't bring himself to voice his fear that the little boy would be terrified of him from now on.

"He's a pretty resilient kid. He might be a little cautious around you for a while, but I think he'll get over it. Now, will you let Chance come in?"

"Why would he want to?"

"Because he's your friend, and he wants to apologize."

"*He* wants to apologize? I'm the one who almost killed him." Her eyes grew round, and he cringed. Better backtrack pronto. "Or broke his nose."

"It wouldn't be the first time." She turned and motioned to her brother, then took Nate's hand and led him farther back into the living room.

Chance got out of the pickup and stopped to get a plastic grocery bag from the backseat. When he walked through the doorway, he paused and checked Nate out. "Are you all right?"

"You know I'm not." Nate's throat clogged up. "But I'm glad to see you. Did I hurt you?"

"Only my pride. You move faster than you used to." Chance handed the bag to Jenna. "Forgive me for teasing you? For not backing off when I could see you were annoyed?"

"Yes." Nate nodded and tried to clear his throat. When he spoke, his voice was still raspy with emotion. "If you'll forgive me."

"You're forgiven." Chance wrapped his

arms around him.

Nate hugged him back. "I'm sorry, man. I don't know what happened. I just lost it."

Chance slapped him lightly on the back, then stepped away. "Better me than somebody who'd have you thrown in jail."

Nate shuddered. "That's one place I never want to go." A tiny smile lifted his mouth.

Chance raised one eyebrow. "What?"

"Trust you to find something good in even the stupidest things."

His friend grinned. "The Bible says all things work together for good for those that love the Lord. Not that he sends bad things our way. But if we ask him for help in times of trouble, I firmly believe he gives it. I'm hoping he's going to use what happened today to knock some sense into that thick skull of yours." His expression sobered. "You have to get some help."

Nate shoved his fingers through his hair, then massaged his sore neck. "I know."

"Nate . . ." Jenna's voice wobbled. When he turned around, she was standing beside the coffee table, her face pale. She pointed to his pistol. "Why do you have your gun out?"

"I took it out of the pickup when I got home and haven't put it away. That's all, honey. I was so tired and cold when I came in that I wrapped up in the afghan and curled up on the couch."

"Cold?" She glanced toward the cover. "It's sixty degrees outside."

"I know. It doesn't make sense to me either, but I was chilled to the bone. I haven't considered suicide, not even an hour ago when I didn't think I had much to live for. I couldn't do that to my folks. Or to you. And I worked too hard to stay alive during the war. The enemy couldn't punch my ticket then, and I'm not about to do it now."

"There's another enemy you have to fight," Chance said quietly. "A spiritual one. And he attacks when you're the most vulnerable. Such as now. You look like you haven't slept in a week."

"Not quite that bad. But the nap I had this morning was the first rest I've had since Sunday. And then it was my usual hour or two."

"How long has that been going on?" Chance pointed toward the kitchen. Jenna picked up the grocery bag. Since they both went into the other room, Nate followed.

"Months. I usually slept in one or two hour chunks in Iraq. Sometimes that was all the sleep we got a night, but more often it was two or three sessions a night. That didn't stop after I got back to the States. Over time, it dwindled down to only a couple of hours a night, until this week, when even that disappeared." He eyed the plastic containers Jenna had removed from the bag. "What's that?"

"Ramona sent your dinner." She opened and closed cabinet doors until she found a covered casserole dish. "She said you weren't in any condition to fix anything for yourself. She's been worrying that you weren't eating good enough since you came home. Gets annoyed when you're working at the ranch and don't join us at noon."

Ramona was so protective of the Callahans that he thought she'd throw something at him if he ever showed his face around the ranch house. Tears misted his eyes again. He had to figure out a way to turn off the faucet. "I was wishin' I'd waited until later to pick a fight. Her spaghetti sure smelled good."

Chance laughed and tossed him a covered plastic bowl. "I'll be sure and mention it to her. She sent some salad too. Start on that. After you eat, the folks would like to come talk to you."

"Is Dub going to fire me?" Nate pried the lid off the bowl and went to the refrigerator for dressing to top the salad. Not a simple salad with a chunk of head lettuce, a token snippet of cucumber, and slice of tomato. No, sir, this one had three kinds of lettuce, spinach, celery, cucumbers, tomatoes, sliced black olives, and marinated artichokes. His stomach rumbled in appreciation.

"He didn't say anything about it." Chance nudged him out of the way. He reached into the refrigerator for the pitcher of iced tea. "Want some?" When Nate nodded, he took two glasses down from the cabinet. "Sis?"

"I'll have water." She dumped the spaghetti into the casserole dish and covered it, then stuck it in the microwave.

Chance retrieved another glass. He filled two with iced tea and the third with cold water from the tap. After setting them on the table, he opened the back door, went across the porch and down the steps.

Nate looked out and shook his head. The pickup door was wide open. Good thing Chance noticed it or he'd be afoot in the morning with a dead battery. He poured dressing on the salad, looking up when his friend came back in. "Guess the door didn't catch. Thanks for shutting it."

Chance laid the keys on the table. "You dropped these on the floorboard."

"Yeah, my hands were shaking a lot."

Nobody made a comment. Chance pulled

out a chair and sat down while Jenna stirred the spaghetti and stuck the dish back in the microwave.

Nate devoured the salad before the microwave beeped again. He looked up to see them watching him with amusement. Still standing by the cabinet, Jenna tore off a paper towel and handed it to him. "I'm glad to see you still have an appetite."

He wiped his mouth. Although his stomach had been talking to him for about half an hour, he was surprised at how hungry he was. "Starving. I've reverted to eating army style too. Shovel everything in as fast as possible 'cause you never know when you're gonna be attacked." He picked up a slice of buttered garlic bread and took a big bite. "I don't think I ate breakfast."

"You don't remember?"

Chew, swallow, and ponder. Uh-oh, there's nothing up yonder.

"No. But I'm making up silly rhymes in my head. I may start laughing hysterically any minute." Due to weariness and need of nourishment. He wouldn't admit it might be the craziness taking over.

Chance and Jenna exchanged a worried glance. Chance took his cell phone from the case attached to his belt and walked into the living room, calling his dad.

She dished up a big plate of spaghetti with at least a dozen meatballs and set it in front of him. "Eat it all."

"No problem." He tested the first bite, sucked in some air to cool it, ate quickly, and drank some iced tea. Blowing on the next bite, he met her gaze across the table as she sat down. "I'm not sure I had supper last night, either. I was pretty worn out when I got home. I think I crashed in the recliner and zoned out."

"But you didn't sleep?"

He shook his head. "Just stared at the television."

"What about lunch yesterday?"

Making an effort not to inhale his food, he chewed slowly and swallowed, then answered. "Definitely had lunch. A peanut butter and jelly sandwich, apple, and four oatmeal raisin cookies." He motioned toward the cabinet. "There are more cookies in the second drawer."

Jenna laughed and rested her forearm on the table. "You can't remember if you ate supper or breakfast, but you know there are cookies in the drawer."

"Gotta keep track of the important stuff. There should be some unless that's what I had for supper and breakfast. Mom sent four dozen home with me on Sunday."

She hopped up and checked the cookie stash. "There are still at least a couple of dozen left." Sitting down again, she pushed another plastic container toward him. "Now you have brownies to go along with them." She pulled off the lid. "Minus one. I need chocolate."

"Eat all you want. As long as you save me a few." After oatmeal raisin, brownies were his favorite.

Chance rejoined them, helped himself to a couple of brownies, and took a big drink of tea. "Mom and Dad will be down in a few minutes. Zach is still asleep, so Will is going to stay with him."

Will had planned to spend the afternoon looking for a bull that liked to wander. And Dub had an appointment with someone from the oil company. Hadn't Sue mentioned going to a Historical Society meeting this afternoon? Or was it something to do with the library? Chance was supposed to be building a house. Could his crew work without him, or would even more people lose time and money because he was loco?

Suddenly, Nate wasn't hungry anymore. He'd ruined everyone's day. He laid his fork on the plate. Pushing the chair back from the table, he picked up his plate and headed to the counter.

"You didn't eat enough." Jenna followed him, standing out of his way.

"You sound like Ramona." He scraped the food back into the casserole dish. There were easily two more meals there. "I'm stuffed. I'll eat the rest for supper." He smiled at her. Or at least he thought he did. When her eyes narrowed, he wasn't so sure. "I'll have a brownie."

"You'd better since I made them."

"Then I'll have two." That earned him a smile. He put the food away and rinsed off his plate and silverware, sticking them into the dishwasher along with the glass, cup, and a spoon that were already there. More proof that he hadn't eaten much lately. If anything. Grabbing a paper towel, he picked up his dessert and nodded toward the living room. "Let's go sit where it's more comfortable."

He made a detour, taking his gun into the bedroom and tucking it into his top dresser drawer instead of on the nightstand where he usually kept it.

Returning to the living room, he watched Jenna wander around, looking at pictures. Some were of his friends and him in Iraq. A few were great shots — even if he did say so himself — of sunsets and sunrises over the desert. He'd picked up some Western prints in a secondhand store and added them to the wall along with a couple of pictures of his folks.

She pointed to the desert scenes. "Did you take these?"

"Yes."

"They're beautiful."

"Thanks." He sat on the loveseat, hoping Jenna would sit beside him. She did. Smiling, Chance claimed the recliner and put his feet up.

They talked about the weather and the price of cotton and how his mom was doing since she'd gone back to work. Chitchat. He figured they wanted him to spill his guts, that they were itching to know what made him the way he was. They had to be curious, but they were too kind to push. Or maybe they were simply waiting for Dub and Sue to arrive so he could tell his sad tale of woe only once.

They would be disappointed. He might talk about some of the general stuff, like the nightmares, but he wasn't going to tell them what he dreamed about. Or the things that rolled through his mind even when he was awake. He couldn't burden them with that; they couldn't handle it. Neither could he. He didn't want to talk about it. He wanted it to go away.

When Dub and Sue arrived, Nate grew nervous again. His hands had cooperated while he ate, but the shakes hit the minute they walked up on the porch. He went to the door anyway to welcome them, hoping he could talk despite his suddenly dry throat.

Sue came in, gave him a hug, and made him all weepy-eyed again when she whispered, "We love you, Nate. Don't you ever forget that."

"Yes, ma'am. I won't." Clearing his throat and blinking his eyes, he turned to Dub. "Thank you for coming, sir. And for stopping me earlier. I couldn't have lived with myself if I'd really hurt Chance or Will."

"I wouldn't have let you." The weathered cowboy smiled and held out his hand. "I still remember how to throw a tackle."

"I expect you do, sir." Nate shook his hand.

Dub surprised him by pulling him into a hug. "Don't give up, son. You don't have to go through this alone."

When he stepped back, Nate looked him in the eye. "You understand about this . . . this craziness?"

"Maybe not all of it. You may have things going on that I didn't have and vice versa. But you need to understand that none of this is your fault. Since we're former military, some of the things we deal with result from our training and being in battle. People in law enforcement go through much the same thing. People who have suffered trauma in other ways have some of the same issues, but not all of them. They probably have ones we don't. It's a normal reaction to the kind of stress you've been under."

Nate wasn't so sure about that. He hadn't been nearly this bad the other times he'd returned from the war zone.

"Let's sit down and visit awhile. You can tell us what's been going on, and we'll share some of what we've learned. Hopefully come up with some ideas that might help, or suggestions of who to see."

Nate sat down beside Jenna, and Dub and Sue took the couch across from him.

Dub spoke first. "There is better understanding of PTSD these days. Better care and more concern from the VA and from civilians. Sue and I struggled for too many years on our own, trying to deal with something we didn't understand. I knew I had problems, like controlling my anger, being jumpy, overreacting to situations, etc. But I didn't know what caused it.

"For me, healing began years after I got home when I read a novel about a helicopter pilot in Nam. Up to then, I'd avoided movies, television shows, or books about the war. The author had been a chopper pilot there a little after I was and in the same general area. I was curious to see how he portrayed it. He was a good writer with excellent descriptions and details. He nailed the characters, the situation, the action perfectly. The minute I started reading, it was as if I'd stepped back in time. I was reliving the whole experience. I made it to page five before I broke down sobbing."

"And scared me half to death," said Sue, curling her hand around his upper arm.

"It brought back memories and emotions that I'd buried, that I didn't even know I had. I'd read awhile and cry awhile, then put it away for a day or two and tell Sue some of the stuff I was dealing with." He met Nate's gaze, understanding in his eyes. "Some things I only talked to God about. And that eventually opened up other ways of healing, mainly through prayer with some close friends and with the pastor. Pastor Brad has been a big help. He's been there — not only in the war but personally dealing with PTSD."

That surprised Nate. From the quick glance between Chance and Jenna, it surprised them too. "I guess I never thought about what the chaplains go through. They're always there for the rest of us, but a lot of the time, they're right in the middle of the fighting." He already admired the preacher, but his respect inched up several notches.

"He's gone through his own struggles, but he was smarter than me," continued Dub. "He figured out pretty quick that he needed treatment. Afterward, he took some training so he could help the rest of us. It will be good for you to talk to him about what's going on now and what you've been through."

"I don't want to talk about what happened over there. I want to forget it."

"That's the irony. The more you hold it inside, the worse it gets. The way to deal with it is to talk about it. I don't understand how it works, but it does. I expect there are a lot of good counselors out there, but the best ones will use Scripture and the guidance of the Holy Spirit to help you cope. Besides the anger, what else is going on?"

"The main thing is not sleeping."

"Nightmares?"

"Yes, sir. Every night. Jumpy too. Every time a cricket chirps, I think somebody is coming in." Best not mention the shadowy figures hiding in the corners of the room, the ghostly al-Qaida or insurgents ready to attack if he let down his guard. "It takes a long time to fall asleep, then I'll have a nightmare and wake up an hour or two later. Lately, it's been really bad. I dread going to sleep, so much that I wind up staying awake all night."

"How long has that been going on?"

"I slept a little Sunday night. Nothing since, except for the nap in the pasture this morning." He tried to smile. "Maybe that's the trick. Sleep in the pickup out in the pasture."

"He's forgetting to eat too." Jenna threaded her fingers through his. "Except maybe for cookies."

"They had oatmeal in them, so they're a little healthy."

She rolled her eyes. "Key word is little."

"I'll admit I'm running on fumes."

"That's stretching it." Jenna's fingers tightened as she frowned at him.

"Hey, give me a little slack. I ate some spaghetti." When she started to say something — probably that he hadn't eaten nearly enough — he quickly added, "And all the salad and some bread. So I'm not totally running on empty."

"Okay, fumes."

"But you are forgetting things," Sue said quietly.

"Yes, ma'am." He sighed. More things than he cared to tell them about. A couple of times he'd driven to town and forgotten why. Other times, he didn't remember coming home from wherever he'd been. He might be aware of working on a particular area of the ranch, or driving to town after something. But he'd find himself pulling up to the house and not remembering the drive home. One evening he'd spent a good half hour talking to Winston before he realized he didn't remember coming home. He had a sneaking suspicion the horse had two apples that night because he didn't recall giving him the first one.

"I've read that the military is doing more psychological evaluations now, both in the field and after servicemen come back to the States. Did you have those?" Sue watched him closely. Did she expect him to lie?

"Yes, ma'am. I had the usual jitters when my unit first came back, but I didn't admit to much. The psychologist picked up on some of it, but I wasn't bad then. I figured it would go away like it always had. Plus I was thinking I would make a career out of the army, and if they see you have problems, it ruins your possibilities for advancement.

Or even your ability to stay in the service. Things were worse when I decided not to reenlist, but I didn't say anything then because I was afraid they wouldn't let me leave. They'd want to keep me in for treatment. I honestly thought everything would settle down and go back to normal once I was home."

"Have you contacted anyone at the Veterans Administration? Or the Disabled American Veterans?"

"No, ma'am." He didn't like where the conversation was going. He didn't like it at all.

"Nate, you need to go to the VA hospital in Big Spring." Sue spoke gently, but her words were bullets through his heart.

Anger and fear ricocheted through him. He jerked his hand from Jenna's. "No, ma'am. I'm not going into a hospital." They'd put him in a psych ward, and he'd be stuck there forever.

"Only to see a doctor, not stay. You have to get something to help you rest to start with. And help with the other things." Sue's face held nothing but kindness. "I'd like to call Pastor Brad. He volunteers at the VA hospital and has good connections. He might be able to get you in to see someone right away."

Nate knew he needed help. But couldn't the local doctor prescribe something to make him sleep? He knew that wouldn't solve his problems, but he still hesitated. Until he felt Jenna lay her hand lightly on his arm. When he looked at her, she simply said, "Please?"

How could one word say so much? *Do it for her. For Zach. For the life you want with them. Most of all, for yourself.*

"You're a warrior, Nate," Dub said softly. "You always will be. But now the battle is for peace of mind."

19

Nate concluded that if his minister hadn't been with him at the VA, they would have strapped him down on a bed and assigned an attendant the size of an NFL linebacker to guard the door. At the beginning of the visit, the doctor was kind but persistent with his questioning. When Nate finally admitted that he'd sought help because he'd had a potentially serious fight with his friends, the physician's primary focus became keeping him from harming others or himself.

Pastor Brad talked fast, assuring him that he would personally bring Nate back early the next morning for a more thorough physical and psychological evaluation. The doctor relented only after Nate promised to take whatever the doctor gave him.

As they walked back to the car, Nate shook his head. "Sheesh, if I wasn't anxious before I went in there, I would be when I came out. With him barking orders, I might as well be back in the army."

Pastor Brad chuckled and rested his hand on Nate's shoulder. "The doctor is a good man, if a little too intense. I think it comes from working in the ER. He's seen too many attempted suicides to simply let someone loose that might be in danger."

The former military chaplain shared some of his recovery experiences with him on the way home. Some sounded okay. A few weren't.

"I'd have a hard time in a group session." Nate's throat went dry at the thought of it.

"They're all vets, most from the War on Terror, though there were a few from Viet Nam. I thought it would be hard too, but after a time or two, I realized that nobody could understand what I'd been through the way they could. The therapist or counselor was there to facilitate the discussion, but most of the help came from the group."

Nate didn't want to sound like a whiner, but he knew he couldn't do it. He'd spent too long trying to hide his feelings from other soldiers. "I don't think I can open up like that to strangers. Maybe if they were Christians and looked at things from a spiritual perspective, it might be easier. But that's not likely, is it?"

"There will probably be some who are

believers, but often the nonbelievers are pretty vocal about not wanting anybody to talk about God. Tell Dr. Silverman how you feel. He's a Christian, so he'll understand where you're coming from. He's good about working one on one with a patient if that's the best thing. After he sees you for a while, I think he'll let me take over the sessions. We could do them in my office, at your house, or out in the middle of nowhere if you want. That way you wouldn't have to keep driving to Big Spring." Pastor Brad flashed him a grin. "And you know we'll include the Lord in the conversation."

Nate smiled for the first time since they left his house. "Then pull every string you can to make it happen."

"Will do." The minister's smile faded. "Getting through this may be hard."

"I know. Though I wouldn't mind a spit and baling wire job."

Brad chuckled. "From your mouth to God's ears. We'll pray that the Lord has an easy fix in mind."

Jenna was playing out in the yard with Zach when Pastor Brad and Nate drove by. *Thank you, Lord, that they let him come home. If they didn't keep him, he must not be real bad, right?*

Zach picked up his little soccer ball and watched the car drive by their house. "That Nate?"

"Yes. He's with Pastor Brad."

"Nate scary."

Jenna's heart dropped. Since waking up from his nap, her son hadn't mentioned Nate or what happened earlier. She'd hoped and prayed that he wouldn't remember it. She picked him up and walked up the steps to the big porch on the old white house, sitting down in a white wicker rocker with Zach on her lap. "Yes, he was scary this morning. But he isn't like that the rest of the time. Except for this morning, he's always been nice, hasn't he?"

Zach nodded, his eyebrows dipping into a tiny frown. "Why he push Uncle Chance down?"

"Uncle Chance said something that made him very angry. Uncle Chance shouldn't have talked to him like that, but Nate shouldn't have thrown him to the floor, either."

"Both bad?"

"Yes, they were both bad. They didn't act nice at all."

"Uncle Will bad too?"

Uh-oh. This was tricky. "Not really. He thought Nate was going to hurt Chance, so he was trying to stop him."

"Nate push him too." Zach examined a dirt streak on his ball.

"Yes, he did. And he shouldn't have. Sometimes people we like do things they shouldn't, but that doesn't mean we stop liking them. Remember when Sara Beth pushed you down on the grass? You didn't like it, and right then you didn't like her much either, did you?"

Zach looked up at her and shook his head. "She not nice."

"No, she wasn't. Not then. But she felt bad about what she did and told you she was sorry. Did that make you feel better?"

"Uh-huh. My her friend."

"Sometimes grownups do bad things too, like this morning. Then they feel bad, and they say they're sorry. That's what Uncle Chance and Nate did while you were asleep. They apologized to each other and forgave each other, so now they're friends again."

"Uncle Will too?"

"I don't think he's talked to Nate yet, but they'll be friends again. If Nate tells you that he's sorry, will you be okay with him?" *Please, Lord.*

His forehead wrinkling in thought, Zach dropped the ball, barely noticing when it bounced across the porch. Concentrating on the question, he played with a rhinestone on her collar. "Nate sorry he scary?"

Jenna hugged him close. "Oh, honey, Nate is very, very sorry he scared you. He loves you very much."

"We go see Nate? He say sorry?"

"I don't know, sweetheart. But I'll call him and ask if we can go over for a few minutes." She carried Zach into the house and pointed him toward his playroom, then she dialed Nate's number.

When he answered, he sounded all wrung out.

After exchanging greetings, she asked, "What did the doctor say?"

"That I should be in a padded room."

"Nate, quit kidding me."

"He didn't use those words, but it's close. He was worried I'd blow up again and hurt somebody or myself. Pastor Brad convinced him that I'm a hotbed of tranquility for now. Too worn out to squish a fly. He gave me some medicine that may help me sleep and ordered me back early tomorrow for further evaluation."

"Do you feel good enough for Zach and me to come by for a few minutes?"

"Are you sure that's a good idea? I scared him awful bad this morning."

"He wants you to say you're sorry. Then I

think he'll be okay."

She heard him catch his breath, then clear his throat. "Then get here quick as you can."

"We're on our way." Jenna hung up and went to get Zach. He was driving a fat little green car around on the carpet. "Let's go see Nate."

Jenna grabbed some CDs she'd laid out along with her car keys and scooped him up, hurrying out the door and trotting down the steps. She secured him in the car seat in record time.

They met Pastor Brad on the way as he was leaving the ranch. She thought he might stop and speak to her, but he merely waved and smiled. When she stopped in front of Nate's house, he stepped out onto the porch.

Zach watched him the whole time Jenna unfastened the straps on the car seat and lifted him out of the pickup. Often Zach preferred to walk these days, but he hung on to her as she carried him up the porch steps.

Nate's sad expression made her want to put her arms around him and tell him not to worry. He studied Zach intently but made no move to reach for him. Her son focused on him just as seriously. "Did I scare you this morning?"

Zach nodded, his expression too somber for such a little boy. "Nate bad."

"Yes, I was. What I did was very wrong. I shouldn't have gotten angry. I'm sorry."

"You sorry you scary?"

Nate flinched, and Jenna shrugged slightly. Evidently, her son needed a little more convincing.

"Very sorry. Will you forgive me?"

"Uh-huh." Zach held out his arms, and Nate took him, holding him close.

He briefly closed his eyes and took a deep breath. "Thank you, Zach."

Zach hugged his neck, then straightened and showed Nate his toy.

"That's a pretty cool car."

"We play cars?"

"Not today, buddy. I'm all worn out. Maybe we can play another time."

"Okay." Zach looked at Jenna, and Nate handed him to her.

"Thanks for coming by."

"Is there anything I can do?" She wanted to stay with him, to assure him that he wasn't alone, but he needed rest, and with Zach around that wouldn't happen.

"Pray for me tonight and tomorrow. Pastor prayed with me before he left, so I don't feel quite as uneasy as I did. But I'm nervous about tomorrow. I thought for a while today that the doctor wasn't going to let me out of there."

"I've been praying for you all afternoon. Actually I pray for you every day."

That brought a tiny smile to his face and a hint of sparkle to his eyes. "You do?"

"Ever since you came home. And a lot of the time while you were overseas, except when I was going through my own troubles. But I'll be especially diligent tonight and tomorrow. I don't think the hospital can keep you unless you consent or they have a court order. It might be different at the VA, but I doubt it."

"You may be right, but the way the doctor talked, he could do whatever he wanted to. He's probably tight with a judge in Howard County."

"We don't live in Howard County. I don't know if that makes a difference, but it might." She laid her hand on his arm. "But we trust in a higher authority than a county judge. God will see you through this, Nate."

"That's what I'm counting on."

"We'll go now and let you rest." She glanced down, confirming that he still had his boots on. "Walk out to the truck with me. I brought you some CDs that helped me when I was depressed and had trouble sleeping."

"Lullabies?" He followed her down the porch steps and across the mainly dirt yard.

"In a way. Instrumental worship songs. Some Celtic, some solo guitar. I found them soothing and relaxing, even if I didn't always recognize the song. They didn't always put me to sleep, but it was a good way to draw close to the Lord and rest in him."

"Thanks. I'll give them a try." He smiled wearily. "Beats watching infomercials any day."

After Jenna left, Nate called Dub, then Chance, and let them know how things stood. He talked to Will too, apologizing for his actions and confirming that his friend was still his friend and wasn't badly injured.

After making peace with Will, Nate walked out to check on the horses. Most of them were grazing in the pasture, within sight of the house but not within easy chasing distance.

Winston had been with the others when Nate came home, but as usual, now he hovered close to the fence in hopes of a little head rub and an apple. He nickered quietly as Nate approached.

"Hi, fellow. Waiting on this?" Nate held out a shiny red apple, smiling when the horse took it from his open hand and began crunching on it. "If you don't eat quieter, your friends are going to wise up, and they'll come beggin' too. Pretty soon, I'll be spending my whole paycheck on apples."

If he continued to get a paycheck. A man wasn't paid when he didn't work. Or at least he shouldn't be. He'd made it clear to Dub that he didn't expect wages for the time he spent going to the doctor. The rancher had grunted and told him not to worry about it, that he wasn't paying him by the hour.

He scratched behind Winston's ears and rested his forehead against the horse's neck. Win made a little noise that sounded as if he was murmuring encouragement, maybe even trying to tell his friend how much he loved him. Whatever he said, Nate found it comforting. "I love you too, boy." He straightened and assessed the other horses, deciding they looked fine. "I gotta call the folks and tell them how messed up I am. 'Course, they probably already know that." With one last pat on the horse's head, he turned and went slowly to the house.

Back inside, he called his mom and dad. Worried about their reaction, he paced across the kitchen twice before his mom picked up the phone. They chatted for a few minutes until he said, "Put the phone on speaker, Mom. I need to talk to you both."

She complied and Nate filled them in on what had been going on the last few weeks and in particular that day. When he finished, they were silent. He pictured them looking at each other across the kitchen table, perplexed and wondering what to say.

Finally his dad cleared his throat. "I'm glad you went to see the doctor, son. We've been worried about you."

His mom spoke up. "We didn't have any idea how bad things were. I'm sorry we didn't realize what you've been going through." She sniffed, and her voice wobbled. Nate almost groaned. He hoped she wouldn't get all weepy on him. He understood her feelings, but he couldn't handle that right now.

"I didn't expect you to, Mom. So don't feel guilty or worry. After talking with Pastor Brad and the doctor, I'm confident they'll get me squared away with the Lord's help. I wanted to let you know what's going on."

"We appreciate that, honey." Her voice sounded stronger, more in control. "What can we do?"

"Pray. And keep it to yourselves. I don't want everybody in town knowing what's going on."

"We can do that, but it doesn't hurt to have other people praying for you."

"I've got a pretty good team lined up with y'all, the Callahans, and Pastor Brad."

"Good enough." His dad paused for a few seconds. "Do you want to move back here, son? So you aren't alone at night?"

"Thanks, but I don't think it would help. I'm too tuned in to every little noise. I think I'd be even more on alert." And he didn't want to scare them out of a night's sleep when he woke up yelling. "I'll let you go. I need to eat some supper and try out one of the doc's miracle pills, see if it will help me sleep." Not that he held out much hope of it acting right away. The physician said it might take awhile of gradually increasing the dosage to become effective.

They said their good-byes, and Nate hung up the phone. They'd reacted better than he thought they might. That was a relief. Having Jenna and the Callahans aware of what was going on lifted a burden too.

He ate another small plate of the spaghetti and had an apple. His mom always stressed the importance of fruit and vegetables along with grains, so he added a couple of her oatmeal cookies to his meal. He thought about turning on the TV and watching the news, then ditched the idea.

Listening to some of Jenna's music would be smarter. He loaded his CD player with all of the albums and turned it on to a low, pleasant volume. The first CD was harp, flute, and fiddle music, with bagpipes joining in on some of the phrases. Nice.

After changing into an old, light gray San Antonio Spurs T-shirt and some lightweight blue sweatpants, he picked up the medicine bottle. The doctor said it was a common generic drug that had been used to treat high blood pressure for years. They had discovered that it also helped control the nightmares in PTSD sufferers. "Lord, the doc didn't think this would help much right at first. But I'm going to trust you to make it happen tonight. I'd be happy with a couple of hours of good rest, but more would be better. Please help me sleep, Jesus. Let me rest in your care."

He took the pill, turned out the lights, and went to bed, stretching out without any covers. Closing his eyes, he focused on the music, silently singing the words of praise that glorified God. The next one was familiar too, and as he silently declared the holiness of Jesus, he gradually felt a sense of peace calm his soul.

By the end of the album he'd almost drifted off to sleep, until the CD player paused and clicked as it turned to the next CD. The click jarred him, causing his heart to race and his muscles to tense. He jumped out of bed and crept to the window, making sure it was locked and that no one lurked outside. The living room was next. Scan the perimeter, check the locks on the doors and windows. Following his normal routine, he covered the kitchen and the spare bedrooms.

He got a drink of water and went back to his bedroom. "So much for resting in you, Lord."

Don't give up. Try again.

Nate lay back down, listening to the music and praying. "God, we prayed for you to send your angels to watch over me. I'm going to believe that they are here protecting me. I know logically that nobody is going to break in here and attack me, but some part of my brain doesn't get the message. I'm asking you to calm that fear, along with being afraid of having a nightmare."

He continued to pray, not for himself but for his family and friends, both locally and some he'd met in the service. Guys he thought might be dealing with the same issues. Keeping his thoughts focused on others seemed to help. He might not be falling asleep, but praying for people had to be a good thing. So he kept going.

He prayed for servicemen and women around the world. For the highway patrolmen; the sheriff and his deputies, specifically his old friend Dalton; the Callahan Crossing constable and the members of the volunteer fire department — including Dub, Will, and Chance — who all kept them safe. Next came the president and others in various levels of the government from national offices on down. About the time he got to the mayor and city council, he fell asleep.

For the first time in weeks, he slept four solid hours.

Without a nightmare.

20

Late the next afternoon, Jenna chopped up celery and onions for a stir-fry and glanced out the kitchen window every few minutes. Nate had called that morning to tell her that he'd had a good night and to thank her for the music, which had helped him relax. He'd still been nervous about seeing the psychiatrist but not quite as worried as the day before. She'd invited him to come have supper with her and Zach if he felt good enough when he got home.

He'd called when he and Pastor Brad left Big Spring, confirming that he'd eat with them. She'd seen them drive by about forty-five minutes earlier on the way to Nate's.

"Quit looking out the window," she muttered. "You won't make him get here any sooner." After checking on Zach, she washed the broccoli pieces and pea pods, then sliced up the chicken. The rice was already cooked, and cubed fresh mango chilled in the refrigerator. She'd baked some banana muffins that morning that would work for dessert and leave some to send home with him.

The way to a man's heart is through his stomach. Jenna hoped he wouldn't think she'd become a cliché. Over the years, plenty of women had tried to entice her brothers with their cooking. "Didn't do them much good, either." Chuckling, she looked out the window again and spotted his dark blue truck coming around the ranch house. Excitement zipped through her. On her way to the door, she took a quick peek in the walnut framed mirror she had rescued from an old dresser. She didn't want to greet him with celery stuck in her teeth or teriyaki sauce splattered on her blouse.

Zach came running over and climbed up in the chair she'd put under the window so he could see outside. He saw Nate getting out of the pickup and looked up at her with a smile.

She opened the door, then jumped over to help Zach down from the chair. He usually made it without any trouble, but he was in a hurry. The second Nate stepped inside, Zach met him with arms uplifted.

Smiling, her tall cowboy bent down and picked him up, giving him a hug. "Hi, buddy."

"Play cars?"

"We'd better check with your mom."

"I'm doing a stir-fry. If you're hungry we can eat right away, or it can wait awhile."

"Let's wait a little bit. I'd like to spend some time with this guy. Zach, you go pick out some cars, and I'll be along in a couple of minutes." He set the boy on the floor, chuckling when he raced into the playroom. "If we could bottle his energy, we'd get rich."

"By selling it to parents and grandparents of other toddlers." Jenna slid her arms around his waist. His eyes widened slightly, and he put his arms around her too. "Welcome to my home."

He grinned and pulled her a little closer. "Is this the way you greet everyone?"

"No. Only special people."

"Ah, so I'm special, huh?" A sparkle lit his eyes.

That was a very good sign. "In a category all your own." He lifted one eyebrow. "The only one I kiss hello."

"I like the sound of that." He kissed her gently. When he raised his head, he sighed softly. "I'm really glad you moved into this house."

Jenna laughed and pulled away. "Me too." Zach came racing back to them, cars in each hand. "No built-in babysitter, but it's definitely going to have some advantages."

Nate followed Zach to his playroom. It had been fun fixing up the room for her son. A little oak table and two chairs sat against one wall. She'd put a small matching bookcase on the floor next to it so he could reach his books. The yellow toy box she'd had as a child sat in the corner. Most of the floor was covered with a low pile rug in mixed shades of blue for a soft place to play with blocks and things. She'd left a stretch of the bare hardwood floor along one side for racing cars. One wall was painted to look like a mini-corral, with oversized boots sitting beside it and a big hat hanging from a post.

Nate stopped in the doorway and surveyed the room. "This is great. Did you do the art?"

"No. That's one of Lindsey's creations. She's developed a nice little side business painting murals. It gives her a good break from her job at the bank."

He turned in the doorway and scanned the living room and country kitchen. "The whole place looks good."

"Thanks. I didn't change things too much. The bedroom furniture, sofa, and chairs are mine. And, of course, the things in Zach's room. The rest either belonged to my grandparents or Mom had picked it up for the guesthouse. I did some painting, but not a whole lot. I'll plop over there in the corner and relax while y'all play."

She followed Nate into the playroom and sat down in the adult-sized, navy blue bean bag chair. There was a matching kid-sized one next to it that Zach occasionally occupied for a minute or two. If he sat there for more than five minutes, it would be a new personal record. Her son considered the room a play area, not a place for resting.

Jenna laughed as Nate pushed a little police car around, making siren noises and chasing Zach's car. They drove up and over a big yellow pillow and under the table — a stretch for Nate but easy for Zach to crawl through when they moved the chairs out of the way. They parked the cars, and the little boy dragged over his barn, which came with animals, people, and a tractor and trailer. Nate helped him load a cow into the trailer. Zach dutifully put the farmer on the tractor seat and drove him "to town."

As she slipped out of the room to finish supper, she heard Nate promising to bring some cotton over to put in the trailer. "Then we can haul it to the gin," he said.

Ten minutes later, she had everything

almost ready. "Y'all wash up. It's time to eat." She heard Zach giggle and looked up to see Nate chasing him down the hall to the bathroom. They joined her a few minutes later, both of their shirts splattered with water spots. "Is there a puddle on the bathroom floor?" she asked with a smile.

"Nope." Nate winked at her son.

Zach grinned. "Nope."

"We cleaned it up." Nate set Zach on the chair in front of the plate she'd already fixed for him. "That looks good. Smells like teriyaki."

"That's right." She tied a bib around Zach's neck. He picked up his cup of milk and had a big drink. When he reached for his fork, she touched his hand. "Wait for us, so we can pray."

Nate helped her with her chair, then sat across the round cherry table from her. Zach dutifully clasped his hands together and bowed his head. It was something he'd just learned, so Jenna prayed quickly before he became rambunctious. "Father, thank you for this food and that Nate can share it with us. Thank you for your many blessings. In Jesus' name, amen."

Two male voices, one deep and one sweetly childish, echoed, "Amen."

She had about half a second to relish the

sound before Zach unfolded his hands and reached for his fork, digging in.

Nate nodded toward the toddler. "That was new."

"This is his third night of actually bowing his head. But whoever is praying has to talk fast."

"Works for me." He spooned a big helping of rice onto his plate, then added the teriyaki chicken and vegetables on top of it. "I worked up an appetite racing all those cars around."

Jenna glanced at Zach. He was eating diligently. "I think somebody else did too. Things must have gone well today."

"Better than I'd expected." Nate dished up some mango in the small bowl by his plate. "Everything they could check today on the regular physical was fine. The results won't come back on some of the blood tests for a few days, but the doctor didn't think there would be anything unusual." He took a bite of the stir-fry. "This is really good."

They ate in silence for a few minutes. "I didn't know you were such an excellent cook. Except for the brownies, I don't think I've eaten anything you've made."

"I botch things now and then, but most of the time it's edible. When Jimmy and I were first married, I didn't have much to do, so I

323

watched a lot of cooking shows. I don't get too gourmet, but I like trying new recipes with fifteen or less ingredients."

"Five's my limit. I even have a cookbook where every recipe has five ingredients or less."

"Chance has one like that. I don't think he's ever opened it. Have you used yours?"

"A couple of times. It's easier to buy frozen dinners at the store and throw them in the microwave. They taste good enough. Sometimes I toss a steak on the grill."

Jenna checked Zach's progress. "Honey, you need to eat some of your vegetables."

"No."

"Yes, you do."

"More chicken." Her little boy smiled sweetly.

"Vegetables first. You like broccoli and pea pods, remember?"

Frowning, Zach poked at a small slice of celery with his fork. "What's that?"

"Celery."

He made a face and shoved it to the side of his plate. Jenna glanced at Nate. He was trying hard to keep from laughing. "You don't need to try the celery this time, but you have to eat some broccoli and peas before you get any more chicken."

"Okay." Sighing, Zach picked up a piece

of pea pod and shoved it in his mouth.

"Chew it good." Satisfied that he wasn't going to try to swallow it whole, she turned her attention back to Nate. His plate was almost empty. Maybe she should admonish him about chewing before swallowing. *Naw.*

"How did you get involved with the Mission?" Nate relaxed against the back of the chair and sipped his iced tea.

"Lindsey volunteered there a couple of afternoons a week. One day another lady was sick, and she'd received a shipment of food from Abilene. She needed help putting it away." Jenna smiled, remembering how her friend had persisted. "And she knew I needed to quit hiding at the ranch and focus on somebody other than myself. She wouldn't take no for an answer. I finally caved in. I'd intended to only help that one time, but she kept asking and I kept going.

"Before long, the director had to retire due to health problems. Nobody else wanted the job, so I took it. It isn't a paid position, which is fine for me. We have a handful of volunteers who work a few hours a month. I try to keep them and everything else organized."

"I'm sure you do a great job." Nate took some more of the stir-fry.

"I give it my best." So far things had run

smoothly, so that must be good enough.

"Chicken." Zach looked at his mom. "Please."

"Oh, good boy." She checked his plate. The celery pieces were pushed together in a neat little pile, but he'd eaten all of the broccoli and a few more pea pods. "You ate some vegetables and remembered to say please. Yes, you may have more chicken."

Nate carefully picked out some small pieces of meat and placed them on Zach's plate. He glanced at Jenna. "Is that enough?"

"Perfect. Thank you."

"T'ank you," added Zach, around a mouthful of food.

"You're welcome." Nate's gaze shifted to Jenna. "Both of you." His smile warmed her clear to her toes.

She wanted to lean her elbow on the table, rest her face on her hand, and simply stare at the sweet, handsome man across from her. But that would be acting like a schoolgirl with a crush. And what she felt for him went way beyond that.

"The Mission is a strong reminder of how blessed I am. To be honest, it makes me feel really good to work there. We're a small community, but it's surprising how many people need a little help sometimes."

"You mentioned a shipment from Abilene earlier. Is that a regular thing?" He started on his second plateful of food.

"Yes. We're associated with the Food Bank of West Central Texas in Abilene. It's part of the Feeding America network, so we benefit from corporate and government donations. Miller's Grocery gives us their surplus too. Between them and the things citizens bring by, we have nonperishable staples, canned goods, meat, dairy products, baked goods, and fresh fruit and vegetables. That's why we're only open for customers two days a week, right after we receive the shipments. All the fresh stuff goes fast. Actually, almost everything goes quickly."

"So locals also contribute the clothes and furniture?"

"Yes. I love it when people clean out closets or their kids outgrow their clothes. Or someone redecorates their house. It's like Christmas anytime of the year."

They moved on to other topics but didn't discuss anything else that had happened at the hospital until supper was over, the dishes were done, and they'd played with Zach for a couple of hours.

After the toddler was tucked into bed and sound asleep, Jenna sat down beside Nate on the pale yellow leather couch, snuggling a little closer when he put his arm around her shoulders. "Do you feel like telling me about the rest of your day?"

"Well, I got up at 6:00 and had water for breakfast. No food because of the blood tests. Brad picked me up, and we drove to Big Spring. Had the physical exam, then I ate. Want to know what I ate?" His eyes twinkled as he tipped his head and looked down at her.

"Not really. Bottom line it, cowboy. What did you think of the psychiatrist? And what did he say?"

"I like Dr. Silverman. He seems to be a good man with a heart for God and for taking care of his patients. He quoted things from various studies, some of them done in the last six months, so he keeps up on all the latest things. According to some research in the last few years, PTSD actually changes the chemistry in the brain, which increases the fight or flight response. So though I passed the regular physical, this weird trip I'm on isn't all a psychological thing. It's partly biological and physiological too.

"He also thinks I had a mild concussion when that house in Iraq blew up. I had a bad headache for several days, ringing in my ears, and dizziness, but I didn't lose consciousness, so I didn't think it was a concussion. I doubt I ever mentioned it. The headache only showed up when the pain meds for the burn and shrapnel wound wore off. It was gone before I got out of the hospital, so I didn't think any more about it.

"But Dr. Silverman specifically asked me if I'd had any of those symptoms after the bomb. He said they've discovered that mild concussions due to a bomb explosion can cause brain injury. Unlike a concussion from a fall, a car wreck, or sports injury, a bomb throws off energy waves that affect the body differently. He said that might be causing some of my problems — or it might not. I don't have the light sensitivity, dizziness, or hearing problems that often go along with a brain injury. I've had a headache for about two weeks, but he agreed that's probably from tension."

"If there is brain damage, can they do anything about it?" Jenna leaned her forehead against his jaw, admiring the subtle fragrance of his light aftershave.

"I don't know. We didn't get into it that much. He said it was something he'd keep an eye on. He believes regular ol' PTSD is my main problem."

"Is that good?"

He shrugged lightly. "Well, it has to be

better than having two things wrong. I sought treatment fairly early, compared to a lot of guys. That will work in my favor. He put me on an antidepressant, which is supposed to help the depression as well as the anxiety. That's in addition to the medicine I'm taking to help with the nightmares. I like his philosophy of starting off with minimal medication and changing it until we find something that works. I'll go see him twice a week for about a month. Hopefully, after that he'll turn me over to Pastor Brad for counseling, with only an occasional visit to Big Spring."

"That would make it easier, plus he's great to talk to. I don't know how many times we stopped in the middle of a visit and prayed for guidance. You've been more relaxed tonight, so are you encouraged after seeing Dr. Silverman?"

"I am. He thinks we have a good probability of getting things under control. He's a strong Christian and definitely believes in God's mercy and healing and the power of prayer. That's a big encouragement right there. I'll have to take medicine for a while, maybe forever. I don't like it, but if that's what it takes to be normal, then I'll do it."

"If you had some other kind of illness that required medication, you'd take that. This is no different."

He tightened his arm around her shoulders. "Thanks. I needed to hear that. I'm very fortunate — make that blessed — to have you, my folks, and your family supporting me. A lot of people don't have that kind of help."

"We come from good stock."

He chuckled and tickled her nose with his fingertip. "Yes, we do."

Footsteps tapped on the back porch, loud enough to warn them someone was coming, but not loud enough to wake Zach. "Sounds like your herd has come to check on us." He leaned down and gave her a lingering kiss. "That's probably the last opportunity we'll get tonight."

Someone knocked lightly on the door.

"I could tell them to go away."

"Honey, you know that would be as useless as a milk bucket under a bull. Go let them in, and I'll hide the banana muffins so those brothers of yours don't eat up my breakfast."

Laughing softly, they tiptoed into the kitchen. Jenna waited for him to stash the muffins in a drawer, then opened the door so her parents and both brothers could come in.

After hushed hellos, they walked quietly

into the living room and sat down. They asked how things had gone, and Nate told about his day all over again. "Well, I got up at 6:00 and had water for breakfast . . ."

Jenna smothered her face in a throw pillow to muffle her laughter and thanked God for his mercy and blessings.

21

Nate initially went to the VA the first week in November. He quickly decided Dub had aptly described what he was going through — a battle for his peace of mind. After that first good night's sleep, he had a couple of bad nights with only a few hours rest and nightmares followed by one with three hours sleep but no bad dreams. Then he started therapy with Dr. Silverman, and he had a solid week of dreams that had him waking up in a sweat, heart pounding. Sometimes he was yelling too.

He blamed it on the doctor's keen insight and ability to encourage Nate to talk, to draw out experiences and feelings he'd deeply buried and never wanted to visit again. At times the anger and frustration were so great that Nate would raise his voice and pound on the arm of the chair. Once, he jumped up and paced around the room, finally picking up a book from the doctor's desk and throwing it against the wall. He'd had no idea that he had so much rage simmering inside.

More often, however, instead of rage, relating his experiences and feelings brought tears, some of grief, some reflecting an emotion he couldn't define. Despite the gut-wrenching aspects of the sessions, he often felt better afterward. Drained, but with the sense that some healing had taken place.

They also spent time discovering how to cope with his thoughts and emotions, what might trigger flashbacks or flares of anger and how to deal with them. Dr. Silverman believed the flashbacks and sudden anger might soon disappear. The sessions always ended in prayer, which he concluded wasn't necessarily the doctor's standard operating procedure with every patient.

Nate continued to work no matter how bad he felt. His appointments were on Tuesday and Thursday afternoons, so he worked those mornings and managed to put in full days the rest of the time.

It had been a hot, rainless fall with plenty of wind. The soil dried out and so did the grass. They gathered up the calves and loaded them into trucks to ship to a pre-condition feed-lot. The animals would have plenty to eat for the next several months before Dub sold them.

With no grass worth eating, they began hauling hay and cottonseed cake to the cattle and horses. They carried feed to each pasture three times a week, rotating through the various areas of the ranch on a daily basis. At the same time, they would inspect the cattle and drive along the fences to look for breaks. The most rugged pastures, with steep hills, low mesas, or many gullies, still required a man on horseback to check the fences and watch for sick or hurt cattle beyond where a pickup could go. Windmill maintenance remained in the work routine too.

The brittle grass and windy weather heightened the fire danger. Keeping on the lookout for smoke and fires became more crucial. Under those conditions, it would only take a spark to start a blaze. Their county, along with most counties in the South Plains and West Texas, declared an outdoor burn ban. It made things a bit difficult for folks living in the country who didn't have garbage pickup and usually burned their trash in burn barrels. But the inconvenience was a small thing compared to staying safe.

There wasn't too much to do at the farm right then, so his dad handled most of it.

They left the cotton stalks in the fields to help hold the topsoil and keep the dust from blowing. Under such dry conditions, they might not break up the land until early spring.

By Thanksgiving week, Nate's medication had kicked in on a regular basis. The nightmares dropped dramatically, and he was sleeping five to six hours most nights, occasionally more.

Catching up on his rest did wonders. The dark circles beneath his eyes faded, and his energy was pretty much back to normal. He was still jumpy sometimes and forgot things occasionally. But he no longer caught glimpses of shadowy al-Qaida figures slinking around the edges of the room.

He thought about Iraq or Afghanistan every day. Sometimes they were good memories; sometimes bad. From what he'd been told and read, that might continue for years. He still had an occasional flashback, and that worried him. Generally, he was feeling better about the situation, but he wasn't as far along as he wanted to be.

On the Tuesday before Thanksgiving, his session with the psychiatrist went longer than usual because the doctor was evaluating his progress. Pastor Brad would be handling his twice-a-week counseling sessions after the holiday, with Nate seeing Dr. Silverman only once a month.

On the way home, he stopped in town at the Boot Stop and picked up two catfish baskets. Each contained three pieces of fish, fries, a hushpuppy, and small container of coleslaw. He planned to eat one order for supper and warm up the other for breakfast. The extra coleslaw would probably sit in the refrigerator until he tossed it.

As he drove by the Callahans, he checked Jenna's house. It was dark except for the back porch light. He expected she was still at the ranch house. Though he wanted to see Jenna and knew he'd be welcome if he stopped by her folks', he was too tired to deal with a lot of people right then.

But neither did he want to go home to his empty house. Since the lights were on at Chance's, he decided to drop in and hang out with him. Nate spotted him in the kitchen as he drove up, so he parked out back and walked up to the door. He'd barely knocked when Chance opened it.

His friend eyed the bag of food. "Did you bring supper?"

"Sure." So much for warming up the fish for breakfast, but he didn't mind sharing.

Chance stepped back out of the way. "I was late comin' in, so I missed eating with the family. I was about to make a scrambled egg sandwich. That won't cut it now that I've smelled catfish."

"There's no comparison." Nate set the food on the kitchen table and shrugged out of his brown leather coat, hanging it on the back of an extra pine ladder-back chair.

"Want some coffee? It's decaf. I got cold out at the building site this afternoon and haven't warmed up yet."

"No, thanks. Do you have any root beer?"

"In the fridge."

Chance offered him a glass, but Nate shook his head. He didn't mind drinking from a can. After retrieving the soda from the shelf in the refrigerator door, he stopped by the kitchen sink and washed his hands, drying them on a paper towel.

"How's the new house coming?" Nate sat down and took their meal out of the paper bag, setting one cardboard basket heaped with food at Chance's place and one at his. Tossing a wrapped set of plastic silverware across to Chance's spot, he kept the other one for himself. He piled the napkins and catsup packets in the middle of the table but divided the tartar sauce cups equally, two for each of them. Otherwise, his friend would hog it.

Chance poured a cup of coffee, added

sugar, and sat down across from Nate. "The foundation is poured. The framers start to work next week. The design has a couple of tricky angles, so it will be a challenge."

"Just what you like."

"Yes, sir. Let's pray." Chance said a short but sincere prayer, asking God to bless the food.

Nate added his amen and grinned.

"What?"

"You Callahans don't mince words when it comes to asking the blessing. Not that I'm complaining." He opened the tartar sauce and dipped the edge of a piece of catfish in it.

"That's because Grandpa Callahan was so long-winded the food got cold. When Daddy moved into his own house, he declared that the prayers would be short and heartfelt and the food hot. He saves his big paragraphs for other times."

Nate chuckled and concentrated on eating for a few minutes. He'd be glad to have Dub Callahan pray for him anytime, long or short.

Chance stuck three fries into his mouth, chewing as he asked, "How did it go today?" When it was only the two of them, they weren't necessarily big on manners.

"Not as good as I'd have liked. Doc gave

me some tests and had me fill out a couple of questionnaires. There are still issues I have to deal with."

"And you'd like to be done with the whole thing."

Nate nodded. "I'm trying to be positive and focus on how far I've come."

"In a short time."

"And I'm thankful for that. Doc says I've made faster progress than many people. I know that's God's grace. I'm trying real hard to trust the Lord to finish the healing and teach me whatever he wants to out of this. I've been spending time in the evening reading the Bible. Plus Pastor Brad gave me some books about getting through this recovery process." He grimaced and picked up his second piece of fish. "That makes me sound like a recovering alcoholic or drug addict. Guess I'd better be careful how I phrase things."

"Not with us. We know what's going on. And I'm betting you haven't told anybody besides your folks and Pastor Brad about this." Chance opened another packet of catsup and squirted it beside the fries in the basket.

"True. But who would I tell? Buster and Ollie? In case you haven't noticed, y'all are the only friends I have around here anymore."

"You could make new ones. Or reconnect with some of the guys we went to school with."

"Don't need to. Unlike you, Mr. Popular, I don't need to have hundreds of friends." He scraped the final bit of tartar sauce out of the last container. When he looked at the little cup across the table, Chance moved it closer to his own plate.

"There's more in the fridge. Second shelf in the door." Chance shrugged and took a sip of coffee. "It helps for a businessman to know lots of people."

"Everyone in town?" Nate found the bottle and returned to the table, dumping some of the tartar sauce into the basket.

"You've known more than half of them all your life. Before long, you'll meet everybody else too. That's the way it is in Callahan Crossing. It's one thing that makes it such a great place to live. Folks here care for each other. Don't forget all those welcome home signs."

"I haven't. For the most part, folks here are good and kind. But it's like most small towns. Gossip is major news."

"Only if you're hearing it. If you're doin' the talkin', it's just plain horseback opinion."

"And people would definitely have an opinion. I don't want everybody and their brother knowing what's going on with me. My actions at the bonfire already generated speculation."

"True, but it died down pretty fast. There are enough vets around here who shrugged it off as a little battle rattle and not a concern to curb the talk."

"You think they know otherwise?"

"Some of them probably do. Those who lived through it, like Dad. But they're keeping it to themselves." Chance polished off his last bites of fish and hushpuppy. The fries had already disappeared.

Nate wasn't far behind. It was past time to change the subject, get the focus off of him. "Since you know everybody in town, probably everybody in two or three counties, why aren't you dating anyone?"

"Slim pickin's, my friend. While I was living the carefree bachelor life, most of the good ones were taken."

"What about Lindsey? She's cute, smart, nice, and a strong Christian."

"No spark. I think she has her eye on our local deputy sheriff."

"Does Dalton know it?"

"Maybe. Maybe not. She's subtle. Jenna says she's had a thing for him since high school. They'd make a good couple. He dated the County Extension agent for a while, but she transferred to a better job in Dallas."

"Learn from his mistake. If you meet someone you like, don't whistle at the moon and give her time to take off."

Chance laughed and gathered up all the trash from supper and dumped it in the wastebasket under the sink. "I'll keep that in mind. Thanks for the meal. That really hit the spot."

"When doesn't fried catfish hit the spot? I would have given a month's pay for some when I was overseas."

"Let's go sit where it's more comfortable. Maybe there's a movie on TV."

"I can't stay too long. I need to hit the hay, so I'll feel like hauling the real stuff early in the morning. The boss man doesn't like the hired hands to be late."

"He doesn't like anybody to be late, including his kids."

Nate followed Chance into the living room. On the far wall, behind a glass door, fire snapped and crackled in the fireplace. Terror spiraled through him. Instantly he was back in Iraq. Flames surrounded him, crawling toward him along the floor, across the ceiling. Smoke filled his lungs and he fought for air.

"Oh, man, I didn't think about the fire." Chance stepped in front of him. "Nate, are you with me? Can you hear me?"

Chance blocked the real dancing flames from his view, and his voice pulled him back to the present. Nate blinked and drew in a deep breath of clean, fresh air. His whole body shook.

"I'm sorry. I forgot that I'd built a fire when I got home. I'm an idiot." Chance shifted his weight from one foot to the other, drawing Nate's gaze. Dancing on the balls of his feet, ready to jump out of the way.

"Don't worry, I'm not going to attack," Nate mumbled. *Keel over maybe, but not fight.*

"Let's go in my office and sit down. You're white as a sheet." Chance lightly touched his arm. When Nate didn't throw him to the ground, he gripped it firmly and turned him around, practically dragging him to his office across the hall.

Nate slumped into a chair in front of the large U-shaped desk, leaned back, and closed his eyes.

"I think I lost you there for a couple of minutes."

"You did. Obviously, I haven't gotten over

the fear of fire."

"Did it trigger a flashback?" Chance sat down in the chair next to him instead of behind the desk.

"Yes. The beginning of one. The good news is you pulled me out of it right away. That's an improvement."

"Do you get them often?"

"Not too much anymore. I had several after the bonfire, but I've figured out most of the things that trigger them."

"Like backfires. And I'd guess fireworks."

Nate nodded and sat up straighter. The shakes had stopped, and he didn't feel so weak. "Haven't tested fireworks, but I figure I'll lay low around New Years. Driving behind a diesel truck can cause one. It takes me right back to being in a convoy. It must have something to do with the truck itself as well as the smell of the diesel. The tractors and cotton stripper at the farm don't bother me. Hearing a helicopter takes me back to a firefight with air support."

"Good thing we don't have many helicopters around here."

"True. I'd be in a world of hurt around an army base. All I've seen is the one that checks the natural gas pipeline every once in a while. I was out in the pasture last week when he flew over. I hit the deck. Scared

Jazzy silly, and she took off. Thankfully, she came back after a few minutes. Or maybe ten or fifteen. I'm not sure how long I was out of it. I'd belly crawled about twenty yards through the grass and ducked down behind some big rocks."

"Whoa, you're lucky you didn't get snake bit."

"If any were out sunning themselves, I scared them off."

"So you need to stay away from fires, avoid diesel trucks and buses — or wear a gas mask — and keep earplugs in your pocket in case you spot a helicopter coming in your direction." Chance rested his hand on Nate's shoulder. "Piece of cake."

"Put me out to pasture. As long as I have earplugs, I'll be fine."

"You'd get lonesome. Especially for a certain redhead and her kid."

"That I would. If she'd been home I would have stopped by there instead of here."

"That tells me where I rate on your priority list." Chance laughed and moved around to the other side of the desk. He nudged a box with his toe. "Want a footrest?"

Nate shook his head and stood. "I need to mosey on home. Will you be working on the ranch tomorrow?"

"Maybe. I have to track down a load of lumber that should have been here already. Only half the shipment arrived yesterday, and the driver didn't have any idea where the rest of it was. The crew can start on Monday, but if the rest of those materials aren't here by Wednesday afternoon, the project will come to a grinding halt." He walked to the kitchen with Nate. "Will we see you on Thanksgiving?"

"I doubt it. We're going to Odessa to Uncle Joe's house."

"He's the petroleum engineer?"

"Yes. Joe Jr. followed in his footsteps. He graduated from A&M last spring and joined his dad's firm. Plus he recently got engaged. Another cousin has a brand new baby. So there will be others for the grandparents, aunts, uncles, and cousins to focus on. Part of the time, at least. They'll fuss over me some, but it'll be good to see them all." Nate put on his coat, peeked at the thermometer outside the kitchen window, and buttoned it up.

"We're having a big crowd too. All the shirttail relations seem to show up at Thanksgiving, whether they're officially invited or not."

"Have a good one, anyway." Nate opened the door and stepped out onto the porch.

"Brrr. It's time to dig out the long johns."

"Now I'm glad I'll be working inside tomorrow. Have a good Turkey Day."

Nate nodded and hustled to the pickup. He didn't bother turning on the heater. It wouldn't warm up before he got home anyway. "Lord, I sure wish you'd get rid of this fire phobia of mine. This would be a perfect night to make use of that fireplace at the house."

As he drove by Jenna's, he spotted a light on in Zach's room. She was probably getting him ready for bed. He imagined Jenna, Zach, and him snuggled together on the big yellow couch in her house, reading a story. Maybe *Dr. Seuss* or something from that little Bible storybook where everything rhymed.

In his daydream, he wasn't a guest. They were a family. He thought she wanted that too. She needed a loving, supportive husband. He could fulfill those requirements, no sweat. But she also needed a man she could rely on. In his current condition, that was like trying to pull a ten-horse load with four Shetland ponies.

22

As usual, Thanksgiving at the Callahans was a zoo. Jenna hadn't been in any shape to see anyone the year before. She and Zach had escaped before anyone arrived, driving to a hotel in Sweetwater so her parents could honestly tell everyone that she was out of town.

She was determined to make up for it this year and help her mom as much as possible. She would also be sweet and friendly to everyone, even if she might not remember who was attached to whom.

Ramona and Ace always spent Thanksgiving and Christmas with their families. They left on Tuesday to visit her parents in San Saba, so Jenna and her mom were in charge of the kitchen. They roasted and carved the turkeys on Wednesday, storing the meat with some broth in plastic containers in the giant spare refrigerator in the laundry room. The cornbread dressing could be made ahead and kept refrigerated. They would bake it on Thanksgiving day while the turkey warmed in the oven. Sue even made the gravy, so their cooking chores the next day would be minimal.

Dub, Will, and Chance set up extra tables and chairs to seat their guests, and a long table to hold all the food. They had learned long ago that buffet style was the only way to handle the thirty-some-odd people who usually showed up.

By ten o'clock Thanksgiving morning, people began to arrive. Even the shirttail relations brought something to contribute to the meal. There were appetizers and relish trays, fruit salads and green salads, make-ahead mashed potatoes and two kinds of sweet potatoes, cheese-broccoli-rice casserole and green bean casserole, homemade rolls and butter, and half a dozen pumpkin and pecan pies and a chocolate cake. With the exception of the cousin who'd made the cake, the single guys contributed soda and sparkling cider.

It was hectic, fun, and exhausting. Zach and Stacy, who was Jenna's cousin's three-year-old daughter, were the stars of the day. Kids and adults alike wanted to play with them. The weather warmed up to the mid-sixties, so the kids were able to play outside.

A couple of the teenage girls volunteered to keep an eye on Zach. Will and Chance organized a touch football game, so most of the guys and a few of the females burned off some of their dinner by racing around the side yard.

At 3:30, one of the girls brought Zach inside for a diaper change. Jenna convinced him to stay in the house and let her dad read him a story. By 4:00 he was worn out. He came into the kitchen looking for her, rubbing his eyes, almost asleep on his feet.

Jenna knelt down in front of him and pulled him into a hug. "You look so tired, sweetheart. Do you want to take a nap?"

"Ye-ah." He leaned his head against her and drooped.

Two aunts who were finishing up the dishes, her mom, and grandmother watched them with tender smiles. "I never saw a child that age admit to needing a nap. Enjoy it while you can. It won't last." Her grandmother leaned down and gently stroked Zach's hair. "You'd better take him home. He'll never get any rest around here."

Jenna picked Zach up and stood, leaning over to give her grandma a kiss. Her grandparents would be staying a few days. "We'll come back over tonight after things settle down."

"We'll look forward to it. We haven't really had a chance to visit with him or you."

"That's because all your other grand-children want to enjoy your company too."

"I'll send Dub over with your things," said her mom. "Sneak out before anybody notices."

She told her aunts good-bye and asked her mom to give her regards to everyone else. "I think I spent a few minutes with almost everybody."

Zach was asleep before she reached her house. She carried him into his bedroom and laid him in bed. Slipping off his shoes, she covered him with a light green blanket and closed the multicolored cowboy-themed curtains. He wiggled around in his sleep, kicking off the blanket and propped one leg up on the low railing of his "big boy" toddler bed. "Sleep well, sweetheart," she whispered.

Her dad knocked on the back door, then opened it and came inside. "Here's the diaper bag. I didn't see anything else lying around."

"Thanks, Dad. If we missed something, I'll find it later." Yawning, she covered her mouth with her hand. "Excuse me."

"You'd better take a nap while you have the chance. I need to get back to the company. And the television. UT has the ball."

"Hook 'em, horns." No self-respecting UT alumni let an opportunity pass without saying the school slogan. "I'll see y'all later. Thanks for bringing this over."

"You're welcome, sugar."

She watched him walk down the drive back toward the ranch house, her heart filled with love. "I'm so blessed to have a wonderful family, Lord. Thank you for each one of them."

Going into the living room, she sat down in her pale green recliner and kicked off her shoes. She raised the footrest, leaned back, and turned on the television, muting the sound. It only took a few minutes to find the football game. Texas had made another touchdown.

Yawning again, she closed her eyes. "I hope Mom gets a chance to do this soon."

She woke up an hour later and peeked in on her son. He'd turned around in the bed but still slept soundly. Looking out the back window, she counted two fewer cars. Still a crowd. It probably wasn't very nice, but she was relieved that Zach would probably take at least a two hour nap.

Settling back in the recliner, she flipped through the latest issue of *Southern Living* magazine. There were plenty of ideas for

Christmas decorations but none of them worked for her. They had some fancy recipes for the holidays, but she was still too full to think about food.

Thinking about Nate was more interesting. And a little scary. She was in love with him. Despite the things he was going through, she loved him. He was the same kind, wonderful guy he'd always been. Maybe a little rough around the edges, but his heart was good. There were still some issues to deal with, but he was working on them, following the doctor's orders, and equally important, drawing closer to the Lord. He'd come a long way since the meltdown at her folks four weeks ago.

She wondered how he was doing. How had he handled the big family get-together? Was he still at his uncle's house in Odessa? Would it be tacky to call him there? She decided it wouldn't hurt to call and wish him a happy Thanksgiving, no matter where he was. He only had a cell phone, so it wasn't as if she could try his house first.

He answered on the third ring. There was a lot of cheering in the background. She peeked at the TV. The Aggies had tied up the game.

"Hi." He was practically shouting. "Let me go outside so I can hear you." The noise gradually faded, and she heard a door close. "Sorry about that. The Aggies around here are going crazy. How's it going?"

"We've had a good day. Stuffed our faces until we waddled. Zach had a blast playing with my cousins and cousins' kids. Chance and Will organized a touch football game. That lasted until the UT-A&M game started."

"Sounds basically like a photocopy of our day. Too much food, a little touch football, a little catching up with the relatives, then piling up in the family room around the big screen TV to watch the game. It's been good, but I miss you."

"I miss you too. My grandparents will be here until about 1:00 on Saturday. Maybe we could go for a ride in the afternoon after they leave? The weather is supposed to be warm."

"I should be caught up on the feeding by then. I'll put it on my calendar. As if I'd have to make a note of a date with you."

"Good. I'll schedule it in too. In other words, con my mom into babysitting. Chance said you stopped by on Tuesday and shared your supper with him. That was nice of you."

"It was good to hang out with him. I meant to call you last night or maybe go see

355

you, but Mom decided I needed to learn how to make pumpkin pies."

Jenna smiled but managed not to laugh out loud. From what she'd gathered, other than cooking breakfast, Nate wasn't real at home in the kitchen. "How'd that go?"

"Not too bad. Mostly I watched her work. I think she wanted to spend some time with me. I did learn how to roll out the pie crust. I didn't get the first one placed in the pan quite right, so it was a little lopsided. But everyone was still impressed when Mom told them I did it. She didn't exactly fib, but it sounded as if I made the whole pie."

"And you didn't set the record straight."

"Didn't want to make her look bad in front of the kinfolk."

Jenna heard Zach start to fuss. "Uh-oh, the boss is beginning to wake up. I'd better go get him before he gets too wound up."

"Give him a hug for me. We probably won't be home until late, but I'll give you a call tomorrow."

"Better yet, stop by. My grandparents would like to see you." They'd known Nate since he was in junior high.

"Will do. Go rescue the kid."

"Okay." She almost said "I love you" but caught herself. She wouldn't push. He needed to make that move first, for her sake

356

and for his own. "Bye."

"Bye, honey." A simple end to the call but spoken with such tenderness that Jenna caught her breath. She clicked off the phone and closed her eyes, treasuring the moment in her heart.

Sometimes the words didn't have to be said to know love was real.

23

On Saturday afternoon, Jenna saddled a palomino named Royal Gold but who had been affectionately called Trigger ever since Dub brought him home. He and Jenna had a special bond, much like the one Nate had with Winston. She rode the gelding to Nate's house, trotting around back to the corrals where he had Ebony saddled and was feeding her an apple.

"Afternoon." He flashed her a smile over the silky black horse's back.

"Hi." She looked over at the pasture fence where Winston was hovering. "Is Win jealous that you're taking Ebony or does he want the treat?"

"Both, I suspect." He reached up and pretended to cover Ebony's ears with his hands. "Don't tell anybody, but he sneaks over here every night for an apple. The other horses haven't caught on to it yet."

Ebony nuzzled Nate's hand.

"He may have company from now on."

"Yeah, he might." Nate untied the reins from the corral railing, stepped back, and swung up into the saddle. He guided Ebony over toward Jenna. Trigger nickered softly, and Ebony greeted him the same way. "See, Eb, I told you Jenna was bringing a friend." The horse shook her head and pranced a little. "She's anxious to move."

"Me too." Jenna turned Trigger around and fell in beside Nate. "How about going over to Aidan's Spring?"

"Sure." It was the right distance for a good run, ending at a cold, clear spring. They walked the horses around the house, then out into the open pasture, slowly increasing their speed until they were galloping across the range side by side.

Nate spent half his time watching where they were going and the other half watching Jenna. He couldn't imagine her living in a city away from the ranch, with no horse to ride, no chance to race the wind. Her face glowed with happiness. He hoped part of it was because she was with him and not only the exhilaration of the ride.

Reining in as they approached the spring, they gradually slowed the horses to a walk. They dismounted beneath a grove of pecan trees and let the horses graze on the grass growing near the spring.

"This is one of the few places that still has grass worth eating." Jenna took off her hat, dropped to her knees, and cupped some cold water in her hands, taking a drink. Nate knelt beside her and did the same. They both had full canteens, but no water on the ranch tasted as pure and good as this.

He wiped his mouth on his sleeve and his hands on his jeans. "It's getting awful dry. The dirt tanks are lower than they were last week." He stood and offered her his hand. She took hold of it, let him help her up, and kept her fingers curled around his.

"We'd be in a world of hurt without the windmills. They've kept the ranch going when others failed during a drought. Daddy says even with them there have been times in the past 130 years that our family almost lost this place.

"I think he's the best manager this ranch has ever had. Of course, I'm prejudiced, but I also keep the books, so I know how he does things. We have records going clear back to the beginning of the ranch, and I've looked through them all at one time or another. Most of my ancestors were pretty conservative with spending, but a few of them blew their money on an elaborate lifestyle. Huge house parties and travel all over the world. Great-great-uncle Jack went to England and basically bought himself an aristocratic bride."

"So that's why those Boston cousins of yours talk funny."

Jenna laughed and playfully swatted him with her hat. Then she admitted, "They do talk funny. I'm not sure their English lineage has much to do with it at this point. Thankfully, my great-great-grandfather bought his brother's share of the ranch to protect it. After that it became family tradition to pass the ranch on to the son best suited to run it, and give everyone else money as their inheritance."

"But Dub's already made all of you partners."

"He figures it will work. I think so too. Chance and I have some say in things, but we both know that Will is the best one to be in charge when Daddy retires. Which will probably be when he's a hundred."

They walked over to a long bench built between a couple of big rocks underneath a large pecan tree. Laying their beige felt hats on one end of the bench, they sat down. Nate ran his finger lightly over the weathered wood. The first Callahan to settle the country had built one like it there for his bride. "What number is this?"

"Ten or eleven. Nobody is quite sure. Some of them have lasted longer than others, depending on the wood and the carpenter." She relaxed against the back of the bench, releasing his hand. He promptly put his arm around her shoulders. "I love it here. I used to dream of having a house right over there." She pointed to a clearing slightly beyond the trees.

"Maybe you should build one."

"I've thought about it, but it's good to be in the compound." Jenna laughed and rested her head on his arm. "That's what it is, you know. We may be grown, but the folks like having us close. And I like being there with them. There's comfort and security with the family, but with each of us having our own place, we have our freedom too. It's good all the way around."

"When Will and Chance get married and have kids, Zach will have playmates right next door. That's a good thing. It gets lonely being out in the country as an only child."

"That's why I take him to day care a couple of days a week."

Maybe we'll give him some brothers and sisters someday. And he'll be mine too. How he wanted to say those words out loud! But he couldn't. Children meant marriage. Until he was straightened out and playing with a full deck, he refused to bring up the subject.

"Chance said you had trouble with the fire on Tuesday night."

What was she doing, reading his mind? "I came out of it pretty fast, thanks to him, but it's clear I still have a big problem there."

"Did it take you back to the building that blew up?"

He nodded. "I definitely won't be using the fireplace at my house anytime soon. And avoiding others. Generally, I'm better than I was, but I think about the war every day. Not intentionally. Thoughts pop into my mind at the weirdest moments. Often there's nothing that triggers them, at least not that I can figure out. I'll be working away, and suddenly I'm thinking about Iraq or Afghanistan."

"Bad things?"

"Sometimes, but not always. We had some good times over there too. Doctor Silverman says those kind of memories are fairly normal, and the every day thing might continue for years. I'm sleeping much better. Those CDs you loaned me have really helped. Which reminds me, I bought some of my own. You can have yours back."

"Are you sure you don't need them?"

"I'm good. I bought the same ones, plus some others."

"Then I'll take them back. I listen to them for enjoyment now, but they helped me through some tough times. I'm glad you're doing so much better." She reached up and caressed his jaw with her fingertips. "I was really worried about you."

"I know. I'm sorry I've put you through this." He caught her hand and kissed her knuckles. "I'm better, but I'm not where I want to be. Not where I should be."

She sat up, studying his face, searching his eyes. "What else is going on?"

"I still forget things sometimes. Get jumpy and irritable."

"I haven't noticed you being irritated."

"The fence posts have."

Jenna laughed and relaxed back beneath his arm. "I don't know anybody who hasn't lost his temper while fixing fence. Those posts and wire don't always cooperate."

"I suppose that's true. There are other things. Yesterday I was coming home from town, and a car was parked beside the road with the hood up. I should have stopped to see if I could help. Even a year ago, I would have.

"But I flashed back to Iraq. Instead of a blond-headed businessman standing beside his car, I saw an Iraqi man in traditional dress. I was terrified that he might be a suicide bomber. I drove clear off the left side of the road in the bar ditch, racing past him as fast as I could. A few minutes later, I realized I wasn't in Iraq. But I was too shaken and embarrassed to go back and see if he needed any help."

"Does the doctor think that will go away?"

"Probably. I called Pastor Brad when I got home. He says he's still nervous if he sees a car beside the road, but he doesn't have flashbacks. And he stops to help. I think that's the trick with cars along the road. If I can block the flashback before it happens, then check to see how I can help — like most men around here would do — maybe that will put a stop to them.

"I've learned good things from the psychiatrist and worked through some stuff, but I honestly think I've benefited the most from our prayer times. It can be a rough session, but when we spend time praying together at the end, I feel the Lord's peace."

"How do people make it without him?"

"I don't know. I sure couldn't have. Next week I start seeing Pastor Brad regularly instead of driving to Big Spring. I only have to check in with Doctor Silverman once a month."

"That's wonderful." She sat up again, an enthusiastic smile lighting up her face. "We know you're better, but that's confirmation you've improved."

"True, though he thinks I'll probably always have some issues." Nate didn't like admitting that, but he needed to be honest with her.

"According to my parents, Dad still deals with some things too." She cupped his face with her hand and met his gaze directly. "Sweetheart, we all have issues. Some may be tougher to handle than others, but we don't have to struggle alone. We have Jesus. And each other. You have me."

She'd called him sweetheart. He'd been so caught up in the thrill of the endearment that her other words barely registered — until he noted the tenderness in her eyes and did a quick replay. *You have me.* He told himself not to jump to conclusions. But his heart started tap-dancing anyway.

"I couldn't have made it this far without my friends," he said carefully, watching her closely.

Disappointment flashed across her face, and she lowered her hand. Sliding back against the seat back, she looked down and took a deep breath. "I thought I was more than a friend."

"Oh, you are." He gently lifted her face so she would look at him. "I fell in love with you when I was fifteen, and you've been in my heart all these years. Since I've been home, I've grown to love you more than ever." A tear ran down her cheek, and he gently brushed it away with his thumb. "Sweetheart, you're the most important person in the world to me. I love you with all my heart."

"I love you too. I think I always have."

He pulled her into his arms, kissing her with half a lifetime of love, rejoicing that he hadn't been wrong, that she loved him too. Lifting her onto his lap, he kissed her again and again, delighting in her eager response and the love in her touch. She caressed his face, curled her fingers in his hair, and then wrapped her arms around his neck.

They both sensed their control slipping at the same time and eased back. He dropped a light kiss on the tip of her nose. "I think we'd better go duck our heads in the spring."

Eyes twinkling, she looked over at the cold water, then back at him. "Go right ahead. I'll watch."

Laughing, he picked her up and set her back on the bench. He noticed the horses gazing at them, ears twitched forward. "I forgot we had an audience."

"They've probably been laughing at us."

"I suppose we did look pretty silly to them." Nate knew she wouldn't like what he was about to say. But he had to do it. Fortifying his resolve, he picked up her hand and brought it to his lips, tenderly kissing the back of it. "Jenna, I love you, and I want to marry you . . ."

"Yes."

He closed his eyes, desperately wishing he'd phrased that differently.

She sat up again. The woman was like one of Zach's bouncy balls. When he looked at her, she was staring at him with narrowed eyes.

"I just said yes, as in yes, I'll marry you. Me, the love of your life. And how do you respond? No hallelujah. Not even a yee-haw or a yippee. Instead you sit there quiet as a sparrow in a hawk's nest. You kinda look like one too, all wide-eyed and searching for a way to escape." She pulled her hand from his. "What's going on?"

He sat up straighter, remembering when they were kids and she would get riled. Jenna hadn't been above taking a swing at her brothers, or occasionally at him. "Honey, I do love you, and I want to marry you, but I can't make a commitment yet."

Jumping to her feet, she put some distance between them, stomping a trail in the scattered pale green grass in the process. Nate breathed a little easier. She spun around and glared at him. "Why not?"

He stood too. As if his height and bulk could intimidate her, which they couldn't. Nor did he want them to. He simply felt more secure on his feet than he did cowering on the bench. "Because I need better proof that the therapy and prayer is going to work. I've only been at it for a month. I won't obligate you to marry me when I could go off my rocker next week. I need a little more time, honey. That's all."

She rubbed the toe of her worn brown boot in the dirt, then emphatically squished a clod. "How much time?"

Since he hadn't planned to tell her that he loved her yet, he hadn't figured that out. *Better pull some number out of the air.* "How about until April 1st?"

"No."

"No?"

"If you propose on April 1st, I won't know if it's real or an April Fool's joke."

"Aw, honey, I wouldn't be that mean."

She glared at him again. Given the way he had botched things in the last five minutes, maybe she had a point.

"Okay, make it April 2nd."

She counted the months on her fingers, clearly not happy with the idea.

Nate thought of something else. "I promised your dad I wouldn't rush you." That was a very loose paraphrase of what he'd said to Dub, but the meaning was the same.

"When?" Her forehead creased in a frown.

"When I went to see him after I got home. When he took your advice and hired me." Judging by her puzzled expression, she was clearly confused. "My senior year, Dub figured out that I was in love with you. Back in September, after I got home, he asked me if I still was. He was worried about you being hurt again."

Her frown faded. "What did you tell him?"

"That I'd always love you as a friend, but I wasn't sure if I was still in love with you. That it would take time to sort out those feelings and to see if God had something more in mind for us than friendship."

He walked toward her. When she didn't move, he stopped in front of her and lightly gripped her shoulders. "Can you give me those four months, Jenna? To take you on dates, sit with you in church, and love you? Time to regain confidence in myself?"

"On one . . . no, two conditions."

"Let's hear them."

"That you make sure all those single women in town who have you in their sights know that you're my guy. We may not be officially engaged, but you belong to me."

"Not a problem. What's number two?"

"If you decide before April that you can make the commitment, you'll go ahead and ask me again. But you'd better wait at least a week because it will take me that long to get over being mad at you."

"Yes, ma'am." When she looked up at him, he swooped down and kissed her.

A minute later, with her arms wrapped around his neck, she murmured, "You don't fight fair."

"Maybe not." He brushed a feathery kiss across her mouth. "But it sure is fun."

24

December was filled with holiday parties and church and town activities. It was chaotic but also the best Christmas season Jenna could remember in years because she and Nate shared so much of it.

They took Zach to the Christmas parade three weeks before Christmas. It was little more than a bunch of tractors with wreaths fastened on the front, a few floats, and the sheriff's posse. The highlight was a cowboy riding a longhorn. The cow's horns were at least six feet wide, and she sported a big red bow around her neck. Santa was last, riding on Callahan Crossing's biggest fire truck. Zach didn't like the boisterous man in the funny-looking red suit. Instead of resting his arm on Nate's shoulder as he usually did, he scooted closer and put one arm around his neck. "Santa too loud."

"Shall we go to the Sonic and get something to eat?"

Zach nodded, but he stayed tucked real close to Nate.

They drove up to the drive-in restaurant, sitting in the pickup to eat the meal. Zach played with a little car while Jenna broke his chicken strips into smaller pieces and blew on them to cool. Nate poured some milk into a spare sippy cup and snapped on the lid. He handed it to Zach through the opening between the seats. "Here you go." After Zach took a big drink of milk, Nate handed him a French fry. "Munch on this until your mom gets the chicken cooled down."

"Almost there, Zach." She glanced back at him. He had half of a French fry sticking out of his mouth and grinned around it. She handed Zach a piece of chicken, took a bite of her hamburger, and met Nate's gaze as he watched her. "What? Do I have mustard on my face?"

He inspected her face, then lightly touched the corner of her mouth. "No, not really."

She laughed and checked to see how Zach was doing. Sometimes Nate came up with the silliest excuses to touch her. And she didn't mind a bit.

"So, Zach, what do you want for Christmas?" Nate peered back at him.

"Horsey."

Jenna blinked and looked at Nate. She really hadn't expected him to say anything. He never had mentioned anything specific before. "Wonder which of my brothers put him up to that," she murmured.

"That's not hard to figure out. If it'd been Chance, he probably would have said a bulldozer."

"Bulldozer!" Zach grinned when they both looked at him.

"You already have one, remember."

"Yeah. Chicken." Zach held out his hand, and Jenna gave him some more lunch.

After they ate, they took him to the park and let him go down the kiddie slide a dozen times. Nate made it easy by lifting him up to the top of the slide instead of him having to climb all the way up the ladder. He played on the swings for a while too, and raced around in the grass as they chased him.

Walking back to the car with Zach riding on his shoulders, Nate looked down at her, his smile wistful. "I could get used to having y'all around all the time."

"Just say the word, cowboy. It's up to you." She knew he wasn't ready yet. But maybe he was getting closer. "How are your sessions with Pastor Brad going?"

"Good. We spend more time praying than

talking, but that's fine with me. I haven't had a nightmare in almost two weeks."

"Fantastic."

"I think I'm seeing light at the end of the tunnel, and it's not a train."

It was an old line, but Jenna expected it spoke volumes about his state of mind.

"Praise the Lord."

"Yes, ma'am. Many times over."

The next day was the children's Christmas program at church. As usual, it was touching, sweet, and funny. And all the more memorable because it was Zach's first foray into performing before a crowd. He enjoyed it immensely. Remembering all the words to "Away in a Manager" was a little tough, but he knew the hand motions. He also wiggled and swayed in perfect time to the music throughout the whole song. Nate snapped a dozen pictures of the little group, most of them zoomed in on Zach.

When the kids bowed and walked down from the stage, her cowboy leaned over and whispered in her ear, "That's our boy." Nate's name might not be on the birth certificate, or even on a marriage certificate yet, but he loved her son as much as any father possibly could.

That afternoon they decorated her big Christmas tree, then went to Nate's and decorated his short, scrawny cedar. When she first spotted it, she stared at it in disbelief. "That's the most pathetic tree I've ever seen. You should get your money back."

"I didn't pay anything for it. I found it over in the pasture, sitting there all alone, looking forlorn. It was in the area Dub is going to clear out in a few months, so I decided its days should end happily instead of being bulldozed into a big pile with all those mesquites and burned."

"Then let's dress it up."

They put so many tiny white lights and ornaments on it that she thought the poor thing might collapse. When they were done and switched on the lights, they both gasped in surprise.

Zach clapped his hands. "Boo-ti-ful."

"Yes, it is." Nate slid his arm around her waist and drew her against his side.

"I think we made it happy."

"Yep." He gave her a light squeeze. "Just like me."

They snuck away in the middle of the week and drove to Abilene to go Christmas shopping. After buying presents for their families and more than they should have for Zach, they split up and shopped for each other. They reunited at the appointed place and time, playfully trying to hide the shopping bags holding their gifts. After stopping for a visit with Nate's grandparents, they headed back home.

On Christmas Eve, both families attended an early candlelight service at church. Then Jenna, Nate, and Zach drove around town for a while, looking at the Christmas lights. They went by the Langleys on the way home, where Zach got to open his first presents. She had no doubt that the older Langleys would make wonderful grandparents when she and Nate were married.

And they would be married. She wasn't going to let him get away. The minute he officially proposed, she intended to haul him to the courthouse, buy a marriage license, and see the preacher as soon as it was legal. She'd have that cowboy roped, hog-tied, and branded before he knew what hit him.

Zach opened a few presents at home on Christmas Eve, ones picked out by Jenna and chosen because they wouldn't excite him too much. He and Nate built a square house with his new building blocks, and Jenna cheered him on as he put together a simple puzzle.

Then they all three snuggled together on the couch, and Nate read the Christmas story from Zach's rhyming Bible using only the tree for light. Jenna thought she might explode with happiness and contentment.

Nate seemed touched too. The dear man choked up and had to clear his throat twice during the story.

Christmas Day was fairly low key, as much as it could be with a two-year-old spoiled rotten by six loving adults. Since Zach told everybody that he wanted a horsey, he got six of them. A small stuffed one to sleep with, a big stuffed one to sit on, a stick horse, two to gallop across the coffee table, and a big rocking horse from Will. There were at least a dozen other toys, including a John Deere riding tractor from Nate and a bulldozer he could ride from Chance.

Her little guy was overwhelmed by so many new things at once.

Jenna opened her presents, delighted with the lovely peach sweater and peach and turquoise flowered skirt from her parents. The supple leather riding gloves from Chance fit perfectly. And the hand-tooled leather Western belt from Will would be great with her nicer jeans. She saved the gift from Nate for last. He did the same with hers.

Smiling, they scooted closer together on the sofa and ignored the chatter around them. Chance was showing Zach how to ride the bulldozer, so he was in good hands.

Nate carefully removed the gold ribbon and bow, then ripped off the shiny red and gold wrapping paper from the box.

Jenna teased him. "You ruined the paper."

"It's not a big enough sheet to recycle next year. And I saved the bow." He leaned close to her ear. "I'm in a hurry to see if it's what I think it is."

It was, but she didn't say so. Camouflaging a box containing a watch wasn't easy.

He opened it carefully, and his face lit up when he saw the gold wristwatch, with a yellow and white gold link band. "Oh, wow. Honey, this is great." He grinned at her. "And it's not one of those five-dollar ones from Walmart."

Not even close. But then he knew that. "I thought you might enjoy something nice to wear when you dress up."

"Yes, ma'am. My old one is fine for everyday, but it's lookin' a little ratty for church. Thank you." The promise in his eyes told her he'd thank her with an extra kiss later. He took the watch out of the box and slipped it on. "It fits perfectly. Great guess on the size of the band. I really like the yellow and white gold combination."

"Good. I was hoping it wouldn't be too small."

Anticipation spiraled through her as she very carefully removed the sparkling, lacy silver bow and dark blue shiny paper from her gift. Judging by the long, narrow box, it was a necklace or bracelet. Or a pen and pencil set.

She eased open the lid to find a beautiful gold bracelet, each link heart-shaped. "Nate, it's beautiful."

"I thought it was appropriate, since you have my heart."

Her eyes stung, but she blinked hard, keeping her emotions under control. Smiling up at him, she said softly, "Thank you for both." Then she stretched up and kissed him lightly.

"You're welcome."

"Okay, you two, quit smoochin' and show us what you gave each other." Chance tossed a wad of green and gold wrapping paper at them, hitting Nate in the chest.

Nate threw it back with a grin. "Take care of your own trash." He held out his arm so everyone could see his present. "My sweet woman gave me a great watch."

While her family commented on the watch, Jenna removed the bracelet from the box and fastened it around her wrist. "And my sweet man gave me this beautiful bracelet."

Her mother's eyes widened, then glistened with a hint of moisture. "Nate, that's exquisite."

"Thank you, ma'am."

Chance grinned at his sister and winked at Nate. "Good job."

Will came over for a closer inspection, nodding in approval. "Looks like I don't have to give you any lessons in the jewelry department. You're doing fine on your own."

Jenna glanced at her dad, expecting to see him smiling his approval. Instead he appeared sad. Was that regret clouding his eyes as he watched them?

He stood suddenly and went into the kitchen, returning a few minutes later with a big plastic trash bag. "Y'all cram all that paper in here, and I'll haul it outside."

As everyone gathered up the trash and crammed it into the bag, Jenna caught her mother's eye. She nodded toward her dad and lifted her eyebrow in question. Her mom shrugged and mouthed, "I don't know."

When Dub left the room with the filled bag, Jenna excused herself and followed him outside. He stood at the end of the porch, his hands resting on the railing, his head bowed. She waited, uncertain if she should intrude. After a few minutes, he raised his head, took a deep breath, and straightened.

Jenna walked over to him. "Daddy, are you all right?"

He turned slightly and shook his head. When she joined him, he put his arm around her shoulders, holding her close. "Forgive me, sugar."

She slipped her arm around his waist and leaned her head against his chest. Apologizing didn't come easy for her dad, though he had done it on occasion. She didn't think, however, that she had ever heard him put it in those terms. "For what?"

"For tellin' Nate years ago that he wasn't good enough for you. For basically running him off."

Jenna pulled away and turned so she could see his face. A shiver rippled through her. "What are you talking about? What did you say to him?"

Dub looked her directly in the eye. "When you were in high school, I could see how much you liked Nate. It was understandable. He was a good-lookin' kid and a nice guy. I figured he was sweet on you too. Who wouldn't be sweet on my darlin' girl? But if he was, he kept it well hidden. I don't know if he was shy or thought you were out of his league or scared of me. Maybe some of all three. I expect he figured I wouldn't approve, and he was right.

"I was too caught up in my own self-importance. I was Dub Callahan. Powerful and particular. My only daughter was going to marry someone important, someone who would make a name for himself, go places in this world."

"That's why you encouraged me to date Jimmy Don." At the time she'd wondered why her dad kept talking him up, practically pushing her to go out with him.

Dub nodded, then looked away, staring across the wide open vistas of his land. "Half the colleges in the country were trying to recruit him in high school. Unless he got hurt, he was a cinch to play pro ball. If something happened to keep him off the ball field, he was a straight-A student. I figured he'd still do well."

Jimmy might have actually done better if he hadn't played pro ball, she thought. *We might have too.* But it didn't matter now. "Back to Nate."

"One day, a month or two before he graduated, I noticed him watching you walk to the house. There was no denying that boy was in love. Hat over boots in love. By then, you were going with Jimmy Don, but I didn't think you were in love with him yet. Nate was a threat to my plans. So I flat told

383

him that he wasn't good enough for you. He wouldn't do anything remarkable or make a name for himself."

"You were wrong about that." Jenna didn't try to hide her resentment. If her father hadn't been so intimidating or interfered, Nate might have been more open with his feelings. If she'd known how much he cared for her, she never would have gone out with Jimmy Don. She certainly wouldn't have married him and gone through so much pain and heartache.

"Yes, I was." Her father sighed heavily and smoothed back her hair. "I was wrong on a lot of things. Because of my pride, I caused you to suffer. And I'll regret that the rest of my days."

"Don't let it eat at you, Daddy. I won't lie and tell you that I don't resent you interfering back then. If I'd had any idea how Nate felt, I would have jumped at the chance to have a life with him. Still, though you encouraged me to go with Jimmy Don, you didn't make me marry him. That was my own choice. I thought I loved him."

"But now you know differently. You've loved Nate all along."

"Yes, sir. I have. But I'm not going to dwell on the past, on what anybody did or didn't do. I did too much of that for too long. Nate and I have a beautiful future ahead of us. That's what is important now." She hugged him tightly. "You're forgiven, Daddy. Let it go."

He held her close. "Thank you, Jenna." He released her and lightly tapped her under the chin with his knuckle. "You'll be the best wife Nate could ever ask for."

"I'm certainly going to try."

"Send him out here. Since I'm eatin' crow, I might as well finish the whole bird."

25

In January, life went back to the normal routine. Feeding the cattle and horses was an everyday chore except on Sunday. For once, it seemed as if they had all the fences squared away. Probably because the whole crew had spent the first two weeks of the month building a fence strong enough to contain Wandering Boy, the nickname they had given the Callahans' prized bull.

Nate spent some time teaching Ebony the intricacies of cutting cattle from a herd. She was a quick learner, with inborn cow sense. The mare would prove her full worth during roundup in the spring.

Saturday night became date night for him and Jenna, with supper out. One week, they went to the Boot Stop, and the next to the Hacienda, a new Mexican restaurant in town. Then they drove to Abilene for seafood.

On warm days, they took horseback rides

when the work was done and they could get away. But the times he enjoyed the most were the evenings she cooked for him. Afterward, they played with Zach until his bedtime, then talked, stole kisses, and dreamed for an hour or two until Nate dragged himself away.

Pastor Brad cut his sessions to once a week, which was fine with Nate. They were seeing progress. The prayers, counseling, and maybe the medication had gone a long way to improving his state of mind. He didn't like taking the meds, but the psychiatrist thought he should stay on them for at least a year. Doctor Silverman anticipated that he might always need to take something for the anxiety and depression due to the likely chemical changes in his brain. Nate agreed to the one year test, then he'd see how things were.

He hadn't had a nightmare in over a month and was sleeping well almost every night. Thoughts of the war still skittered through his mind several times a day. Intermittently, he fought battles all over again, not exactly in a flashback but in his memories.

Cars beside the road still bothered him. He tried to head off a flashback or panic attack when he first spotted the vehicle by reminding himself, often out loud, that he was in Texas. Usually, it was a rancher checking a stock tank across the fence, or an oil company rep inspecting some equipment. Folks stopped for other reasons were far and few between. If he saw someone who might need assistance, he'd pray for guidance and control and pull in behind them. Once a radiator had overheated. Another time, a very pregnant lady had a flat tire.

Then there were the tourists who barely spoke English. They were looking for the "cows with twenty foot wide horns" that some guy in Dallas had told them about. They wanted to take a picture standing beside one. He tried to explain that twenty feet was an exaggeration even for longhorns, but he wasn't sure they understood. Finally, he sent them about thirty miles down the road to a ranch with a Texas longhorn herd. Then he called the rancher — the same one who'd ridden the longhorn in the Christmas parade — and warned him that he was about to have company.

Buster came up behind him one day to ask a question and startled him. When Nate spun around and almost punched him, word got around town to approach him from the front or make a lot of noise if coming from behind. To his relief, nobody seemed to think he was weird because of it. Or if they did, they didn't spout off where he could hear it.

He was better, but not good enough yet to be a husband and father.

Since the week after Christmas, the temperature had been unusually warm, with fairly low humidity, moderate winds, and not a drop of rain. The stock tanks without windmills were barely more than mud. The creeks were empty, and Buster declared that the catfish were wearing flea collars.

The Callahans, along with the rest of the volunteer fire department, were called out to fight three grass fires in one week. Due to their quick response and a drop in the wind, those fires had remained fairly small, only burning a total of 150 acres. One shed was lost, but they saved the farmhouse nearby.

Folks were nervous, watchful, and extra careful.

On the last Tuesday in January, the National Weather Service issued a Red Flag Warning for a large part of West Texas, advising of critical fire weather conditions. The temperature was expected to reach the high seventies by the afternoon with humidity below 15 percent. They predicted winds twenty-five to thirty miles per hour with gusts up to forty-five. As far as the eye could see, the land was a tinderbox.

Chance went to his job site but was prepared to leave at a moment's notice. Dub and Will stayed close to the house in case they were called out. They checked the water level in the two large portable spray tanks kept on the ranch and made sure the tires on the trailers had the right amount of air. If the Callahans were gone, Ollie and Ace would be in charge of keeping fire watch on the ranch. If anything happened, Buster would man one spray rig with Ace driving the pickup. Ollie and Ethel would handle the other one.

The fire departments in thirty counties readied their equipment and put their fire crews on notice.

Though he felt bad about it, Nate knew he couldn't help fight a fire. He and Buster went to feed the cattle. They distributed a load of hay and one of cottonseed cake, counted the cattle in the pasture, and made a quick drive-by of the fence line.

Jenna was meeting Lindsey in town for lunch and had a hair appointment at 2:00. Without her at the ranch house for the meal, Nate planned to fix himself a sandwich and pay his bills. He dropped Buster off at the barn for his truck and went home to eat. The older cowboy always took a short rest after lunch, so Nate also spent a few minutes in his recliner before going back to meet him.

Dub's and Will's pickups were still at the house when they drove by to get another load of feed. Hopefully, they'd still be there at quitting time.

Nate and Buster rotated positions on the feeding job. It was Nate's turn to drive slowly across the pasture while Buster tossed the hay bales off the truck every twenty feet or so. This kind of driving wasn't exactly a mental challenge. Watch for potholes and check on his partner every few minutes to make sure he hadn't fallen off the truck. It gave a man time for his mind to wander.

He glanced at the clock on the dash. Jenna's stylist should be snipping away at her pretty red hair. They were probably both laughing and talking up a storm. After the appointment, she intended to go by the Mission and sort through some donations. That kind of thing went better on the afternoons that they weren't open for customers.

Zach had the sniffles, so playtime with his little friends at the day care had been nixed.

He was spending the day with Grandma.

Three quarters of the way through the load, Buster pounded on the top of the cab. Nate stopped and stuck his head out the window to see what he wanted.

"You better come up here and take a look-see."

Nate turned off the engine, hopped out of the cab, and climbed onto the back bumper and the open tailgate into the truck bed. A gust of wind caught his cap bill, almost blowing it off his head. He shoved it down tighter. "What's up?"

"Look over yonder." Buster pointed to the northwest. A wide, thick plume of smoke rose high in the pale blue sky.

"That looks like a bad one." Nate scanned the pasture, noting their position and that of the smoke, which expanded rapidly. He estimated the fire to be about four miles, maybe less, southwest of Callahan Crossing.

And the wind was out of the southwest.

His blood ran cold. "That's headed right toward town."

Buster nodded, the color draining from his face. "Lord have mercy."

"We gotta go." Nate threw a bale of hay over the side of the truck. Buster grabbed one and tossed it over the other side. Nate pushed the last one off the back and jumped down. Buster was right behind him. Nate slid into the driver's seat, taking off as Buster slammed his door closed.

Dub had bought some two-way radios the previous summer. Though they hadn't been cheap, they'd never achieved the twenty-mile range advertised, not even in a flat, grassy pasture. In some places they worked well for keeping in touch with someone less than a mile or two away. But in this part of the ranch, the walkie-talkies were worthless.

They sped across the pasture, their heads smacking the ceiling of the cab a couple of times when Nate drove over bumps instead of avoiding them. Buster tried twice to press the right number on his cell phone before he succeeded. His wife was at the high school.

"Nadine, there's a fire headed toward town. Get out of there right now." Shaking his head as he listened, he grabbed the armrest when they hit another bump. "Honey, don't wait till everybody —" He jerked the phone away from his ear, staring at it. For the first time in his life, Nate heard Buster swear. The older man dialed again.

Nate couldn't manage the phone and driving through the rough pasture at the same time. After he crossed the cattle guard and turned onto the dirt road, he pushed number two, the speed dial for Jenna. He got a fast busy signal. Buster was trying again. "I think the circuits are overloaded. Or the cell towers are already down."

"Nadine said they're evacuating the school, but she won't leave until all the kids are gone. I know that's the right thing for her to do, but I don't like her being there. The buses pick up the little kids first. I ain't goin' to sit home and wait for her to come in the door."

Nate dropped Buster off at his pickup, then raced to the ranch house and skidded to a stop. As expected, Dub and Will were gone. Jenna's car wasn't there or at her house. Shifting into park, he left the engine running and jogged to the back door.

He burst into the kitchen, startling Ramona as she walked in from the dining room. She shrieked and threw a blue dishtowel in the air. "Have you heard from Jenna?"

"No. We've been trying, but the phone lines are down."

Carrying her purse, Sue hurried into the kitchen. She already had her keys out. "Cell phones are down too."

"I know. Stay here with Zach," ordered Nate. "And keep an eye on that fire. If the wind shifts, get out of here. I'll go to town and find Jenna. What's the name of the beauty shop?"

"Joanie's Cut and Clip. It's on Twelfth between Fir and Elm. But try the Mission first. Even if she stayed for the haircut, she should be done by now."

Nate ran back to the pickup. Judging by the trail of dust on the main ranch road, Buster was almost to the highway. He hoped the other man planned to put the pedal to the metal because he had no intention of worrying about the speed limit.

He covered the distance to the highway in record time. When he pulled onto the blacktop, there was no sign of Buster. Nate floored it until he hit ninety. The dark line of smoke had grown to terrifying proportions. "Lord, protect the people who are fighting that fire. Especially Dub, Will, and Chance. Please protect anyone in its way."

He topped a hill and saw the blaze, an inferno a mile wide and only a couple of miles from town. The wind whipped it into a leaping, dancing frenzy, devouring everything in its path. The smoke rolled before it, covering the countryside and blocking his view of the flames. "Father God, please don't let anybody get hurt."

Red lights flashed amid the smoke. There

had to be at least fifty or sixty vehicles trying to get ahead of the blaze. Trucks and firemen from half a dozen counties rushing to the battle. He didn't see how a battalion of fire trucks could stop it.

Half a mile from town, Nate crossed into the forty mile per hour zone and began to slow down. The speed limit would drop to twenty-five shortly. No matter his fear and haste, he couldn't risk plowing into somebody. He met a highway patrolman going the other way, lights flashing, siren on and doing at least seventy. He suspected they were closing the road to keep people out. "Thanks, Lord, for letting me get here first."

The Mission was on the west side of town. He turned left on Main and met a stream of cars and pickups headed east. The siren at the downtown fire station blasted continuously. From the noise level, the one at the stadium sounded the same warning.

Two people hurried from the drugstore to their cars. The insurance man rushed out of his office, carrying a box of files to his pickup. Next door, the realtor hauled out his computer and went back to lock the door. Across the street, Bob Hunter carried a box from Maisie's store and put it in the back of his pickup, which was already almost full of antiques. He supposed Bob could always order more sporting goods, but according to Jenna, many things in Maisie's shop were irreplaceable.

Nate drove three blocks and turned up Maple, going to Third Street. Jenna's truck was parked at the side of the Mission. Relief swept through him. She was safe. But not for long. Heavy smoke darkened the sky, and he thought he spotted flames at the edge of town. He shook his head, not letting himself dwell on the image.

As he pulled up next to her pickup, she came out of the building, carrying a big, full plastic trash bag. He jumped out and ran to help her. He took the bag, noting through the slight gap in the top that it held clothes. He threw it in the back of her truck, adding to the large pile already there. "Honey, you have to leave."

She glanced at the red glow in the west as smoke swirled around them. "We have time to get a few more things. There are two boxes of unsorted clothes in the back. You get those, and I'll grab the rest of the coats." Nate did as she asked, wedging the big boxes in the truck bed.

When she came out with the coats, he asked, "Where are you going to put those?"

"The backseat."

He opened the back door, deciding there

was enough room for the coats on top of the stacks of canned goods and bags of beans and rice. She stuffed them in the truck while he ran back inside. Grabbing a big empty box, he swept a tableful of shoes and boots into it.

Jenna met him on the way out. She coughed and wiped her eyes. "I'll get the record books. This will have to do."

He shoved some of the bags around to make room for the shoes. There were still boxes of canned goods in the building, and his truck was empty, but they'd run out of time. The wind swirled sand down the street, and the smoke irritated his eyes.

She ran out a few minutes later, locking the door behind her. "Maybe it won't reach here."

But they both knew it would. He took the records from her and crammed them into the only empty spot in the backseat. As she fastened her seat belt and started the engine, a roar drew their attention to the west. The cotton gin had gone up in flames. "Nate, let's go!"

"I'll follow you." He ran to his truck and pulled out behind her on Maple. The smoke was getting thicker. Instead of continuing on Maple to get out of town, she whipped right on Third. "What the . . . ?"

He pulled up beside her on the left side of the street. She stopped and lowered her window. He lowered his right one. "What are you doing?"

"I just remembered that Mrs. Dodd was supposed to come home last night. She doesn't have a car. We have to check on her."

Nate stared down the street at the fire clearly in view. Sweat broke out on his forehead, and his hands grew clammy. *Help me, Jesus.* Forcing his gaze away from the sight, he focused on Jenna. Mrs. Dodd was eighty years old and used a walker. "Lead the way. I don't know where she lives."

Nodding, the love of his life took off down the street, toward the firestorm. Nate was right behind her, praying furiously all the way. Three blocks later, he spotted the tiny, frail, white-haired lady. She stood in her front yard, leaning on the walker with one hand, holding the garden hose in the other, spraying water on her yard and house. The old girl wasn't going to go down without a fight. A house at the other end of the block exploded into flames.

Jenna screeched to a halt and ran to her.

Nate stopped behind Jenna's truck — and froze. The flames slithered through the rubble on both sides of the street and swept across the grass. They leaped up the front of an old blue Victorian directly beyond the empty lot next door. The noise was unlike anything he'd ever heard. A window exploded. Then another.

Flames were everywhere.

Lt. Myers was on the floor.

"No!" With every ounce of his will, Nate forced the memory aside. The flames held him captive. He couldn't move. "Jesus, set me free!" Barely a whisper, but a cry from the depths of his soul. "Help me!"

Suddenly, God's peace flowed through him. The terror vanished. He looked around. Jenna was trying to help Mrs. Dodd to her pickup, but the old lady moved at a snail's pace. The flames were closing in. Unclenching his hands from the steering wheel, he threw open the door and leaped from the truck, running to them. The heat was almost unbearable. He swept the woman up in his arms. "Get the walker."

Jenna grabbed the walker and ran ahead of him, opening the passenger door, then she sprinted to his truck and tossed it in the back. He quickly slid Mrs. Dodd onto the seat.

"My cat!" She pointed toward her house. "She's on the porch."

He could barely hear the animal's terrified wail above the roar of the fire. Embers landed on Mrs. Dodd's roof. Through the thick smoke, he spotted the silhouette of a cat carrier on the porch. He looked back to check on Jenna. She was in the driver's seat. "Go! I'll bring the cat."

"Hurry." He shut the passenger door, and she turned the pickup around, heading east on Third.

Nate ducked low, shielding his mouth and nose with his hand as he ran. The smoke was so thick he could hardly breathe. His eyes stung and watered. The fire raced toward the house. But he hadn't been an All Region wide receiver for nothing. Wondering where that silly thought came from, he dashed up the sidewalk and grabbed the carrier. A box sat beside it, and he scooped that up too.

The cat screamed and clawed at the screened window of the small crate, but Nate's hand was out of reach on the handle. Entering the driver's side of the truck, he heaved the cat carrier into the passenger seat and dropped the box on the floor.

He shifted into drive as he closed the door and made a U-turn, pushing the gas pedal to the floorboard. He was a block away when he checked the rearview mirror and saw Mrs. Dodd's house go up in flames.

Once he had a little breathing room, he

slowed down, afraid he would run into someone in the heavy smoke. The houses were scattered in that area, but he tried to watch for anyone, any movement as he passed. He spotted faint headlights several blocks up, then taillights close ahead. Nate hoped they were Jenna's until they turned bright red to indicate the vehicle was stopping. "Now what's she doing?"

The woman was going to give him a heart attack.

The pickup coming toward them stopped beside her. Nate slowed even more.

The cat yowled.

"Quiet."

Meooooow!

Another female who didn't take orders.

"It's okay, kitty. You're safe." He tried to use his most soothing voice, but it came out gravelly from the smoke. Coughing, he glanced in the rearview mirror again. "For about five minutes."

He stopped behind Jenna. She was talking to Chance. When she started moving again, Nate eased forward. "You're headed the wrong way."

"I went by the Mission to check on Jenna, then was going to see about Mrs. Dodd. The judge sent us to town to make sure everyone is out." Chance coughed and

402

wiped his eyes.

The cat yowled again.

"What's that awful noise?"

"Dodd's cat." Two fire trucks and a police car went past on the next street, sirens wailing.

Chance leaned out the window, looking behind him. "They're trying to get ahead of the fire. Going to make a stand on the northwest side of town, try to stop it there."

Which meant the loss of whole blocks of homes.

The fire was growing closer, louder. Between it and the cat, Chance had to shout. "Did you see anyone else on this street?"

"No, and I looked. I need to take Mrs. Dodd's walker and her cat out to the ranch, then I'll be back to help. Where do I report?"

"Are you up for that?"

"Yes." When Chance appeared concerned — and with good reason — Nate said simply, "I can handle it. Jesus worked a miracle at Mrs. Dodd's. I'm free of the fire problem." He didn't know about the other stuff, but that was a big one.

"Hallelujah! There's a command post at the high school. Check there for an assignment."

"Will do. Stay safe."

"You too."

After Nate drove away, Chance turned around and went east to the next street, taking a left on Hickory. Nate was once again the charge-ahead guy Chance had always known. The kid who intervened when a bully picked on someone smaller. The cowboy who rode into the thickest brush and came out with the orneriest cow. The soldier — and now civilian — who risked his life to save someone else.

Regarding Mrs. Dodd, however, he gathered that Jenna had led the way. He needed to have a serious talk with his little sister about putting herself in jeopardy.

Chance clicked on the walkie-talkie that connected him to his dad and brother. They were helping clear the town too. "Dad, Will, can you hear me?"

"Go ahead, bro."

"I hear you, son."

"I just talked to Jenna and Nate on Third. They rescued Mrs. Dodd before I could get to her house. She and Jenna are headed to the ranch. Nate is taking her walker and her cat out there, then he's coming back in to help."

"Praise God, they're all safe." Dub's voice cracked over the radio.

"Is Nate okay?" asked Will.

"Yes. He said God worked a miracle. He

isn't any more scared of the fire than the rest of us."

"Then he's shaking in his boots," said Dub. "Gotta go. I see a woman, little girl, and a puppy running down the street. I'll pick them up."

"Do you need help?" asked Will.

"No, they've spotted me and are waiting. Check with you later."

Chance laid the walkie-talkie on the seat, thanking God for keeping his family, Nate, Mrs. Dodd, and the unknown woman and little girl free from harm. With the cell phones down, they hadn't known Jenna's status and hadn't had time to look for her until now. They'd been worried about her but trusted her good sense.

He scanned each side of the street, driving as slowly as he dared with the fire only a couple of blocks away. It broke his heart to look behind him and to the west. Part of downtown blazed, but the wind was driving most of the fire into the more residential neighborhoods. He prayed that everyone had gotten out.

Crossing Tenth Street, he relaxed minutely because he was farther north and out of the immediate line of the fire. The three houses on the corner looked empty. He glanced across the street toward the old museum as he drove past. It had been closed for at least ten years. A while back his mom had mentioned the possibility of it reopening, but he didn't remember her saying anything else about it.

"Wait a minute." Was that a vehicle behind the building? Stopping, he backed up. A light blue van was parked outside the back door. He pulled over, peering through the smoke. The electricity was off, but he caught a glimmer of a light through the museum window. Flashlight.

Leaving the motor running, he grabbed his own flashlight and ran up the driveway. A young woman dressed in a blue T-shirt, jeans, and tennis shoes stepped out the door, staggering under the weight of a heavy box. He rushed over and took it. He didn't recognize her. "Ma'am, you need to evacuate."

"We have to save the pictures and old records." She pointed to approximately a dozen boxes already in the van. He spotted a desk computer and monitor in one corner. Right behind the front seat were a pile of clothes, a large suitcase, and a laptop.

"There's more inside we need to get." Spinning around, she hurried back into the building. Chance followed. They had fifteen minutes max, and that was cutting it too close for comfort.

"Shut the door. We need to try to keep out the smoke as much as possible."

Yes, ma'am. She wasn't exactly bossy but concerned about the building contents. He pulled the door closed. Shining the flashlight ahead of him, he followed her into what appeared to be a conference room. He hadn't been in the museum since junior high.

"If you'll work on those boxes, I'll start on these." She went into a small room and began pulling books off a shelf, gathering up as many as she could carry.

After setting the heavy-duty flashlight upward on a table and softly illuminating the room, he stacked two of the six boxes on top of each other and picked them up. And earned an admiring glance from the pretty blonde.

Amazing how a man's mind worked, he mused, carrying the boxes outside. Here he was worrying about a fire that might destroy their whole town, but he still noticed how attractive she was. Light blonde hair, good figure, about five-six. Maybe blue eyes. He couldn't tell in the dim light. She had to be new in town, or he would have already heard about her. If not seen her himself. Sliding the boxes into her van, he straightened and checked the eerie red glow in the smoke-blackened sky.

She added her pile of books and looked upward. "Do we have more time?"

"Not much." Hustling back inside, he grabbed two more boxes while she scooped up books. "What are those?"

"Old City Council minutes and who knows what else. This is the records storage room, so they must be important."

They carried that load out and ran back in for the last of the books and boxes. After they put them into the van, Chance gently caught her arm. "We can't stay any longer."

She looked wistfully at the door and hesitated. Her face was so expressive that he knew the instant she made up her mind. "All right. I don't know what else to try to save anyway. I'll lock the door in case the fire misses it."

She ran to the door and locked it, then rested her hand on the wall of the museum and bowed her head slightly. She spoke softly and rapidly. The only words he made out were at the end. "In Jesus' name."

He assumed she was asking the Lord to save the museum. He added a silent amen to her prayer.

When she rejoined him by the van, he asked, "Do you have a place to go?"

"No. I thought I'd head east until I came

to a town."

Definitely new to the area. Chance shook his head. "You don't need to. Go to Oak Street and turn right."

"Three blocks that way?" She pointed to the east.

"Four. Turn right on Oak and head south. The fire missed that part of town. After you cross Main Street, follow the highway. Go fifteen miles to the Callahan Ranch. You can't miss it. Turn left and follow the dirt road two miles to the ranch house. Tell Mrs. Callahan that Chance sent you and said to take good care of you."

"And she'll know who you are?"

He smiled for one of the few times that afternoon. "She'd better. She's my mom. Now, get movin'."

"Okay. Thanks." She ran around to the driver's side of the van.

Chance started to his truck, turned around, and jogged back up the driveway. "What's your name?"

"Emily Rose Denny."

He nodded toward the museum. "Thank you."

Jogging back to his pickup, he decided her name was as pretty as she was.

26

Jenna and Nate had Mrs. Dodd and Ginger the cat comfortably settled into a recliner when a blue van pulled up in front of the house. "Who's that?"

Nate looked out the window. "Don't recognize her."

Jenna's mom glanced out on her way to the front door. "Oh! It's the curator from San Antonio, the one who's going to revamp our museum. I'd completely forgotten that she was supposed to arrive over the weekend." She hurried down the sidewalk.

A few minutes later she ushered the young woman inside and introduced her to everyone. Emily was windblown and reeked of smoke like anyone else who'd been in town, but she was attractive. Jenna glanced at her hand. No ring.

Her mom motioned toward one of the couches, and Emily sat down. Sue joined her. "I'm so glad Chance sent you out here."

Jenna glanced at Nate. He wiggled his eyebrows ever so slightly, making her smile.

"Where did you run into him?"

"I was at the museum, and he saw my van. He stopped to order me to evacuate and helped me rescue the boxes of records and pictures before he sent me out here." She focused on Jenna's mom. "We took all the books from the record storage room too. Safer to grab everything than miss something important. I wish we could have gathered up some of the other things, but there wasn't time."

They all stared at her, even Mrs. Dodd. Sue blinked and glanced at Ramona, who had come out of the kitchen to meet the new arrival. The housekeeper's mouth hung open. Jenna's mom cleared her throat and turned back to Emily. "You stayed in town to save our historical records?"

When nobody else thought of it. Nobody said anything out loud, but Jenna bet it crossed their minds. Of course, everybody else in town was worried about their families, homes, and businesses. Still . . .

Emily's cheeks grew pink. "It is what you hired me to do. I kept a close eye on the fire." Shrugging lightly, she crossed her arms. "I guess I'm a little obsessive about old things. Especially records that tell the

411

history of a place."

"Bless your heart." Jenna's mom leaned over and hugged her. "Thank you."

Emily's face turned bright red. "You're welcome, ma'am. Be sure and thank your son too. I couldn't have gotten it all by myself."

"We will." Sue stood, then looked down at Emily with a frown of renewed concern. "You're staying in Maybelle's rental house?"

"Was," said Mrs. Dodd. "That house was two blocks west of mine. There's nothing left over there." She sighed heavily, her expression grim. "Like on my block." With a hoarse but quiet meow, Ginger stretched up, resting her head against the elderly lady's neck. Mrs. Dodd gently petted her. "But those are just things. What's important is right here." She gave Jenna and Nate a wobbly smile. "Thanks to you two."

"I thought it probably burned, which is a shame," said Emily. "It was a lovely little house. It was furnished, so I only brought clothes and personal things with me from San Antonio. They're in the van."

"Thank goodness for that. Now, can we fix you something to eat? I'm sure you need something to drink. Or shall I show you to a guest room first?"

"Some iced tea or soda would be nice.

My throat is a little raw. But I can get it."
She started to stand up, but Sue waved her
hand, motioning for her to stay put.

"You stay right there and rest." She peered
out the front window again. "Dub's home,
and he brought some folks with him. Jenna,
would you get Emily's tea?"

"Sure." But she doubted her mom heard
her. She was already out the door, running
to meet her husband. He held her close for
a minute before turning to help a woman
and little girl from the truck. And a cute
brown, floppy-eared puppy. All three of
them appeared shaken and tired.

Nate glanced at the dog, then the cat.
"This may get interesting. Mrs. Dodd, how
does your cat get along with puppies?"

"Ignores 'em."

"Good. I'll go see if Dub needs help
unloading anything." Nate went out the
front door.

Emily stood and walked over to Jenna. "I
don't expect y'all to wait on me. Point me
toward the bathroom. I'll wash up and help
in the kitchen if it's needed."

"I like you already. The bathroom is down
the hall, first door on the right." She heard
a whimper come from Zach's old room. "I'll
go that way too. My little guy is waking up."

I wonder how Ginger gets along with kids?

413

At 6:00, Jenna and Emily Rose took the back roads, circling around to the northeast side of Callahan Crossing. Her mom followed in her SUV. Their goal was to try to enter town from that direction near Grace Community Church. One of the television stations in Abilene had been giving reports on the fire every half hour, so they knew that part of town had been spared.

Their church had plans established to be a shelter during a community crisis. They'd implemented them once five years earlier when an ice storm hit the region during the Christmas holidays and stranded travelers.

Before Dub came out to the ranch earlier, he had talked to Pastor Brad. County Judge Coleman, who was in charge of coordinating the firefighting and evacuation efforts, had given his preliminary approval to open the shelter, contingent on the winds dying way down. They started dropping around 5:00.

Sue, Ramona, and Ollie's wife, Ethel, had started cooking and baking around 3:00, ever since the first news report revealed how bad things were. So had their neighbors, including Nate's mom. Fortunately, she'd had the day off and hadn't been in town. They brought their food to the ranch under the assumption that if anyone could get into town, it would be the Callahans.

Nate and Dub had gone back to town together shortly after her dad brought Jill Harmon and her ten-year-old daughter, Kim, to the ranch. Her husband was a long-haul trucker, currently on a run to Pennsylvania. Somehow, Dub had managed for her to get a message to him via the Red Cross. They didn't know if their house had survived or not.

Jill was a school bus driver and had run her route north of town after the early dismissal, taking Kim with her. Some parents had picked up their children, so the trip was shorter than usual. The volunteer guarding the road had allowed them back in to return the bus and pick up her car at the bus barn, which was near the high school.

If they'd gotten the car and left, they would have been fine. But they couldn't bear to leave the puppy behind. While they were in the house, a big monster truck skidded around the corner and hit her car, smashing the back fender so badly that the tire wouldn't turn. She didn't think the driver realized they were home when he drove off. They had no choice but to try to get out on foot.

Kim and Zach had taken to each other right away. He adored the puppy and had been oh-so-careful when he petted him. Playing with the little boy helped keep Kim's mind off the fire.

Ethel was about the same size as Jill, and her daughter was only a little bigger than Kim. When Ace went to Ethel's house and asked if they could spare some clothes for them, they were glad to help. Jenna had given Mrs. Dodd some pink Capri pants with a drawstring waist and a pretty rose knit top. The snazzy outfit, as the elderly lady called it, seemed to cheer her up a little.

Ramona and Ace planned to stay the night at the ranch house. They would take good care of their guests and Zach, which freed Jenna and Sue to try to help out in town.

And hopefully get news of their menfolk.

Jenna slowly approached the sheriff's car parked across the road, its blue lights flashing. The officer shielded his eyes against her dimmed headlights. A wall of flame lit the night sky on the other side of town, and she shuddered. *Please, God, protect the people fighting that monster.*

"The fire isn't moving as fast," Emily said

quietly. "I don't think the flames are as high."

Jenna picked up the two-way radio from a pocket on the console and pressed the talk button. "Looks like Dalton is manning the roadblock, Mom."

"Good. We'll have a better chance of getting through."

Jenna stopped, and he walked toward her. She lowered the window as he approached. "Hi, Dalton. How's it going?"

"Evenin', Jenna." He looked across the cab at Emily and nodded slightly. "Ma'am."

Sue got out of the SUV and walked up to join them. "How are you holding up, Dalton?"

"A lot better than the guys on the fire line. I hear a few of them have been treated for smoke inhalation. None of your men," he added quickly. "As far as we know, there haven't been any serious injuries or fatalities.

"Actually, it's boring out here. Other than the Red Cross and Salvation Army, y'all are the first people to come along in an hour. I wish I was in there helping them."

"Someone has to guard the town. Some people are ornery enough to try to sneak in and loot."

"I turned away a few guys who didn't have

any business here. I didn't have to talk hard. They took one look at the fire and decided it wasn't a good place to be.

"We have firefighters from dozens of volunteer fire districts in there now. And engine companies from as far away as Midland and Abilene. They're having better success establishing a control line now that the wind has died down, but it's going to be a long night. The Texas Forest Service sent in a couple of bulldozers to build a firebreak. Chance hauled his dozer out there and is working alongside them."

He peeked into the back of Jenna's truck. "I suppose y'all want to go in and help at the church."

"Nate and I took some clothes and food from the Mission this afternoon." Jenna hesitated, then voiced the question she'd been dreading to ask. "Is the Mission gone?"

"Yes, Jenna, it is. I'm sorry. But what you salvaged will be a big help to people."

Jenna's mom reached up and curled her hand around her arm in comfort. "I have a truckload of food. Folks out our way have been bringing it by all afternoon. Things to eat now and supplies to take. Even if nobody stays at the shelter, we can feed the fire-fighters. Have you had any supper?"

"No, ma'am." He took off his hat and

sifted his fingers through his hair. "I haven't felt much like eating. I lost my place too."

"Oh, Dalton! We're so sorry." Sue put her arms around the tall deputy, etching a crack in his professional facade. He let her hug him briefly, then eased away.

"Thanks." He cleared his throat and wiped his eyes with the side of his index finger. "Reckon I needed that." He shrugged and put his hat back on. "I have good insurance. I can rebuild. Dad rescued the horses and took them to his place. He was trapped in the pasture by the fire. Had to cut the fence to get away. But he's safe, and so are my animals. That counts more than anything."

"Will you be staying with your folks?"

"No, ma'am. Grandma is living with them, so they don't have room. Will invited me to bunk at his place as long as I need to."

"Good. Now, come back here, and I'll give you some food. You need to eat."

He followed her and returned to Jenna's truck a few minutes later, holding a paper plate filled with fried chicken and rolls. A sandwich-sized bag of cookies dangled from one hand. "I'll pull over so y'all can go by. Don't go anywhere other than the church."

"We won't. Thank you, Dalton." Jenna's

heart ached for her friend. He was putting on a brave front — like Mrs. Dodd and Jill Harmon — but losing his home must cause a great big hole in his heart. He'd only built it a couple of years ago and had done a lot of the work himself.

While she was waiting for him to move the car, she heard her mom on the radio.

"Dub, can you hear me?"

Thirty seconds later, he answered. There was a lot of noise in the background, or static on the radio. Jenna wasn't sure which.

"I hear you, Sue. Are you at the church?"

"Almost. We're waiting for Dalton to move his car and let us through. How are you?"

"Tired and hungry. The Salvation Army and Red Cross folks brought us some sandwiches awhile ago, but that wore off already."

"I can barely hear you."

"Hang on." There was a pause. "I moved back from the fire line a little." There wasn't as much noise now. "Is that better?"

"Yes. I have a truckload of food. If you can, come by the church and rest a spell. Get something to eat. How are the boys?"

"Tired like everybody else. But they don't let up for a minute. I'm mighty proud of them. Jenna, you on here too?"

"Yes, Daddy. How's Nate?"

"Handling a fire shovel like he's been doin' it all his life. He's doing good. Real good."

"Tell him I love him. And to stay safe. That goes for all of you. I have to go now. Dalton is waving us through."

"Y'all be careful."

"You too."

Her mom signed off as Jenna drove past the deputy's car, waving at Dalton. For somebody who wasn't very hungry, he sure was gnawing on a chicken leg.

27

Pastor Brad and a couple of other men had already set up the twenty cots the church owned. The Red Cross had provided twenty more. Some were in classrooms, the rest were in the sanctuary in the open areas at the back and across the front. So far, only five people had come to stay the night, a family who had no place else to go.

Sue and the rest of the kitchen crew fed them and comforted them. They kept a few casseroles warm but put everything else in the commercial-sized refrigerator and waited.

Grace Community had the biggest fellowship hall in town. Jenna, her mom, Pastor Brad, and a couple of the Emergency Committee members decided to divide it in half, with one end set up for meals and the other as a food and clothing distribution center. The North Side Baptist church a few blocks over would use their fellowship hall as a distribution center for household goods, appliances, and furniture. And the Presbyterians offered space for any overflow.

Jenna and Emily began sorting the clothing that came from the Mission, organizing it by size, type, and gender where appropriate. Lindsey showed up to help. Misty Dumont, the woman who had made a play for Nate at church back in October, arrived a few minutes later.

Jenna had a little trouble with that. Was Misty there to try to impress somebody? Maybe some of the firefighters if they came in? But Misty pitched in and worked hard unpacking canned goods and organizing them on portable shelves someone had brought in. Her heart seemed to be in the right place, and Jenna chided herself for judging her.

At 8:00, a Salvation Army semitruck arrived with more clothes, food, and water. "Tomorrow or the next day is when you'll really start needing the groceries and clothing," said Captain Carrie Carpenter, who was already in town to coordinate their efforts. "Whenever the authorities start letting people back into town."

They had a crew of volunteers with them who started unloading the truck. Jenna was surprised and touched when they deferred to her on where to put things. They were the experts. But they respected her as the local person in charge, right then, at least.

Half an hour later, a Walmart semi arrived, filled with pallets of bottled water, Gatorade, batteries, ready-to-eat food like canned ravioli, peanut butter and crackers, Vienna sausages, and even pudding cups. Jenna was floored. She'd read about the company's response during hurricanes along the coast, but it never occurred to her that they would come to Callahan Crossing.

That's when the magnitude of her community's loss hit her.

Overcome with emotion, she sought sanctuary in a corner of the room used to store decorations and props from plays they'd performed over the years. Curled up on the floor next to a life-sized wooden donkey, she began to cry.

Nate found her there ten minutes later. When he opened the door, she scrambled to her feet and threw herself into his arms, holding him as tight as she could. How she loved this man — dirt, smoke, sweat, and all.

He embraced her for a minute, then wheezed, "Honey, you're squeezing the stuffing out of me."

"Oh, sorry." She eased her hold and took

a good look at him. Dirt and soot covered him from head to toe, except for slightly paler ovals around his eyes. "You've been wearing glasses."

"Tinted safety glasses. Dub had an extra pair." He was hoarse.

She drew him farther into the room and listened to his breathing. The wheezing hadn't been merely because she was squeezing him. She'd made it worse, but there was a definite raspy whistle. "Your poor voice. And you're wheezing. I can hear it. Did you let a medic check you out?"

"Yes. She had me breathe some oxygen with something in it to open up the airways. It's only minor smoke inhalation. She said I'll be fine, but I need to stay away from the smoke."

"Which you're going to do, right?"

"Right. At least right at the fire. That's the worst. But the whole town is full of it."

She gently put her arms around him, though she realized she was getting filthy. He rested his hand at her waist and leaned against the wall. "I'm proud of you for fighting the fire, but I'm so glad you won't be going back out there. Is it contained?"

"Almost. There's a stretch where they're still trying to get the control line in place. Chance was moving his dozer ahead of it when I left. He's something to see on that thing. I was amazed at how he could operate it."

"He's even better with a backhoe. Total precision. So they're all doing okay? Dad, Will, Chance?"

"They are. The crews are going to rotate taking an hour or two break. Come in and eat and rest."

"I'd better get in there and help."

"They can handle it for a few minutes." He brushed a grimy finger along her jaw, then made a face. "I'm getting you dirty."

"I don't care. I don't mind your dirt."

He smiled, his teeth shining white against his smoky skin. "You sayin' a Saturday night bath is all I need to take?"

"No. Not at all. I don't mind you getting a little of your dirt on me right now."

"Got it." He leaned down and kissed her slowly and thoroughly.

Maybe they didn't need her in the kitchen after all.

He lifted his head, searching her eyes. "I love you."

"I love you too." She wanted so badly to give him a little nudge in the marriage direction. Thanks to Jesus, he had faced and conquered his biggest nightmare that day.

Surely the other PTSD issues paled next to that.

"I don't want to waste any more time. I'm sayin' the word, honey. Will you marry me?"

Tears of joy stung her eyes. "You know I will. But I'm not waiting for a big wedding. Been there, done that. Don't need it."

"You're sure?"

"Positive."

He took a deep breath and relaxed. "Good. I don't want to wait long enough to plan anything big."

"Me, either. We can run over to the courthouse tomorrow and get the license."

A wide grin slowly lit his face. "That quick, huh?"

"Yes, sir. And we'll corner Pastor Brad and ask him to keep Saturday afternoon free." She hadn't thought his smile could get any wider, but it did. "Your immediate family and mine. Well, the grandparents too. But that's it. And Lindsey. She's been too good a friend since I came home to leave her out. And we have to invite Dalton because he'll be staying with Will."

"And the folks on the ranch. They'd be hurt if we didn't invite them."

"True. But that's it. I don't want a lot of fuss and bother. It doesn't seem right in the midst of all this, for one thing. I want it done and over with and you for my husband."

"And Zach's daddy."

"He's going to be thrilled."

"Does he know what a daddy is?"

"He knows his friends have them. Thankfully, he's never asked me why he doesn't have one. Dad and my brothers have tried hard to fill that hole. And you have too." She stood on tiptoe and kissed him again. "I really should go help in the kitchen. You need to go wash up and find a cot to stretch out on. Get some rest."

Nate shook his head, his countenance as sad as a country song. "We haven't even committed matrimony yet, and you're ordering me around."

She winked and sashayed out the door. "I'm the boss lady, remember?"

The fire was contained by midnight but not yet under control Wednesday morning. Nate and Jenna shared their plans with their delighted families. They took Zach with them when they drove to the county seat to pick up the marriage license. But instead of going back toward the ranch, Nate headed toward Sweetwater.

"You missed a turn back there."

Nate grinned and patted her hand. "Are

you questioning my driving, soon-to-be Mrs. Langley?"

"Mostly wondering what you're up to."

"Going to the jewelry store."

Her eyes lit up. "Really? And is there a special reason for that?"

"Need a new battery for my watch."

"Oh, I see."

"What you see?" called Zach from the backseat.

Jenna chuckled and scanned the scenery for something that might interest a two-year-old. "That big ol' barn over there. See it?"

"Yeah." He didn't sound that impressed. He saw a bigger one every day.

"Keep looking, maybe you'll see a tractor."

When they got to the jewelry store, Nate glanced at his watch. "Why, look at that, it's working." Carrying Zach, he deftly guided her toward the engagement and wedding rings. "I've had my eye on one for a while, but since we're here, you can tell me what you think of it."

"Sweet man, I'd be happy with anything. Well, maybe not something from the quarter toy machines at the grocery store."

"They're probably up to fifty cents by now anyway." He smiled at the middle-aged clerk who walked up behind the counter. "Could we see that one in the middle, please?"

The clerk unlocked the case and removed the ring, a beautiful diamond solitaire in a yellow gold band. Jenna was no diamond expert, but she thought it might be about half a carat in size. Too much money for her cowboy to spend, though he had a nice savings.

But then, he was marrying someone with a hefty bank account, she thought with a smile. She was secure enough in their love and in him to know he would love her just as much if she didn't have a cent. So she wasn't going to question him on the expense.

The clerk held it out toward them. It caught the light, sparkling more than any other ring she'd ever seen. The ring Jimmy Don had given her had been bigger, but it hadn't been as bright or finely cut.

"Like it?"

"It's beautiful. I've never seen one that sparkles so much."

"It has to do with the cut and the clarity of the diamond," said the clerk. "Would you like to try it on?"

When she hesitated, Nate leaned closer, carefully holding Zach so he wouldn't kick the glass case. "See if it fits, sweetheart."

"It probably will. I haven't tried on a standard size one yet that didn't." She met his gaze. "But if I put it on and it fits, I don't want to take it off."

Nate laughed and glanced at the smiling clerk. "Is there someplace where we can sit down so I can hold this little guy and slip a diamond on my girl's hand at the same time?"

"Of course. Come right over here." She led them to a table with two chairs in front and one in back, obviously for displaying jewelry in a more comfortable setting.

Nate sat down and settled Zach on his lap. "You need to sit real still for a minute, okay? I have to use both hands."

Zach nodded, looking up at some expensive figurines on a nearby shelf. Good thing Nate was hanging on to him, otherwise her inquisitive son would be trying to figure out how to get his little hands on them.

Nate looked at the clerk, and she handed him the ring. Jenna held out her left hand, and he took it in his. "Do I need to ask again?" He gave her the lopsided smile that had won her heart at fourteen.

"No, not again." Jenna glanced at the benignly smiling clerk. "I've already said yes twice."

Nate chuckled and winked at the clerk.

"And one time I wasn't even asking."

That made the serene woman laugh.

Nate slipped the ring on Jenna's finger. He didn't propose again or tell her he loved her out loud. But he said it with his eyes, his touch, the tenderness of his smile.

It fit perfectly.

"I think it works." If he grinned any bigger, he'd bust something.

"That, my love, is the understatement of the year." She leaned up and kissed him.

A minute later, the clerk cleared her throat. When they looked up at her, she smiled brightly. "Will that be cash or charge?"

"Debit card." Nate handed Zach to Jenna and shifted on the seat, pulling his wallet from his back pocket. She entertained her son by showing him how the pretty ring sparkled. Nate handed the woman the card and grumbled when she walked away. "Talk about ruining the moment."

Jenna caressed his jaw. "Nothing could ruin that moment, sweetheart."

He smiled, kissed her palm, and jumped to his feet. "Ma'am, wait. We need to look at wedding bands too."

After returning to the ranch, they ate a sandwich, played with Zach for a little while, and took him over to the ranch house. Kim was happy to play with him until time for his nap.

Ramona agreed to watch him while they went to town. "I can't go in there yet. I'll do my part for now by cooking."

Jenna's mom and Emily had gone back to the church midmorning. Her dad and brothers came in about ten minutes after Nate and Jenna arrived. They had stayed in town all night, catching a few hours sleep at the shelter, then going back out again to work the fire line.

"We have it controlled," said Dub, "though they haven't made the official announcement yet. There are still some hot spots here and there, a few homes still burning. Some fresh crews from other counties came in about half an hour ago. They'll take care of things now."

The people who had been fighting the fire for twenty-four hours could go home and rest. Or in the case of many members of the Callahan Crossing volunteer fire department, see if they still had a home left.

"The boys and I are going to drive around a little, want to double-check things one last time." He sighed heavily, resting his arm across Sue's shoulder. "And take a look in the daylight at what we'll be facing in the days ahead. Judge Coleman said y'all could go with us if you want to. Knowing how things are might help you prepare a little better when folks come back in."

Nate and Jenna rode with Chance and Will. She felt her parents needed time alone to deal with the disaster together. Emily seemed to sense the same thing and politely declined when her mom asked if she wanted to go along. But when Chance asked if she wanted to go in his truck, she changed her mind.

Will wasn't too tired to pick up on the vibes between his brother and the cute blonde. He surprised Jenna when he squeezed into the backseat with her and Nate.

They followed Dub down Oak to Main Street. The businesses in the heart of downtown hadn't been touched by the actual fire, only the heavy smoke that still hung in the air. That would cause damage, but at least the buildings were intact.

By the time they reached Maple, the buildings began to show scars from the fire. Jenna glanced up the side street and drew in a sharp breath. Where only part of the stores at that point on Main had been scorched, there appeared to be nothing but rubble from First Street north. The smoke was so thick, they couldn't tell how far it went.

"It came in at an angle," Chance said quietly. "That's why it hit the streets north of here harder. The wind must have shifted a little about the time it got to Fourth. It moved mainly north from there."

Between Maple and the next street, Hickory, the damage increased dramatically. Beyond Hickory were only ashes and rubble as far as they could see.

As they slowly wound through the streets, the devastation stunned them. The cotton gin, five businesses, the Mission, and more homes than they could count had been completely destroyed.

To her surprise, Jenna didn't cry when she saw the ashes of the Mission. But she wept as they passed block after block of burned-out homes. A lone chimney stood here. A burned car there. A child's swing set in a backyard, scorched but standing while the ruins of the home still smoldered.

"Look at the trees." Emily pointed to a big elm tree. The trunk was burned halfway up, the lower branches looked like charcoal, but a few dried leaves still clung to the uppermost branches. Many others were the same way.

At the museum, the section that housed

the office, conference room, and records storage room was a blackened, gaping hole. The main portion of the building was still intact, though no doubt heavily smoke damaged.

From her spot in the backseat, Jenna glanced at Emily in the front. Tears streamed down her face. A few minutes earlier, she, too, had been crying for the families who had lost their homes. But these were fresh tears, perhaps of thanksgiving because she'd had the foresight to take the records. Perhaps gratitude that the whole building wasn't gone.

Chance stopped in the street to give them a good look. After a moment, he reached over and gently squeezed Emily's hand. "You did a good thing yesterday, Emily Rose."

She squeezed his hand back. "We did a good thing, Chance."

Will winked at Jenna but wisely kept his mouth shut.

When they got back to the shelter, they learned that the judge and fire chief had a partial list of the damage. In addition to the things they had seen downtown, ninety-eight homes in town and two farmhouses along with their barns had been destroyed.

They hadn't tallied the burned cars scattered throughout the southwest and west part of town. In the farm and ranch area where the fire started, it would take days, perhaps weeks, to determine how many cattle had been lost or miles of fencing burned.

The firefighters had thoroughly searched the burned areas and found no sign that anyone had died in the fire. Nor had there been any serious injuries.

At 3:00, the authorities allowed the townspeople back into Callahan Crossing. As the news spread through announcements on the radio and television and by word of mouth, cars slowly streamed into town. Thick smoke still hung in the air, making it difficult to see. With street signs burned and landmarks gone, some folks had trouble finding where they had lived.

Those whose homes were intact, like Jill Harmon's, comforted those who had lost everything. In the areas where the rubble had cooled enough, people sifted through the ashes with rakes, looking for keepsakes and anything that could be salvaged. They found little. The fire had burned so hot that appliances were mere piles of twisted and melted metal.

Mrs. Dodd's son arrived from Austin and took her to see the ashes of the home she had lived in for fifty years. The only thing they found worth keeping was a pocketknife that had belonged to her late husband.

Jenna, Nate, Sue, Emily, and Lindsey worked at the shelter alongside others from their church and other churches in town. They served meals to those who had begun trying to clean up, handed out clothes and food supplies to those who needed it. Often they simply sat down and listened to stories of heartache and bravery and gave someone a shoulder to cry on.

People from FEMA, along with volunteers from the Salvation Army and Red Cross, were also there to help with financial assistance and how to get other aid. Insurance claims adjusters arrived practically in a caravan.

Members of all the churches in town organized to provide meals for the weeks to come, bringing the food to Grace Community on each church's designated day and also working in the kitchen. Church folk from other towns brought food too, and came in to help. Cleanup would take awhile, and people had to eat.

The Baptist church filled up with donated appliances, furniture, towels, sheets, and other household goods. They quickly had to start sending people to the Presbyterian church with the overflow.

Money poured in from all across the nation, some through aid agencies and some into the disaster fund established at the Callahan Crossing National Bank. A committee was established to handle the funds at the bank and disburse them fairly and to those most in need.

Through it all, despite all the material loss, everyone thanked God that no lives had been lost, nor anyone seriously injured. The whole town hadn't been destroyed. They would build again. Callahan Crossing had always been a close-knit community. It was even more so now.

On Saturday afternoon, in the bright, warm West Texas sunshine, Nate and Jenna stood beneath the old pecan trees at Aidan's Spring. She wore her pretty peach sweater and calf-length turquoise and peach flowered skirt with white cowboy boots. The lovely gold heart-link bracelet and a sparkling diamond ring were her only jewelry.

Nate wore his best Sunday jeans, a new silver-gray shirt his folks had gotten him for Christmas, and his best pair of cowboy boots. And a fancy yellow and white gold watch that he kept checking every few minutes before the service started.

Lindsey stood up with Jenna. Chance served as Nate's best man. With Pastor Brad officiating, Jenna and Nate pledged themselves to each other before family, friends, and their God.

Dressed in his finest Western shirt and jeans, Zach watched from his grandfather's arms. "What they doing?"

"They're getting married," whispered Dub.

"What's that?" His little voice rang out loud and clear in the quiet afternoon.

"I'll tell you later."

"Why?"

Waiting for their pastor and friend to finish the ceremony, Jenna and Nate looked into each other's eyes and laughed.

"I now pronounce you husband and wife." Pastor Brad beamed them a smile. "Nate, you may kiss your bride."

When Nate took her in his arms on this most special of days and kissed her, Jenna knew how it felt to be loved and cherished.

"Why they kissin'?"

Laughing, Jenna and Nate ended the kiss.

"It's not like you haven't seen it before, buddy." Nate turned and reached for the little boy. Dub handed his grandchild to his new son-in-law and wiped a tear from his eye.

Zach looked around at all the people with a tiny frown as if he was trying to figure out why they were laughing.

"Are you wondering why Nate kissed me in front of everybody?"

"Uh-huh." Her son focused on her.

"Nate and I just got married. Like Grandma and Papa are married. And Ramona and Ace. That means we belong together now. He's going to stay with us all the time. He's going to live at our house."

Zach grinned and looked at Nate. "You live at our house?"

"Yes. I'm going to be your daddy."

Out of the corner of her eye, Jenna saw Chance nudge Will. "Does he even know what that means?"

Will shrugged. "I don't know."

"My daddy?" Zach's eyes were wide as saucers.

"Is that okay with you?"

Zach started wiggling in excitement and threw his arms around Nate's neck. "Yeah!"

Jenna looked at her brothers. "Guess he knows what it means."

"We're a family now, Zach. The three of us. What do you think of that?"

Zach released Nate's neck and sat up, resting his hand on his new daddy's shoulder. He thought for a minute and threw his hands up in the air. "Awesome!"

Jenna knew she would love this brave, battle-scarred, and honorable man for the rest of her life. The healing the Lord brought to her broken heart was now complete.

Nate was not only the hometown hero.

He was hers.

ABOUT THE AUTHOR

Sharon Gillenwater was born and raised in west Texas, and loves to write about her native state. The author of nineteen novels, including ten for the Christian market, she is a member of American Christian Fiction Writers and Romance Writers of America. When she's not writing, she and her husband enjoy spending time with their son, daughter-in-law, and two adorable grandchildren.